PENGUIN WEIRD FICTION

Weird Fiction: An Anthology

Sometime around the turn of the twentieth century, something happened, something . . . *weird*. In the dark halls of ivy-clad manors, in the ancient woodland escapes of New England, a generation of authors was inspired to radically reinterpret the horror and fantasy writing of the past. In place of vampires and werewolves were atmospheres of breathless dread, terrifying visions of long-forgotten gods and unexplainable, writhing monsters. The strange and extraordinary work from that time remains incredibly influential on all aspects of literature today. **Penguin Weird Fiction** is a celebration of the very best of this writing, a store of novels and tales that for generations have delighted and horrified.

Weird Fiction: An Anthology

PENGUIN BOOKS

PENGUIN BOOKS

UK | USA | Canada | Ireland | Australia
India | New Zealand | South Africa

Penguin Books is part of the Penguin Random House group of companies whose addresses can be found at global.penguinrandomhouse.com.

Penguin Random House UK,
One Embassy Gardens, 8 Viaduct Gardens, London SW11 7BW

penguin.co.uk
global.penguinrandomhouse.com

First published in Penguin Books 2024
003

Typeset by Jouve (UK), Milton Keynes
Printed and bound in Great Britain by Clays Ltd, Elcograf S.p.A.

The authorized representative in the EEA is Penguin Random House Ireland, Morrison Chambers, 32 Nassau Street, Dublin D02 YH68

A CIP catalogue record for this book is available from the British Library

ISBN: 978-1-405-97290-1

MIX
Paper | Supporting responsible forestry
FSC® C018179
FSC www.fsc.org

Penguin Random House is committed to a sustainable future for our business, our readers and our planet. This book is made from Forest Stewardship Council® certified paper.

Contents

The Masque of the Red Death

Edgar Allan Poe

The 'Red Death' had long devastated the country. No pestilence had ever been so fatal, or so hideous. Blood was its Avatar and its seal – the redness and the horror of blood. There were sharp pains, and sudden dizziness, and then profuse bleeding at the pores, with dissolution. The scarlet stains upon the body and especially upon the face of the victim, were the pest ban which shut him out from the aid and from the sympathy of his fellow-men. And the whole seizure, progress, and termination of the disease, were the incidents of half an hour.

But the Prince Prospero was happy and dauntless and sagacious. When his dominions were half depopulated, he summoned to his presence a thousand hale and light-hearted friends from among the knights and dames of his court, and with these retired to the deep seclusion of one of his castellated abbeys. This was an extensive and magnificent structure, the creation of the prince's own eccentric yet august taste. A strong and lofty wall girdled it in. This wall had gates of iron. The courtiers, having entered, brought furnaces and massy hammers and welded the bolts. They resolved to leave means neither of ingress nor egress to the sudden impulses of despair or of frenzy from within. The abbey was amply provisioned. With such precautions the courtiers might bid defiance to contagion. The external world could take care of itself. In the meantime it was folly to grieve, or to think. The prince had provided all the appliances of pleasure. There were buffoons, there were improvisatori, there were ballet-dancers, there were musicians, there was Beauty, there was wine. All these and security were within. Without was the 'Red Death'.

It was toward the close of the fifth or sixth month of his seclusion, and while the pestilence raged most furiously abroad, that the Prince Prospero entertained his thousand friends at a masked ball of the most unusual magnificence.

It was a voluptuous scene, that masquerade. But first let me tell of the rooms in which it was held. There were seven – an imperial suite. In many palaces, however, such suites form a long and straight vista, while the folding doors slide back nearly to the walls on either hand, so that the view of the whole extent is scarcely impeded. Here the case was very different; as might have been expected from the duke's love of the *bizarre*. The apartments were so irregularly disposed that the vision embraced but little more than one at a time. There was a sharp turn at every twenty or thirty yards, and at each turn a novel effect. To the right and left, in the middle of each wall, a tall and narrow Gothic window looked out upon a closed corridor which pursued the windings of the suite. These windows were of stained glass whose color varied in accordance with the prevailing hue of the decorations of the chamber into which it opened. That at the eastern extremity was hung, for example, in blue – and vividly blue were its windows. The second chamber was purple in its ornaments and tapestries, and here the panes were purple. The third was green throughout, and so were the casements. The fourth was furnished and lighted with orange – the fifth with white – the sixth with violet. The seventh apartment was closely shrouded in black velvet tapestries that hung all over the ceiling and down the walls, falling in heavy folds upon a carpet of the same material and hue. But in this chamber only, the color of the windows failed to correspond with the decorations. The panes here were scarlet – a deep blood color. Now in no one of the seven apartments was there any lamp or candelabrum, amid the profusion of golden ornaments that lay scattered to and fro or depended from the roof. There was no light of any kind emanating from lamp or candle within the suite of chambers. But in the corridors that followed the suite, there stood, opposite to each window, a heavy tripod, bearing a brazier of fire, that projected its rays through the tinted glass and so glaringly illumined the room. And thus were produced a multitude of gaudy and fantastic appearances. But in the western or black chamber the effect of the firelight that streamed upon the dark hangings through the blood-tinted panes was ghastly in the extreme, and produced so wild a look upon the countenances of those who entered, that there were few of the company bold enough to set foot within its precincts at all.

It was in this apartment, also, that there stood against the western wall, a gigantic clock of ebony. Its pendulum swung to and fro with a dull, heavy, monotonous clang; and when the minute-hand made the circuit of the face, and the hour was to be stricken, there came from the brazen lungs of the clock a sound which was clear and loud and deep and exceedingly musical, but of so peculiar a note and emphasis that, at each lapse of an hour, the musicians of the orchestra were constrained to pause, momentarily, in their performance, to hearken to the sound; and thus the waltzers perforce ceased their evolutions; and there was a brief disconcert of the whole gay company; and, while the chimes of the clock yet rang, it was observed that the giddiest grew pale, and the more aged and sedate passed their hands over their brows as if in confused revery or meditation. But when the echoes had fully ceased, a light laughter at once pervaded the assembly; the musicians looked at each other and smiled as if at their own nervousness and folly, and made whispering vows, each to the other, that the next chiming of the clock should produce in them no similar emotion; and then, after the lapse of sixty minutes (which embrace three thousand and six hundred seconds of the Time that flies), there came yet another chiming of the clock, and then were the same disconcert and tremulousness and meditation as before.

But, in spite of these things, it was a gay and magnificent revel.

The tastes of the duke were peculiar. He had a fine eye for colors and effects. He disregarded the *decora* of mere fashion. His plans were bold and fiery, and his conceptions glowed with barbaric lustre. There are some who would have thought him mad. His followers felt that he was not. It was necessary to hear and see and touch him to be *sure* that he was not.

He had directed, in great part, the movable embellishments of the seven chambers, upon occasion of this great *fête*; and it was his own guiding taste which had given character to the masqueraders. Be sure they were grotesque. There were much glare and glitter and piquancy and phantasm – much of what has been since seen in 'Hernani'. There were arabesque figures with unsuited limbs and appointments. There were delirious fancies such as the madman fashions. There were much of the beautiful, much of the wanton, much of the *bizarre*, something of the terrible, and not a little of that which might have excited disgust. To and fro in the seven chambers there stalked, in fact, a multitude of dreams. And these – the dreams – writhed in and about, taking hue from the rooms, and causing the wild music of the orchestra to seem as the echo of their steps. And, anon, there strikes the ebony clock which stands in the hall of the velvet. And then, for a moment, all is still, and all is silent save the voice of the clock. The dreams are stiff-frozen as they stand. But the echoes of the chime die away – they have endured but an instant – and a light, half-subdued laughter floats after them as they depart. And now again the music swells, and the dreams live, and writhe to and fro more merrily than ever, taking hue from the many-tinted windows through which stream the rays from the tripods. But to the chamber which lies most westwardly of the seven there are now none of the maskers who venture; for the night is waning away; and there flows a ruddier light through the blood-colored panes; and the blackness of the sable drapery appals; and to him whose foot falls upon the sable carpet, there comes from the near clock of ebony a muffled peal more solemnly emphatic than any which reaches *their* ears who indulge in the more remote gaieties of the other apartments.

But these other apartments were densely crowded, and in them beat feverishly the heart of life. And the revel went whirlingly on, until at length there commenced the sounding of midnight upon the clock. And then the music ceased, as I have told; and the evolutions of the waltzers were quieted; and there was an uneasy cessation of all things as before. But now there were twelve strokes to be sounded by the bell of the clock; and thus it happened, perhaps that more of thought crept, with more of time, into the meditations of the thoughtful among those who revelled. And thus too, it happened, perhaps, that before the last echoes of the last chime had utterly sunk into silence, there were many individuals in the crowd who had found leisure to become aware of the presence of a masked figure which had arrested the attention of no single individual before. And the rumor of this new presence having spread itself whisperingly around, there arose at length from the whole company a buzz, or murmur, expressive of disapprobation and surprise – then, finally, of terror, of horror, and of disgust.

In an assembly of phantasms such as I have painted, it may well be supposed that no ordinary appearance could have excited such sensation. In truth the masquerade license of the night was nearly unlimited; but the figure in question had out-Heroded Herod, and gone beyond the bounds of even the prince's indefinite decorum. There are chords in the hearts of the most reckless which cannot be touched without emotion. Even with the utterly lost, to whom life and death are equally jests, there are matters of which no jest can be made. The whole company, indeed, seemed now deeply to feel that in the costume and bearing of the stranger neither wit nor propriety existed. The figure was tall and gaunt, and shrouded from head to foot in the habiliments of the grave. The mask which concealed the visage was made so nearly to resemble the countenance of a stiffened corpse that the closest scrutiny must have had difficulty in detecting the cheat. And yet all this might have been endured, if not approved, by the mad revellers around. But the mummer had gone so far as to assume the type of the Red Death. His vesture was dabbled in *blood* – and his broad brow, with all the features of the face, was besprinkled with the scarlet horror.

When the eyes of Prince Prospero fell upon this spectral image (which, with a slow and solemn movement, as if more fully to sustain its *rôle*, stalked to and fro among the waltzers) he was seen to be convulsed, in the first moment, with a strong shudder either of terror or distaste; but, in the next, his brow reddened with rage.

'Who dares' – he demanded hoarsely of the courtiers who stood near him – 'who dares insult us with this blasphemous mockery? Seize him and unmask him – that we may know whom we have to hang, at sunrise, from the battlements!'

It was in the eastern or blue chamber in which stood the Prince Prospero as he uttered these words. They rang throughout the seven rooms loudly and clearly, for the prince was a bold and robust man, and the music had become hushed at the waving of his hand.

It was in the blue room where stood the prince, with a group of pale courtiers by his side. At first, as he spoke, there was a slight rushing movement of this group in the direction of the intruder, who, at the moment was also near at hand, and now, with deliberate and stately step, made closer approach to the speaker. But from a certain nameless awe with which the mad assumptions of the mummer had inspired the whole party, there were found none who put forth hand to seize him; so that, unimpeded, he passed within a yard of the prince's person; and, while the vast assembly, as if with one impulse, shrank from the centres of the rooms to the walls, he made his way uninterruptedly, but with the same solemn and measured step which had distinguished him from the first, through the blue chamber to the purple – through the purple to the green – through the green to the orange – through this again to the white – and even thence to the violet, ere a decided movement had been made to arrest him. It was then, however, that the Prince Prospero, maddening with rage and the shame of his own momentary cowardice, rushed hurriedly through the six chambers, while none followed him on account of a deadly terror that had seized upon all. He bore aloft a drawn dagger, and had approached, in rapid impetuosity, to within three or four feet of the retreating figure, when the latter, having attained the extremity of the velvet apartment, turned suddenly and confronted his pursuer. There was a sharp cry – and the dagger dropped gleaming upon the sable carpet, upon which, instantly afterward, fell prostrate in death the Prince Prospero. Then, summoning the wild courage of despair, a throng of the revellers at once threw themselves into the black apartment, and, seizing the mummer, whose tall figure stood erect and motionless within the shadow of the ebony clock, gasped in unutterable horror at finding the grave cerements and corpse-like mask, which they handled with so violent a rudeness, untenanted by any tangible form.

And now was acknowledged the presence of the Red Death. He had come like a thief in the night. And one by one dropped the revellers in the blood-bedewed halls of their revel, and died each in the despairing posture of his fall. And the life of the ebony clock went out with that of the last of the gay. And the flames of the tripods expired. And Darkness and Decay and the Red Death held illimitable dominion over all.

The Monkey's Paw

W. W. Jacobs

I

Without, the night was cold and wet, but in the small parlour of Laburnam Villa the blinds were drawn and the fire burned brightly. Father and son were at chess, the former, who possessed ideas about the game involving radical changes, putting his king into such sharp and unnecessary perils that it even provoked comment from the white-haired old lady knitting placidly by the fire.

'Hark at the wind,' said Mr White, who, having seen a fatal mistake after it was too late, was amiably desirous of preventing his son from seeing it.

'I'm listening,' said the latter, grimly surveying the board as he stretched out his hand. 'Check.'

'I should hardly think that he'd come to-night,' said his father, with his hand poised over the board.

'Mate,' replied the son.

'That's the worst of living so far out,' bawled Mr White, with sudden and unlooked-for violence; 'of all the beastly, slushy, out-of-the-way places to live in, this is the worst. Pathway's a bog, and the road's a torrent. I don't know what people are thinking about. I suppose because only two houses in the road are let, they think it doesn't matter.'

'Never mind, dear,' said his wife, soothingly; 'perhaps you'll win the next one.'

Mr White looked up sharply, just in time to intercept a knowing glance between mother and son. The words died away on his lips, and he hid a guilty grin in his thin grey beard.

'There he is,' said Herbert White, as the gate banged to loudly and heavy footsteps came toward the door.

The old man rose with hospitable haste, and opening the door, was heard condoling with the new arrival. The new arrival also condoled with himself, so that Mrs White said, 'Tut, tut!' and coughed gently as her husband entered the room, followed by a tall, burly man, beady of eye and rubicund of visage.

'Sergeant-Major Morris,' he said, introducing him.

The sergeant-major shook hands, and taking the proffered seat by the fire, watched contentedly while his host got out whiskey and tumblers and stood a small copper kettle on the fire.

At the third glass his eyes got brighter, and he began to talk, the little family circle regarding with eager interest this visitor from distant parts, as he squared his broad shoulders in the chair and spoke of wild scenes and doughty deeds; of wars and plagues and strange peoples.

'Twenty-one years of it,' said Mr White, nodding at his wife and son. 'When he went away he was a slip of a youth in the warehouse. Now look at him.'

'He don't look to have taken much harm,' said Mrs White, politely.

'I'd like to go to India myself,' said the old man, 'just to look round a bit, you know.'

'Better where you are,' said the sergeant-major, shaking his head. He put down the empty glass, and sighing softly, shook it again.

'I should like to see those old temples and fakirs and jugglers,' said the old man. 'What was that you started telling me the other day about a monkey's paw or something, Morris?'

'Nothing,' said the soldier, hastily. 'Leastways nothing worth hearing.'

'Monkey's paw?' said Mrs White, curiously.

'Well, it's just a bit of what you might call magic, perhaps,' said the sergeant-major, offhandedly.

His three listeners leaned forward eagerly. The visitor absent-mindedly put his empty glass to his lips and then set it down again. His host filled it for him.

'To look at,' said the sergeant-major, fumbling in his pocket, 'it's just an ordinary little paw, dried to a mummy.'

He took something out of his pocket and proffered it. Mrs White drew back with a grimace, but her son, taking it, examined it curiously.

'And what is there special about it?' inquired Mr White as he took it from his son, and having examined it, placed it upon the table.

'It had a spell put on it by an old fakir,' said the sergeant-major, 'a very holy man. He wanted to show that fate ruled people's lives, and that those who interfered with it did so to their sorrow. He put a spell on it so that three separate men could each have three wishes from it.'

His manner was so impressive that his hearers were conscious that their light laughter jarred somewhat.

'Well, why don't you have three, sir?' said Herbert White, cleverly.

The soldier regarded him in the way that middle age is wont to regard presumptuous youth. 'I have,' he said, quietly, and his blotchy face whitened.

'And did you really have the three wishes granted?' asked Mrs White.

'I did,' said the sergeant-major, and his glass tapped against his strong teeth.

'And has anybody else wished?' persisted the old lady.

'The first man had his three wishes. Yes,' was the reply; 'I don't know what the first two were, but the third was for death. That's how I got the paw.'

His tones were so grave that a hush fell upon the group.

'If you've had your three wishes, it's no good to you now, then, Morris,' said the old man at last. 'What do you keep it for?'

The soldier shook his head. 'Fancy, I suppose,' he said, slowly. 'I did have some idea of selling it, but I don't think I will. It has caused enough mischief already. Besides, people won't buy. They think it's a fairy tale; some of them, and those who do think anything of it want to try it first and pay me afterward.'

'If you could have another three wishes,' said the old man, eyeing him keenly, 'would you have them?'

'I don't know,' said the other. 'I don't know.'

He took the paw, and dangling it between his forefinger and thumb, suddenly threw it upon the fire. White, with a slight cry, stooped down and snatched it off.

'Better let it burn,' said the soldier, solemnly.

'If you don't want it, Morris,' said the other, 'give it to me.'

'I won't,' said his friend, doggedly. 'I threw it on the fire. If you keep it, don't blame me for what happens. Pitch it on the fire again like a sensible man.'

The other shook his head and examined his new possession closely. 'How do you do it?' he inquired.

'Hold it up in your right hand and wish aloud,' said the sergeant-major, 'but I warn you of the consequences.'

'Sounds like the *Arabian Nights*,' said Mrs White, as she rose and began to set the supper. 'Don't you think you might wish for four pairs of hands for me?'

Her husband drew the talisman from pocket, and then all three burst into laughter as the sergeant-major, with a look of alarm on his face, caught him by the arm.

'If you must wish,' he said, gruffly, 'wish for something sensible.'

Mr White dropped it back in his pocket, and placing chairs, motioned his friend to the table. In the business of supper the talisman was partly forgotten, and afterward the three sat listening in an enthralled fashion to a second instalment of the soldier's adventures in India.

'If the tale about the monkey's paw is not more truthful than those he has been telling us,' said Herbert, as the door closed behind their guest, just in time for him to catch the last train, 'we sha'nt make much out of it.'

'Did you give him anything for it, father?' inquired Mrs White, regarding her husband closely.

'A trifle,' said he, colouring slightly. 'He didn't want it, but I made him take it. And he pressed me again to throw it away.'

'Likely,' said Herbert, with pretended horror. 'Why, we're going to be rich, and famous and happy. Wish to be an emperor, father, to begin with; then you can't be henpecked.'

He darted round the table, pursued by the maligned Mrs White armed with an antimacassar.

Mr White took the paw from his pocket and eyed it dubiously. 'I don't know what to wish for, and that's a fact,' he said, slowly. 'It seems to me I've got all I want.'

'If you only cleared the house, you'd be quite happy, wouldn't you?' said Herbert, with his hand on his shoulder. 'Well, wish for two hundred pounds, then; that 'll just do it.'

His father, smiling shamefacedly at his own credulity, held up the talisman, as his son, with a solemn face, somewhat marred by a wink at his mother, sat down at the piano and struck a few impressive chords.

'I wish for two hundred pounds,' said the old man distinctly.

A fine crash from the piano greeted the words, interrupted by a shuddering cry from the old man. His wife and son ran toward him.

'It moved,' he cried, with a glance of disgust at the object as it lay on the floor. 'As I wished, it twisted in my hand like a snake.'

'Well, I don't see the money,' said his son as he picked it up and placed it on the table, 'and I bet I never shall.'

'It must have been your fancy, father,' said his wife, regarding him anxiously.

He shook his head. 'Never mind, though; there's no harm done, but it gave me a shock all the same.'

They sat down by the fire again while the two men finished their pipes. Outside, the wind was higher than ever, and the old man started nervously at the sound of a door banging upstairs. A silence unusual and depressing settled upon all three, which lasted until the old couple rose to retire for the night.

'I expect you'll find the cash tied up in a big bag in the middle of your bed,' said Herbert, as he bade them good-night, 'and something horrible squatting up on top of the wardrobe watching you as you pocket your ill-gotten gains.'

He sat alone in the darkness, gazing at the dying fire, and seeing faces in it. The last face was so horrible and so simian that he gazed at it in amazement. It got so vivid that, with a little uneasy laugh, he felt on the table for a glass containing a little water to throw over it. His hand grasped the monkey's paw, and with a little shiver he wiped his hand on his coat and went up to bed.

II

In the brightness of the wintry sun next morning as it streamed over the breakfast table he laughed at his fears. There was an air of prosaic wholesomeness about the room which it had lacked on the previous night, and the dirty, shrivelled little paw was pitched on the sideboard with a carelessness which betokened no great belief in its virtues.

'I suppose all old soldiers are the same,' said Mrs White. 'The idea of our listening to such nonsense! How could wishes be granted in these days? And if they could, how could two hundred pounds hurt you, father?'

'Might drop on his head from the sky,' said the frivolous Herbert.

'Morris said the things happened so naturally,' said his father, 'that you might if you so wished attribute it to coincidence.'

'Well, don't break into the money before I come back,' said Herbert as he rose from the table. 'I'm afraid it'll turn you into a mean, avaricious man, and we shall have to disown you.'

His mother laughed, and following him to the door, watched him down the road; and returning to the breakfast table, was very happy at the expense of her husband's credulity. All of which did not prevent her from scurrying to the door at the postman's knock, nor prevent her from referring somewhat shortly to retired sergeant-majors of bibulous habits when she found that the post brought a tailor's bill.

'Herbert will have some more of his funny remarks, I expect, when he comes home,' she said, as they sat at dinner.

'I dare say,' said Mr White, pouring himself out some beer; 'but for all that, the thing moved in my hand; that I'll swear to.'

'You thought it did,' said the old lady soothingly.

'I say it did,' replied the other. 'There was no thought about it; I had just— What's the matter?'

His wife made no reply. She was watching the mysterious movements of a man outside, who, peering in an undecided fashion at the house, appeared to be trying to make up his mind to enter. In mental connection with the two hundred pounds, she noticed that the stranger was well dressed, and wore a silk hat of glossy newness. Three times he paused at the gate, and then walked on again. The fourth time he stood with his hand upon it, and then with sudden resolution flung it open and walked up the path. Mrs White at the same moment placed her hands behind her, and hurriedly unfastening the strings of her apron, put that useful article of apparel beneath the cushion of her chair.

She brought the stranger, who seemed ill at ease, into the room. He gazed at her furtively, and listened in a preoccupied fashion as the old lady apologized for the appearance of the room, and her husband's coat, a garment which he usually reserved for the garden. She then waited as patiently as her sex would permit, for him to broach his business, but he was at first strangely silent.

'I – was asked to call,' he said at last, and stooped and picked a piece of cotton from his trousers. 'I come from "Maw and Meggins".'

The old lady started. 'Is anything the matter?' she asked, breathlessly. 'Has anything happened to Herbert? What is it? What is it?'

Her husband interposed. 'There, there, mother,' he said, hastily. 'Sit down, and don't jump to conclusions. You've not brought bad news, I'm sure, sir'; and he eyed the other wistfully.

'I'm sorry –' began the visitor.

'Is he hurt?' demanded the mother, wildly.

The visitor bowed in assent. 'Badly hurt,' he said, quietly, 'but he is not in any pain.'

'Oh, thank God!' said the old woman, clasping her hands. 'Thank God for that! Thank—'

She broke off suddenly as the sinister meaning of the assurance dawned upon her and she saw the awful confirmation of her fears in the other's perverted face. She caught her breath, and turning to her slower-witted husband, laid her trembling old hand upon his. There was a long silence.

'He was caught in the machinery,' said the visitor at length in a low voice.

'Caught in the machinery,' repeated Mr White, in a dazed fashion, 'yes.'

He sat staring blankly out at the window, and taking his wife's hand between his own, pressed it as he had been wont to do in their old courting-days nearly forty years before.

'He was the only one left to us,' he said, turning gently to the visitor. 'It is hard.'

The other coughed, and rising, walked slowly to the window. 'The firm wished me to convey their sincere sympathy with you in your great loss,' he said, without looking round. 'I beg that you will understand I am only their servant and merely obeying orders.'

There was no reply; the old woman's face was white, her eyes staring, and her breath inaudible; on the husband's face was a look such as his friend the sergeant might have carried into his first action.

'I was to say that Maw and Meggins disclaim all responsibility,' continued the other. 'They admit no liability at all, but in consideration of your son's services, they wish to present you with a certain sum as compensation.'

Mr White dropped his wife's hand, and rising to his feet, gazed with a look of horror at his visitor. His dry lips shaped the words, 'How much?'

'Two hundred pounds,' was the answer.

Unconscious of his wife's shriek, the old man smiled faintly, put out his hands like a sightless man, and dropped, a senseless heap, to the floor.

III

In the huge new cemetery, some two miles distant, the old people buried their dead, and came back to a house steeped in shadow and silence. It was all over so quickly that at first they could hardly realize it, and remained in a state of expectation as though of something else to happen – something else which was to lighten this load, too heavy for old hearts to bear.

But the days passed, and expectation gave place to resignation – the hopeless resignation of the old, sometimes miscalled, apathy. Sometimes they hardly exchanged a word, for now they had nothing to talk about, and their days were long to weariness.

It was about a week after that the old man, waking suddenly in the night, stretched out his hand and found himself alone. The room was in darkness, and the sound of subdued weeping came from the window. He raised himself in bed and listened.

'Come back,' he said, tenderly. 'You will be cold.'

'It is colder for my son,' said the old woman, and wept afresh.

The sound of her sobs died away on his ears. The bed was warm, and his eyes heavy with sleep. He dozed fitfully, and then slept until a sudden wild cry from his wife awoke him with a start.

'*The paw!*' she cried wildly. 'The monkey's paw!'

He started up in alarm. 'Where? Where is it? What's the matter?'

She came stumbling across the room toward him. 'I want it,' she said, quietly. 'You've not destroyed it?'

'It's in the parlour, on the bracket,' he replied, marvelling. 'Why?'

She cried and laughed together, and bending over, kissed his cheek.

'I only just thought of it,' she said, hysterically. 'Why didn't I think of it before? Why didn't *you* think of it?'

'Think of what?' he questioned.

'The other two wishes,' she replied, rapidly. 'We've only had one.'

'Was not that enough?' he demanded, fiercely.

'No,' she cried, triumphantly; 'we'll have one more. Go down and get it quickly, and wish our boy alive again.'

The man sat up in bed and flung the bedclothes from his quaking limbs. 'Good God, you are mad!' he cried, aghast.

'Get it,' she panted; 'get it quickly, and wish— Oh, my boy, my boy!'

Her husband struck a match and lit the candle. 'Get back to bed,' he said, unsteadily. 'You don't know what you are saying.'

'We had the first wish granted,' said the old woman, feverishly; 'why not the second?'

'A coincidence,' stammered the old man.

'Go and get it and wish,' cried his wife, quivering with excitement.

The old man turned and regarded her, and his voice shook. 'He has been dead ten days, and besides he – I would not tell you else, but – I could only recognise him by his clothing. If he was too terrible for you to see then, how now?'

'Bring him back,' cried the old woman, and dragged him toward the door. 'Do you think I fear the child I have nursed?'

He went down in the darkness, and felt his way to the parlour, and then to the mantelpiece. The talisman was in its place, and a horrible fear that the unspoken wish might bring his mutilated son before him ere he could escape from the room seized upon him, and he caught his breath as he found that he had lost the direction of the door. His brow cold with sweat, he felt his way round the table, and groped along the wall until he found himself in the small passage with the unwholesome thing in his hand.

Even his wife's face seemed changed as he entered the room. It was white and expectant, and to his fears seemed to have an unnatural look upon it. He was afraid of her.

'*Wish!*' she cried, in a strong voice.

'It is foolish and wicked,' he faltered.

'*Wish!*' repeated his wife.

He raised his hand. 'I wish my son alive again.'

The talisman fell to the floor, and he regarded it fearfully. Then he sank trembling into a chair as the old woman, with burning eyes, walked to the window and raised the blind.

He sat until he was chilled with the cold, glancing occasionally at the figure of the old woman peering through the window. The candle-end, which had burned below the rim of the china candlestick, was throwing pulsating shadows on the ceiling and walls, until, with a flicker larger than the rest, it expired. The old man, with an unspeakable sense of relief at the failure of the talisman, crept back to his bed, and a minute or two afterward the old woman came silently and apathetically beside him.

Neither spoke, but lay silently listening to the ticking of the clock. A stair creaked, and a squeaky mouse scurried noisily through the wall. The darkness was oppressive, and after lying for some time screwing up his courage, he took the box of matches, and striking one, went downstairs for a candle.

At the foot of the stairs the match went out, and he paused to strike another; and at the same moment a knock, so quiet and stealthy as to be scarcely audible, sounded on the front door.

The matches fell from his hand and spilled in the passage. He stood motionless, his breath suspended until the knock was repeated. Then he turned and fled swiftly back to his room, and closed the door behind him. A third knock sounded through the house.

'*What's that?*' cried the old woman, starting up.

'A rat,' said the old man in shaking tones – 'a rat. It passed me on the stairs.'

His wife sat up in bed listening. A loud knock resounded through the house.

'It's Herbert!' she screamed. 'It's Herbert!'

She ran to the door, but her husband was before her, and catching her by the arm, held her tightly.

'What are you going to do?' he whispered hoarsely.

'It's my boy; it's Herbert!' she cried, struggling mechanically. 'I forgot it was two miles away. What are you holding me for? Let go. I must open the door.

'For God's sake don't let it in,' cried the old man, trembling.

'You're afraid of your own son,' she cried, struggling. 'Let me go. I'm coming, Herbert; I'm coming.'

There was another knock, and another. The old woman with a sudden wrench broke free and ran from the room. Her husband followed to the landing, and called after her appealingly as she hurried downstairs. He heard the chain rattle back and the bottom bolt drawn slowly and stiffly from the socket. Then the old woman's voice, strained and panting.

'The bolt,' she cried, loudly. 'Come down. I can't reach it.'

But her husband was on his hands and knees groping wildly on the floor in search of the paw. If he could only find it before the thing outside got in. A perfect fusillade of knocks reverberated through the house, and he heard the scraping of a chair as his wife put it down in the passage against the door. He heard the creaking of the bolt as it came slowly back, and at the same moment he found the monkey's paw, and frantically breathed his third and last wish.

The knocking ceased suddenly, although the echoes of it were still in the house. He heard the chair drawn back, and the door opened. A cold wind rushed up the staircase, and a long loud wail of disappointment and misery from his wife gave him courage to run down to her side, and then to the gate beyond. The street lamp flickering opposite shone on a quiet and deserted road.

'Oh, Whistle, and I'll Come to You, My Lad'

M. R. James

'I suppose you will be getting away pretty soon, now Full term is over, Professor,' said a person not in the story to the Professor of Ontography, soon after they had sat down next to each other at a feast in the hospitable hall of St James's College.

The Professor was young, neat, and precise in speech.

'Yes,' he said; 'my friends have been making me take up golf this term, and I mean to go to the East Coast – in point of fact to Burnstow – (I dare say you know it) for a week or ten days, to improve my game. I hope to get off tomorrow.'

'Oh, Parkins,' said his neighbour on the other side, 'if you are going to Burnstow, I wish you would look at the site of the Templars' preceptory, and let me know if you think it would be any good to have a dig there in the summer.'

It was, as you might suppose, a person of antiquarian pursuits who said this, but, since he merely appears in this prologue, there is no need to give his entitlements.

'Certainly,' said Parkins, the Professor: 'if you will describe to me whereabouts the site is, I will do my best to give you an idea of the lie of the land when I get back; or I could write to you about it, if you would tell me where you are likely to be.'

'Don't trouble to do that, thanks. It's only that I'm thinking of taking my family in that direction in the Long, and it occurred to me that, as very few of the English preceptories have ever been properly planned, I might have an opportunity of doing something useful on off-days.'

The Professor rather sniffed at the idea that planning out a preceptory could be described as useful. His neighbour continued:

'The site – I doubt if there is anything showing above ground – must be down quite close to the beach now. The sea has encroached tremendously, as you know, all along that bit of coast. I should think, from the map, that it must be about three-quarters of a mile from the Globe Inn, at the north end of the town. Where are you going to stay?'

'Well, *at* the Globe Inn, as a matter of fact,' said Parkins; 'I have engaged a room there. I couldn't get in anywhere else; most of the lodging-houses are shut up in winter, it seems; and, as it is, they tell me that the only room of any size I can have is really a double-bedded one, and that they haven't a corner in which to store the other bed, and so on. But I must have a fairly large room, for I am taking some books down, and mean to do a bit of work; and though I don't quite fancy having an empty bed – not to speak of two – in what I may call for the time being my study, I suppose I can manage to rough it for the short time I shall be there.'

'Do you call having an extra bed in your room roughing it, Parkins?' said a bluff person opposite. 'Look here, I shall come down and occupy it for a bit; it'll be company for you.'

The Professor quivered, but managed to laugh in a courteous manner.

'By all means, Rogers; there's nothing I should like better. But I'm afraid you would find it rather dull; you don't play golf, do you?'

'No, thank Heaven!' said rude Mr Rogers.

'Well, you see, when I'm not writing I shall most likely be out on the links, and that, as I say, would be rather dull for you, I'm afraid.'

'Oh, I don't know! There's certain to be somebody I know in the place; but, of course, if you don't want me, speak the word, Parkins; I shan't be offended. Truth, as you always tell us, is never offensive.'

Parkins was, indeed, scrupulously polite and strictly truthful. It is to be feared that Mr Rogers sometimes practised upon his knowledge of these characteristics. In Parkins's breast there was a conflict now raging, which for a moment or two did not allow him to answer. That interval being over, he said:

'Well, if you want the exact truth, Rogers, I was considering whether the room I speak of would really be large enough to accommodate us both comfortably; and also whether (mind, I shouldn't have said this if you hadn't pressed me) you would not constitute something in the nature of a hindrance to my work.'

Rogers laughed loudly.

'Well done, Parkins!' he said. 'It's all right. I promise not to interrupt your work; don't you disturb yourself about that. No, I won't come if you don't want me; but I thought I should do so nicely to keep the ghosts off.' Here he might have been seen to wink and to nudge his next neighbour. Parkins might also have been seen to become pink. 'I beg pardon, Parkins,' Rogers continued; 'I oughtn't to have said that. I forgot you didn't like levity on these topics.'

'Well,' Parkins said, 'as you have mentioned the matter, I freely own that I do *not* like careless talk about what you call ghosts. A man in my position,' he went on, raising his voice a little, 'cannot, I find, be too careful about appearing to sanction the current beliefs on such subjects. As you know, Rogers, or as you ought to know; for I think I have never concealed my views –'

'No, you certainly have not, old man,' put in Rogers *sotto voce*.

'– I hold that any semblance, any appearance of concession to the view that such things might exist is equivalent to a renunciation of all that I hold most sacred. But I'm afraid I have not succeeded in securing your attention.'

'Your *undivided* attention, was what Dr Blimber actually *said*,'*

* Mr Rogers was wrong, *vide Dombey and Son*, Chapter xii.

Rogers interrupted, with every appearance of an earnest desire for accuracy. 'But I beg your pardon, Parkins; I'm stopping you.'

'No, not at all,' said Parkins. 'I don't remember Blimber; perhaps he was before my time. But I needn't go on. I'm sure you know what I mean.'

'Yes, yes,' said Rogers, rather hastily – 'just so. We'll go into it fully at Burnstow, or somewhere.'

In repeating the above dialogue I have tried to give the impression which it made on me, that Parkins was something of an old woman – rather hen-like, perhaps, in his little ways; totally destitute, alas! of the sense of humour, but at the same time dauntless and sincere in his convictions, and a man deserving of the greatest respect. Whether or not the reader has gathered so much, that was the character which Parkins had.

On the following day Parkins did, as he had hoped, succeed in getting away from his college, and in arriving at Burnstow. He was made welcome at the Globe Inn, was safely installed in the large double-bedded room of which we have heard, and was able before retiring to rest to arrange his materials for work in apple-pie order upon a commodious table which occupied the outer end of the room, and was surrounded on three sides by windows looking out seaward; that is to say, the central window looked straight out to sea, and those on the left and right commanded prospects along the shore to the north and south respectively. On the south you saw the village of Burnstow. On the north no houses were to be seen, but only the beach and the low cliff backing it. Immediately in front was a strip – not considerable – of rough grass, dotted with old anchors, capstans, and so forth; then a broad path; then the beach. Whatever may have been the original distance between the Globe Inn and the sea, not more than sixty yards now separated them.

The rest of the population of the inn was, of course, a golfing one, and included few elements that call for a special description.

The most conspicuous figure was, perhaps, that of an *ancien militaire*, secretary of a London club, and possessed of a voice of incredible strength, and of views of a pronouncedly Protestant type. These were apt to find utterance after his attendance upon the ministrations of the Vicar, an estimable man with inclinations towards a picturesque ritual, which he gallantly kept down as far as he could out of deference to East Anglian tradition.

Professor Parkins, one of whose principal characteristics was pluck, spent the greater part of the day following his arrival at Burnstow in what he had called improving his game, in company with this Colonel Wilson: and during the afternoon – whether the process of improvement were to blame or not, I am not sure – the Colonel's demeanour assumed a colouring so lurid that even Parkins jibbed at the thought of walking home with him from the links. He determined, after a short and furtive look at that bristling moustache and those incarnadined features, that it would be wiser to allow the influences of tea and tobacco to do what they could with the Colonel before the dinner-hour should render a meeting inevitable.

'I might walk home tonight along the beach,' he reflected – 'yes, and take a look – there will be light enough for that – at the ruins of which Disney was talking. I don't exactly know where they are, by the way; but I expect I can hardly help stumbling on them.'

This he accomplished, I may say, in the most literal sense, for in picking his way from the links to the shingle beach his foot caught, partly in a gorse-root and partly in a biggish stone, and over he went. When he got up and surveyed his surroundings, he found himself in a patch of somewhat broken ground covered with small depressions and mounds. These latter, when he came to examine them, proved to be simply masses of flints embedded in mortar and grown over with turf. He must, he quite rightly concluded, be on the site of the preceptory he had promised to look at. It seemed not unlikely to reward the spade of the explorer; enough of the foundations was probably left at no great depth to throw a good deal of light on the general plan. He remembered vaguely that the Templars, to whom this site had belonged, were in the habit of building round churches, and he thought a particular series of the humps or mounds near him did appear to be arranged in something of a circular form. Few people can resist the temptation to try a little amateur research in a department quite outside their own, if only for the satisfaction of showing how successful they would have been had they only taken it up seriously. Our Professor, however, if he felt something of this mean desire, was also truly anxious to oblige Mr Disney. So he paced with care the circular area he had noticed, and wrote down its rough dimensions in his pocket-book. Then he proceeded to examine an oblong eminence which lay east of the centre of the circle, and seemed to his thinking likely to be the base of a platform or altar. At one end of it, the northern, a patch of the turf was gone – removed by some boy or other creature *ferae naturae*. It might, he thought, be as well to probe the soil here for evidences of masonry, and he took out his knife and began scraping away the earth. And now followed another little discovery: a portion of soil fell inward as he scraped, and disclosed a small cavity. He lighted one match after another to help him to see of what nature the hole was, but the wind was too strong for them all. By tapping and scratching the sides with his knife, however, he was able to make out that it must be an artificial hole in masonry. It was rectangular, and the sides, top, and bottom, if not actually plastered, were smooth and regular. Of course it was empty. No! As he withdrew the knife he heard a metallic clink, and when he introduced his hand it met with a cylindrical object lying on the floor of the hole. Naturally enough, he picked it up, and when he brought it into the light, now fast fading, he could see that it, too, was of man's making – a metal tube about four inches long, and evidently of some considerable age.

By the time Parkins had made sure that there was nothing else in this odd receptacle, it was too late and too dark for him to think of undertaking any further search. What he had done had proved so unexpectedly interesting that he determined to sacrifice a little more of the daylight on the morrow to archaeology. The object which he now had safe in his pocket was bound to be of some slight value at least, he felt sure.

Bleak and solemn was the view on which he took a last look before starting homeward. A faint yellow light in the west showed the links, on which a few figures moving towards the club-house were still visible, the squat martello tower, the lights of Aldsey village, the pale ribbon of sands intersected at intervals by black wooden groynes, the dim and murmuring sea. The wind was bitter from the north, but was at his back when he set out for the Globe. He quickly rattled and clashed through the shingle and gained the sand, upon which, but for the groynes which had to be got over every few yards, the going was both good and quiet. One last look behind, to measure the distance he had made since leaving the ruined Templars' church, showed him a prospect of company on his walk, in the shape of a rather indistinct personage, who seemed to be making great efforts to catch up with him, but made little, if any, progress. I mean that there was an appearance of running about his movements, but that the distance between him and Parkins did not seem materially to lessen. So, at least, Parkins thought, and decided that he almost certainly did not know him, and that it would be absurd to wait until he came up. For all that, company, he began to think, would really be very welcome on that lonely shore, if only you could choose your companion. In his unenlightened days he had read of meetings in such places which even now would hardly bear thinking of. He went on thinking of them, however, until he reached home, and particularly of one which catches most people's fancy at some time of their childhood. 'Now I saw in my dream that Christian had gone but a very little way when he saw a foul fiend coming over the field to meet him.' 'What should I do now,' he thought, 'if I looked back and caught sight of a black figure sharply defined against the yellow sky, and saw that it had horns and wings? I wonder whether I should stand or run for it. Luckily, the gentleman behind is not of that kind, and he seems to be about as far off now as when I saw him first. Well, at this rate he won't get his dinner as soon as I shall; and, dear me! it's within a quarter of an hour of the time now. I must run!'

Parkins had, in fact, very little time for dressing. When he met the Colonel at dinner, Peace – or as much of her as that gentleman could manage – reigned once more in the military bosom; nor was she put to flight in the hours of bridge that followed dinner, for Parkins was a more than respectable player. When, therefore, he retired towards twelve o'clock, he felt that he had spent his evening in quite a satisfactory way, and that, even for so long as a fortnight or three weeks, life at the Globe would be supportable under similar conditions – 'especially,' thought he, 'if I go on improving my game.'

As he went along the passages he met the boots of the Globe, who stopped and said:

'Beg your pardon, sir, but as I was a-brushing your coat just now there was somethink fell out of the pocket. I put it on your chest of drawers, sir, in your room, sir – a piece of a pipe or somethink of that, sir. Thank you, sir. You'll find it on your chest of drawers, sir – yes, sir. Good night, sir.'

The speech served to remind Parkins of his little discovery of that afternoon. It was with some considerable curiosity that he turned it over by the light of his candles. It was of bronze, he now saw, and was shaped very much after the manner of the modern dog-whistle; in fact it was – yes, certainly it was – actually no more nor less than a whistle. He put it to his lips, but it was quite full of a fine, caked-up sand or earth, which would not yield to knocking, but must be loosened with a knife. Tidy as ever in his habits, Parkins cleared out the earth on to a piece of paper, and took the latter to the window to empty it out. The night was clear and bright, as he saw when he had opened the casement, and he stopped for an instant to look at the sea and note a belated wanderer stationed on the shore in front of the inn. Then he shut the window, a little surprised at the late hours people kept at Burnstow, and took his whistle to the light again. Why, surely there were marks on it, and not merely marks, but letters! A very little rubbing rendered the deeply-cut inscription quite legible, but the Professor had to confess, after some earnest thought, that the meaning of it was as obscure to him as the writing on the wall to Belshazzar. There were legends both on the front and on the back of the whistle. The one read thus:

FLA
FUR BIS
FLE

The other:

QUIS EST ISTE QUI VENIT

'I ought to be able to make it out,' he thought; 'but I suppose I am a little rusty in my Latin. When I come to think of it, I don't believe I even know the word for a whistle. The long one does seem simple enough. It ought to mean, "Who is this who is coming?" Well, the best way to find out is evidently to whistle for him.'

He blew tentatively and stopped suddenly, startled and yet pleased at the note he had elicited. It had a quality of infinite distance in it, and, soft as it was, he somehow felt it must be audible for miles round. It was a sound, too, that seemed to have the power (which many scents possess) of forming pictures in the brain. He saw quite clearly for a moment a vision of a wide, dark expanse at night, with a fresh wind blowing and in the midst a lonely figure – how employed, he could not tell. Perhaps he would have seen more had not the picture been broken by the sudden surge of a gust of wind against his casement, so sudden that it made him look up, just in time to see the white glint of a sea-bird's wing somewhere outside the dark panes.

The sound of the whistle had so fascinated him that he could not help trying it once more, this time more boldly. The note was little, if at all, louder than before, and repetition broke the illusion – no picture followed, as he had half hoped it might. 'But what is this? Goodness! what force the wind can get up in a few minutes! What a tremendous gust! There! I knew that window-fastening was no use! Ah! I thought so – both candles out. It's enough to tear the room to pieces.'

The first thing was to get the window shut. While you might count twenty Parkins was struggling with the small casement, and felt almost as if he were pushing back a sturdy burglar, so strong was the pressure. It slackened all at once, and the window banged to and latched itself. Now to relight the candles and see what damage, if any, had been done. No, nothing seemed amiss; no glass even was broken in the casement. But the noise had evidently roused at least one member of the household: the Colonel was to be heard stumping in his stockinged feet on the floor above, and growling.

Quickly as it had risen, the wind did not fall at once. On it went, moaning and rushing past the house, at times rising to a cry so desolate that, as Parkins disinterestedly said, it might have made fanciful people feel quite uncomfortable; even the unimaginative, he thought after a quarter of an hour, might be happier without it.

Whether it was the wind, or the excitement of golf, or of the researches in the preceptory that kept Parkins awake, he was not sure. Awake he remained, in any case, long enough to fancy (as I am afraid I often do myself under such conditions) that he was the victim of all manner of fatal disorders: he would lie counting the beats of his heart, convinced that it was going to stop work every moment, and would entertain grave suspicions of his lungs, brain, liver, etc. – suspicions which he was sure would be dispelled by the return of daylight, but which until then refused to be put aside. He found a little vicarious comfort in the idea that someone else was in the same boat. A near neighbour (in the darkness it was not easy to tell his direction) was tossing and rustling in his bed, too.

The next stage was that Parkins shut his eyes and determined to give sleep every chance. Here again over-excitement asserted itself in another form – that of making pictures. *Experto crede*, pictures do come to the closed eyes of one trying to sleep, and are often so little to his taste that he must open his eyes and disperse them.

Parkins's experience on this occasion was a very distressing one. He found that the picture which presented itself to him was continuous. When he opened his eyes, of course, it went; but when he shut them once more it framed itself afresh, and acted itself out again, neither quicker nor slower than before. What he saw was this:

A long stretch of shore – shingle edged by sand, and intersected at short intervals with black groynes running down to the water – a scene, in fact, so like that of his afternoon's walk that, in the absence of any landmark, it could not be distinguished therefrom. The light was obscure, conveying an impression of gathering storm, late winter evening, and slight cold rain. On this bleak stage at first no actor was visible. Then, in the distance, a bobbing black object appeared; a moment more, and it was a man running, jumping, clambering over the groynes, and every few seconds looking eagerly back. The nearer he came the more obvious it was that he was not only anxious, but even terribly frightened, though his face was not to be distinguished. He was, moreover, almost at the end of his strength. On he came; each successive obstacle seemed to cause him more difficulty than the last. 'Will he get over this next one?' thought Parkins; 'it seems a little higher than the others.' Yes; half-climbing, half throwing himself, he did get over, and fell all in a heap on the other side (the side nearest to the spectator). There, as if really unable to get up again, he remained crouching under the groyne, looking up in an attitude of painful anxiety.

So far no cause whatever for the fear of the runner had been shown; but now there began to be seen, far up the shore, a little flicker of something light-coloured moving to and fro with great swiftness and irregularity. Rapidly growing larger, it, too, declared itself as a figure in pale, fluttering draperies, ill-defined. There was something about its motion which made Parkins very unwilling to see it at close quarters. It would stop, raise arms, bow itself toward the sand, then run stooping across the beach to the water-edge and back again; and then, rising upright, once more continue its course forward at a speed that was startling and terrifying. The moment came when the pursuer was hovering about from left to right only a few yards beyond the groyne where the runner lay in hiding. After two or three ineffectual castings hither and thither it came to a stop, stood upright, with arms raised high, and then darted straight forward towards the groyne.

It was at this point that Parkins always failed in his resolution to keep his eyes shut. With many misgivings as to incipient failure of eyesight, overworked brain, excessive smoking, and so on, he finally resigned himself to light his candle, get out a book, and pass the night waking, rather than be tormented by this persistent panorama, which he saw clearly enough could only be a morbid reflection of his walk and his thoughts on that very day.

The scraping of match on box and the glare of light must have startled some creatures of the night – rats or what not – which he heard scurry across the floor from the side of his bed with much rustling. Dear, dear! the match is out! Fool that it is! But the second one burnt better, and a candle and book were duly procured, over which Parkins pored till sleep of a wholesome kind came upon him, and that in no long space. For about the first time in his orderly and prudent life he forgot to blow out the candle, and when he was called next morning at eight there was still a flicker in the socket and a sad mess of guttered grease on the top of the little table.

After breakfast he was in his room, putting the finishing touches to his golfing costume – fortune had again allotted the Colonel to him for a partner – when one of the maids came in.

'Oh, if you please,' she said, 'would you like any extra blankets on your bed, sir?'

'Ah! thank you,' said Parkins. 'Yes, I think I should like one. It seems likely to turn rather colder.'

In a very short time the maid was back with the blanket.

'Which bed should I put it on, sir?' she asked.

'What? Why, that one – the one I slept in last night,' he said, pointing to it.

'Oh yes! I beg your pardon, sir, but you seemed to have tried both of 'em; leastways, we had to make 'em both up this morning.'

'Really? How very absurd!' said Parkins. 'I certainly never touched the other, except to lay some things on it. Did it actually seem to have been slept in?'

'Oh yes, sir!' said the maid. 'Why, all the things was crumpled and throwed about all ways, if you'll excuse me, sir – quite as if anyone 'adn't passed but a very poor night, sir.'

'Dear me,' said Parkins. 'Well, I may have disordered it more than I thought when I unpacked my things. I'm very sorry to have given you the extra trouble, I'm sure. I expect a friend of mine soon, by the way – a gentleman from Cambridge – to come and occupy it for a night or two. That will be all right, I suppose, won't it?'

'Oh yes, to be sure, sir. Thank you, sir. It's no trouble, I'm sure,' said the maid, and departed to giggle with her colleagues.

Parkins set forth, with a stern determination to improve his game.

I am glad to be able to report that he succeeded so far in this enterprise that the Colonel, who had been rather repining at the prospect of a second day's play in his company, became quite chatty as the morning advanced; and his voice boomed out over the flats, as certain also of our own minor poets have said, 'like some great bourdon in a minster tower'.

'Extraordinary wind, that, we had last night,' he said. 'In my old home we should have said someone had been whistling for it.'

'Should you, indeed!' said Parkins. 'Is there a superstition of that kind still current in your part of the country?'

'I don't know about superstition,' said the Colonel. 'They believe in it all over Denmark and Norway, as well as on the Yorkshire coast; and my experience is, mind you, that there's generally something at the bottom of what these country-folk hold to, and have held to for generations. But it's your drive' (or whatever it might have been: the golfing reader will have to imagine appropriate digressions at the proper intervals).

When conversation was resumed, Parkins said, with a slight hesitancy:

'Apropos of what you were saying just now, Colonel, I think I ought to tell you that my own views on such subjects are very strong. I am, in fact, a convinced disbeliever in what is called the "supernatural".'

'What!' said the Colonel, 'do you mean to tell me you don't believe in second-sight, or ghosts, or anything of that kind?'

'In nothing whatever of that kind,' returned Parkins firmly.

'Well,' said the Colonel, 'but it appears to me at that rate, sir, that you must be little better than a Sadducee.'

Parkins was on the point of answering that, in his opinion, the Sadducees were the most sensible persons he had ever read of in the Old Testament; but, feeling some doubt as to whether much mention of them was to be found in that work, he preferred to laugh the accusation off.

'Perhaps I am,' he said; 'but – Here, give me my cleek, boy! – Excuse me one moment, Colonel.' A short interval. 'Now, as to whistling for the wind, let me give you my theory about it. The laws which govern winds are really not at all perfectly known – to fisher-folk and such, of course, not known at all. A man or woman of eccentric habits, perhaps, or a stranger, is seen repeatedly on the beach at some unusual hour, and is heard whistling. Soon afterwards a violent wind rises; a man who could read the sky perfectly or who possessed a barometer could have foretold that it would. The simple people of a fishing-village have no barometers, and only a few rough rules for prophesying weather. What more natural than that the eccentric personage I postulated should be regarded as having raised the wind, or that he or she should clutch eagerly at the reputation of being able to do so? Now, take last night's wind: as it happens, I myself was whistling. I blew a whistle twice, and the wind seemed to come absolutely in answer to my call. If anyone had seen me –'

The audience had been a little restive under this harangue, and Parkins had, I fear, fallen somewhat into the tone of a lecturer; but at the last sentence the Colonel stopped.

'Whistling, were you?' he said. 'And what sort of whistle did you use? Play this stroke first.' Interval.

'About that whistle you were asking, Colonel. It's rather a curious one. I have it in my – No; I see I've left it in my room. As a matter of fact, I found it yesterday.'

And then Parkins narrated the manner of his discovery of the whistle, upon hearing which the Colonel grunted, and opined that, in Parkins's place, he should himself be careful about using a thing that had belonged to a set of Papists, of whom, speaking generally, it might be affirmed that you never knew what they might not have been up to. From this topic he diverged to the enormities of the Vicar, who had given notice on the previous Sunday that Friday would be the Feast of St Thomas the Apostle, and that there would be a service at eleven o'clock in the church. This and other similar proceedings constituted in the Colonel's view a strong presumption that the Vicar was a concealed Papist, if not a Jesuit; and Parkins, who could not very readily follow the Colonel in this region, did not disagree with him. In fact, they got on so well together in the morning that there was no talk on either side of their separating after lunch.

Both continued to play well during the afternoon, or, at least, well enough to make them forget everything else until the light began to fail them. Not until then did Parkins remember that he had meant to do some more investigating at the preceptory; but it was of no great importance, he reflected. One day was as good as another; he might as well go home with the Colonel.

As they turned the corner of the house, the Colonel was almost knocked down by a boy who rushed into him at the very top of his speed, and then, instead of running away, remained hanging on to him and panting. The first words of the warrior were naturally those of reproof and objurgation, but he very quickly discerned that the boy was almost speechless with fright. Inquiries were useless at first. When the boy got his breath he began to howl, and still clung to the Colonel's legs. He was at last detached, but continued to howl.

'What in the world is the matter with you? What have you been up to? What have you seen?' said the two men.

'Ow, I seen it wive at me out of the winder,' wailed the boy, 'and I don't like it.'

'What window?' said the irritated Colonel. 'Come, pull yourself together, my boy.'

'The front winder it was, at the 'otel,' said the boy.

At this point Parkins was in favour of sending the boy home, but the Colonel refused; he wanted to get to the bottom of it, he said; it was most dangerous to give a boy such a fright as this one had had, and if it turned out that people had been playing jokes, they should suffer for it in some way. And by a series of questions he made out this story: The boy had been playing about on the grass in front of the Globe with some others; then they had gone home to their teas, and he was just going, when he happened to look up at the front winder and see it a-wiving at him. *It* seemed to be a figure of some sort, in white as far as he knew – couldn't see its face; but it wived at him, and it warn't a right thing – not to say not a right person. Was there a light in the room? No, he didn't think to look if there was a light. Which was the window? Was it the top one or the second one? The seckind one it was – the big winder what got two little uns at the sides.

'Very well, my boy,' said the Colonel, after a few more questions. 'You run away home now. I expect it was some person trying to give you a start. Another time, like a brave English boy, you just throw a stone – well, no, not that exactly, but you go and speak to the waiter, or to Mr Simpson, the landlord, and – yes – and say that I advised you to do so.'

The boy's face expressed some of the doubt he felt as to the likelihood of Mr Simpson's lending a favourable ear to his complaint, but the Colonel did not appear to perceive this, and went on:

'And here's a sixpence – no, I see it's a shilling – and you be off home, and don't think any more about it.'

The youth hurried off with agitated thanks, and the Colonel and Parkins went round to the front of the Globe and reconnoitred. There was only one window answering to the description they had been hearing.

'Well, that's curious,' said Parkins; 'it's evidently my window the lad was talking about. Will you come up for a moment, Colonel Wilson? We ought to be able to see if anyone has been taking liberties in my room.'

They were soon in the passage, and Parkins made as if to open the door. Then he stopped and felt in his pockets.

'This is more serious than I thought,' was his next remark. 'I remember now that before I started this morning I locked the door. It is locked now, and, what is more, here is the key.' And he held it up. 'Now,' he went on, 'if the servants are in the habit of going into one's room during the day when one is away, I can only say that – well, that I don't approve of it at all.' Conscious of a somewhat weak climax, he busied himself in opening the door (which was indeed locked) and in lighting candles. 'No,' he said, 'nothing seems disturbed.'

'Except your bed,' put in the Colonel.

'Excuse me, that isn't my bed,' said Parkins. 'I don't use that one. But it does look as if someone has been playing tricks with it.'

It certainly did: the clothes were bundled up and twisted together in a most tortuous confusion. Parkins pondered.

'That must be it,' he said at last: 'I disordered the clothes last night in unpacking, and they haven't made it since. Perhaps they came in to make it, and that boy saw them through the window; and then they were called away and locked the door after them. Yes, I think that must be it.'

'Well, ring and ask,' said the Colonel, and this appealed to Parkins as practical.

The maid appeared, and, to make a long story short, deposed that she had made the bed in the morning when the gentleman was in the room, and hadn't been there since. No, she hadn't no other key. Mr Simpson he kep' the keys; he'd be able to tell the gentleman if anyone had been up.

This was a puzzle. Investigation showed that nothing of value had been taken, and Parkins remembered the disposition of the small objects on tables and so forth well enough to be pretty sure that no pranks had been played with them. Mr and Mrs Simpson furthermore agreed that neither of them had given the duplicate key of the room to any person whatever during the day. Nor could Parkins, fair-minded man as he was, detect anything in the demeanour of master, mistress, or maid that indicated guilt. He was much more inclined to think that the boy had been imposing on the Colonel.

The latter was unwontedly silent and pensive at dinner and throughout the evening. When he bade good night to Parkins, he murmured in a gruff undertone:

'You know where I am if you want me during the night.'

'Why, yes, thank you, Colonel Wilson, I think I do; but there isn't much prospect of my disturbing you, I hope. By the way,' he added, 'did I show you that old whistle I spoke of? I think not. Well, here it is.'

The Colonel turned it over gingerly in the light of the candle.

'Can you make anything of the inscription?' asked Parkins, as he took it back.

'No, not in this light. What do you mean to do with it?'

'Oh, well, when I get back to Cambridge I shall submit it to some of the archaeologists there, and see what they think of it; and very likely, if they consider it worth having, I may present it to one of the museums.'

''M!' said the Colonel. 'Well, you may be right. All I know is that, if it were mine, I should chuck it straight into the sea. It's no use talking, I'm well aware, but I expect that with you it's a case of live and learn. I hope so, I'm sure, and I wish you a good night.'

He turned away, leaving Parkins in act to speak at the bottom of the stair, and soon each was in his own bedroom.

By some unfortunate accident, there were neither blinds nor curtains to the windows of the Professor's room. The previous night he had thought little of this, but tonight there seemed every prospect of a bright moon rising to shine directly on his bed, and probably wake him later on. When he noticed this he was a good deal annoyed, but, with an ingenuity which I can only envy, he succeeded in rigging up, with the help of a railway-rug, some safety-pins, and a stick and umbrella, a screen which, if it only held together, would completely keep the moonlight off his bed. And shortly afterwards he was comfortably in that bed. When he had read a somewhat solid work long enough to produce a decided wish for sleep, he cast a drowsy glance round the room, blew out the candle, and fell back upon the pillow.

He must have slept soundly for an hour or more, when a sudden clatter shook him up in a most unwelcome manner. In a moment he realised what had happened: his carefully constructed screen had given way, and a very bright frosty moon was shining directly on his face. This was highly annoying. Could he possibly get up and reconstruct the screen? or could he manage to sleep if he did not?

For some minutes he lay and pondered over the possibilities; then he turned over sharply, and with all his eyes open lay breathlessly listening. There had been a movement, he was sure, in the empty bed on the opposite side of the room. Tomorrow he would have it moved, for there must be rats or something playing about in it. It was quiet now. No! the commotion began again. There was a rustling and shaking: surely more than any rat could cause.

I can figure to myself something of the Professor's bewilderment and horror, for I have in a dream thirty years back seen the same thing happen; but the reader will hardly, perhaps, imagine how dreadful it was to him to see a figure suddenly sit up in what he had known was an empty bed. He was out of his own bed in one bound, and made a dash towards the window, where lay his only weapon, the stick with which he had propped his screen. This was, as it turned out, the worst thing he could have done, because the personage in the empty bed, with a sudden smooth motion, slipped from the bed and took up a position, with outspread arms, between the two beds, and in front of the door. Parkins watched it in a horrid perplexity. Somehow, the idea of getting past it and escaping through the door was intolerable to him; he could not have borne – he didn't know why – to touch it; and as for its touching him, he would sooner dash himself through the window than have that happen. It stood for the moment in a band of dark shadow, and he had not seen what its face was like. Now it began to move, in a stooping posture, and all at once the spectator realised, with some horror and some relief, that it must be blind, for it seemed to feel about it with its muffled arms in a groping and random fashion. Turning half away from him, it became suddenly conscious of the bed he had just left, and darted towards it, and bent over and felt the pillows in a way which made Parkins shudder as he had never in his life thought it possible. In a very few moments it seemed to know that the bed was empty, and then, moving forward into the area of light and facing the window, it showed for the first time what manner of thing it was.

Parkins, who very much dislikes being questioned about it, did once describe something of it in my hearing, and I gathered that what he chiefly remembers about it is a horrible, an intensely horrible, face *of crumpled linen*. What expression he read upon it he could not or would not tell, but that the fear of it went nigh to maddening him is certain.

But he was not at leisure to watch it for long. With formidable quickness it moved into the middle of the room, and, as it groped and waved, one corner of its draperies swept across Parkins's face. He could not – though he knew how perilous a sound was – he could not keep back a cry of disgust, and this gave the searcher an instant clue. It leapt towards him upon the instant, and the next moment he was half-way through the window backwards, uttering cry upon cry at the utmost pitch of his voice, and the linen face was thrust close into his own. At this, almost the last possible second, deliverance came, as you will have guessed: the Colonel burst the door open, and was just in time to see the dreadful group at the window. When he reached the figures only one was left. Parkins sank forward into the room in a faint, and before him on the floor lay a tumbled heap of bedclothes.

Colonel Wilson asked no questions, but busied himself in keeping everyone else out of the room and in getting Parkins back to his bed; and himself, wrapped in a rug, occupied the other bed for the rest of the night. Early on the next day Rogers arrived, more welcome than he would have been a day before, and the three of them held a very long consultation in the Professor's room. At the end of it the Colonel left the hotel door carrying a small object between his finger and thumb, which he cast as far into the sea as a very brawny arm could send it. Later on the smoke of a burning ascended from the back premises of the Globe.

Exactly what explanation was patched up for the staff and visitors at the hotel I must confess I do not recollect. The Professor was somehow cleared of the ready suspicion of delirium tremens, and the hotel of the reputation of a troubled house.

There is not much question as to what would have happened to Parkins if the Colonel had not intervened when he did. He would either have fallen out of the window or else lost his wits. But it is not so evident what more the creature that came in answer to the whistle could have done than frighten. There seemed to be absolutely nothing material about it save the bedclothes of which it had made itself a body. The Colonel, who remembered a not very dissimilar occurrence in India, was of opinion that if Parkins had closed with it it could really have done very little, and that its one power was that of frightening. The whole thing, he said, served to confirm his opinion of the Church of Rome.

There is really nothing more to tell, but, as you may imagine, the Professor's views on certain points are less clear cut than they used to be. His nerves, too, have suffered: he cannot even now see a surplice hanging on a door quite unmoved, and the spectacle of a scarecrow in a field late on a winter afternoon has cost him more than one sleepless night.

A Wicked Voice

Vernon Lee

They have been congratulating me again to-day upon being the only composer of our days – of these days of deafening orchestral effects and poetical quackery – who has despised the newfangled nonsense of Wagner, and returned boldly to the traditions of Handel and Gluck and the divine Mozart, to the supremacy of melody and the respect of the human voice.

O cursed human voice, violin of flesh and blood, fashioned with the subtle tools, the cunning hands, of Satan! O execrable art of singing, have you not wrought mischief enough in the past, degrading so much noble genius, corrupting the purity of Mozart, reducing Handel to a writer of high-class singing-exercises, and defrauding the world of the only inspiration worthy of Sophocles and Euripides, the poetry of the great poet Gluck? Is it not enough to have dishonoured a whole century in idolatry of that wicked and contemptible wretch the singer, without persecuting an obscure young composer of our days, whose only wealth is his love of nobility in art, and perhaps some few grains of genius?

And then they compliment me upon the perfection with which I imitate the style of the great dead masters; or ask me very seriously whether, even if I could gain over the modern public to this bygone style of music, I could hope to find singers to perform it. Sometimes, when people talk as they have been talking to-day, and laugh when I declare myself a follower of Wagner, I burst into a paroxysm of unintelligible, childish rage, and exclaim, 'We shall see that some day!'

Yes; some day we shall see! For, after all, may I not recover from this strangest of maladies? It is still possible that the day may come when all these things shall seem but an incredible nightmare; the day when *Ogier the Dane* shall be completed, and men shall know whether I am a follower of the great master of the Future or the miserable singing-masters of the Past. I am but half-bewitched, since I am conscious of the spell that binds me. My old nurse, far off in Norway, used to tell me that were-wolves are ordinary men and women half their days, and that if, during that period, they become aware of their horrid transformation they may find the means to forestall it. May this not be the case with me? My reason, after all, is free, although my artistic inspiration be enslaved; and I can despise and loathe the music I am forced to compose, and the execrable power that forces me.

Nay, is it not because I have studied with the doggedness of hatred this corrupt and corrupting music of the Past, seeking for every little peculiarity of style and every biographical trifle merely to display its vileness, is it not for this presumptuous courage that I have been overtaken by such mysterious, incredible vengeance?

And meanwhile, my only relief consists in going over and over again in my mind the tale of my miseries. This time I will write it, writing only to tear up, to throw the manuscript unread into the fire. And yet, who knows? As the last charred pages shall crackle and slowly sink into the red embers, perhaps the spell may be broken, and I may possess once more my long-lost liberty, my vanished genius.

It was a breathless evening under the full moon, that implacable full moon beneath which, even more than beneath the dreamy splendour of noontide, Venice seemed to swelter in the midst of the waters, exhaling, like some great lily, mysterious influences, which make the brain swim and the heart faint – a moral malaria, distilled, as I thought, from those languishing melodies, those cooing vocalisations which I had found in the musty music-books of a century ago. I see that moonlight evening as if it were present. I see my fellow-lodgers of that little artists' boarding-house. The table on which they lean after supper is strewn with bits of bread, with napkins rolled in tapestry rollers, spots of wine here and there, and at regular intervals chipped pepper-pots, stands of toothpicks, and heaps of those huge hard peaches which nature imitates from the marble-shops of Pisa. The whole *pension*-full is assembled, and examining stupidly the engraving which the American etcher has just brought for me, knowing me to be mad about eighteenth century music and musicians, and having noticed, as he turned over the heaps of penny prints in the square of San Polo, that the portrait is that of a singer of those days.

Singer, thing of evil, stupid and wicked slave of the voice, of that instrument which was not invented by the human intellect, but begotten of the body, and which, instead of moving the soul, merely stirs up the dregs of our nature! For what is the voice but the Beast calling, awakening that other Beast sleeping in the depths of mankind, the Beast which all great art has ever sought to chain up, as the archangel chains up, in old pictures, the demon with his woman's face? How could the creature attached to this voice, its owner and its victim, the singer, the great, the real singer who once ruled over every heart, be otherwise than wicked and contemptible? But let me try and get on with my story.

I can see all my fellow-boarders, leaning on the table, contemplating the print, this effeminate beau, his hair curled into *ailes de pigeon*, his sword passed through his embroidered pocket, seated under a triumphal arch somewhere among the clouds, surrounded by puffy Cupids and crowned with laurels by a bouncing goddess of fame. I hear again all the insipid exclamations, the insipid questions about this singer: – 'When did he live? Was he very famous? Are you sure, Magnus, that this is really a portrait,' &c. &c. And I hear my own voice, as if in the far distance, giving them all sorts of information, biographical and critical, out of a battered little volume called *The Theatre of Musical Glory; or, Opinions upon the most Famous Chapel-masters and Virtuosi of this Century*, by Father Prosdocimo Sabatelli, Barnalite, Professor of

Eloquence at the College of Modena, and Member of the Arcadian Academy, under the pastoral name of Evander Lilybæan, Venice, 1785, with the approbation of the Superiors. I tell them all how this singer, this Balthasar Cesari, was nicknamed Zaffirino because of a sapphire engraved with cabalistic signs presented to him one evening by a masked stranger, in whom wise folk recognised that great cultivator of the human voice, the devil; how much more wonderful had been this Zaffirino's vocal gifts than those of any singer of ancient or modern times; how his brief life had been but a series of triumphs, petted by the greatest kings, sung by the most famous poets, and finally, adds Father Prosdocimo, 'courted (if the grave Muse of history may incline her ear to the gossip of gallantry) by the most charming nymphs, even of the very highest quality'.

My friends glance once more at the engraving; more insipid remarks are made; I am requested – especially by the American young ladies – to play or sing one of this Zaffirino's favourite songs – 'For of course you know them, dear Maestro Magnus, you who have such a passion for all old music. Do be good, and sit down to the piano.' I refuse, rudely enough, rolling the print in my fingers. How fearfully this cursed heat, these cursed moonlight nights, must have unstrung me! This Venice would certainly kill me in the long-run! Why, the sight of this idiotic engraving, the mere name of that coxcomb of a singer, have made my heart beat and my limbs turn to water like a love-sick hobbledehoy.

After my gruff refusal, the company begins to disperse; they prepare to go out, some to have a row on the lagoon, others to saunter before the *cafés* at St Mark's; family discussions arise, gruntings of fathers, murmurs of mothers, peals of laughing from young girls and young men. And the moon, pouring in by the wide-open windows, turns this old palace ballroom, nowadays an inn dining-room, into a lagoon, scintillating, undulating like the other lagoon, the real one, which stretches out yonder furrowed by invisible gondolas betrayed by the red prow-lights.

At last the whole lot of them are on the move. I shall be able to get some quiet in my room, and to work a little at my opera of *Ogier the Dane*. But no! Conversation revives, and, of all things, about that singer, that Zaffirino, whose absurd portrait I am crunching in my fingers.

The principal speaker is Count Alvise, an old Venetian with dyed whiskers, a great check tie fastened with two pins and a chain; a threadbare patrician who is dying to secure for his lanky son that pretty American girl, whose mother is intoxicated by all his mooning anecdotes about the past glories of Venice in general, and of his illustrious family in particular. Why, in Heaven's name, must he pitch upon Zaffirino for his mooning, this old duffer of a patrician?

'Zaffirino, – ah yes, to be sure! Balthasar Cesari, called Zaffirino,' snuffles the voice of Count Alvise, who always repeats the last word of every sentence at least three times. 'Yes, Zaffirino, to be sure! A famous singer of the days of my forefathers; yes, of my forefathers, dear lady!' Then a lot of rubbish about the former greatness of Venice, the glories of old music, the former Conservatoires, all mixed up with anecdotes of Rossini and Donizetti, whom he pretends to have known intimately. Finally, a story, of course containing plenty about his illustrious family: – 'My great grand-aunt, the Procuratessa Vendramin, from whom we have inherited our estate of Mistrà, on the Brenta' – a hopelessly muddled story, apparently, fully of digressions, but of which that singer Zaffirino is the hero. The narrative, little by little, becomes more intelligible, or perhaps it is I who am giving it more attention.

'It seems,' says the Count, 'that there was one of his songs in particular which was called the "Husbands' Air" – *L'Aria dei Mariti* – because they didn't enjoy it quite as much as their better-halves . . . My grand-aunt, Pisana Renier, married to the Procuratore Vendramin, was a patrician of the old school, of the style that was getting rare a hundred years ago. Her virtue and her pride rendered her unapproachable. Zaffirino, on his part, was in the habit of boasting that no woman had ever been able to resist his singing, which, it appears, had its foundation in fact – the ideal changes, my dear lady, the ideal changes a good deal from one century to another! – and that his first song could make any woman turn pale and lower her eyes, the second make her madly in love, while the third song could kill her off on the spot, kill her for love, there under his very eyes, if he only felt inclined. My grand-aunt Vendramin laughed when this story was told her, refused to go to hear this insolent dog, and added that it might be quite possible by the aid of spells and infernal pacts to kill a *gentildonna*, but as to making her fall in love with a lackey – never! This answer was naturally reported to Zaffirino, who piqued himself upon always getting the better of anyone who was wanting in deference to his voice. Like the ancient Romans, *parcere subjectis et debellare superbos*. You American ladies, who are so learned, will appreciate this little quotation from the divine Virgil. While seeming to avoid the Procuratessa Vendramin, Zaffirino took the opportunity, one evening at a large assembly, to sing in her presence. He sang and sang and sang until the poor grand-aunt Pisana fell ill for love. The most skilful physicians were kept unable to explain the mysterious malady which was visibly killing the poor young lady; and the Procuratore Vendramin applied in vain to the most venerated Madonnas, and vainly promised an altar of silver, with massive gold candlesticks, to Saints Cosmas and Damian, patrons of the art of healing. At last the brother-in-law of the Procuratessa, Monsignor Almorò Vendramin, Patriarch of Aquileia, a prelate famous for the sanctity of his life, obtained in a vision of Saint Justina, for whom he entertained a particular devotion, the information that the only thing which could benefit the strange illness of his sister-in-law was the voice of Zaffirino. Take notice that my poor grand-aunt had never condescended to such a revelation.

'The Procuratore was enchanted at this happy solution; and his lordship the Patriarch went to seek Zaffirino in person, and carried him in his own coach to the Villa of Mistrà, where the Procuratessa was residing. On being told what was about to happen, my poor grand-aunt went into fits of rage, which were succeeded immediately by equally violent fits of joy. However, she never forgot what was due to her great position. Although sick almost unto death, she had herself arrayed with the greatest pomp, caused her face to be painted, and put on all her diamonds: it would seem as if she were anxious to affirm her full dignity before this singer. Accordingly she received Zaffirino reclining on a sofa which had been placed in the great ballroom of the Villa of Mistrà, and beneath the princely canopy; for the Vendramins, who had intermarried with the house of Mantua, possessed imperial fiefs and were princes of the Holy Roman Empire. Zaffirino saluted her with the most profound respect, but not a word passed between them. Only, the singer inquired from the Procuratore whether the illustrious lady had received the Sacraments of the Church. Being told that the Procuratessa had herself asked to be given extreme unction from the hands of her brother-in-law, he declared his readiness to obey the orders of His Excellency, and sat down at once to the harpsichord.

'Never had he sung so divinely. At the end of the first song the Procuratessa Vendramin had already revived most extraordinarily; by the end of the second she appeared entirely cured and beaming with beauty and happiness; but at the third air – the *Aria dei Mariti*, no doubt – she began to change frightfully; she gave a dreadful cry, and fell into the convulsions of death. In a quarter of an hour she was dead! Zaffirino did not wait to see her die. Having finished his song, he withdrew instantly, took post-horses, and travelled day and night as far as Munich. People remarked that he had presented himself at Mistrà dressed in mourning, although he had mentioned no death among his relatives; also that he had prepared everything for his departure, as if fearing the wrath of so powerful a family. Then there was also the extraordinary question he had asked before beginning to sing, about the Procuratessa having confessed and received extreme unction . . . No, thanks, my dear lady, no cigarettes for me. But if it does not distress you or your charming daughter, may I humbly beg permission to smoke a cigar?'

And Count Alvise, enchanted with his talent for narrative, and sure of having secured for his son the heart and the dollars of his fair audience, proceeds to light a candle, and at the candle one of those long black Italian cigars which require preliminary disinfection before smoking.

. . . If this state of things goes on I shall just have to ask the doctor for a bottle; this ridiculous beating of my heart and disgusting cold perspiration have increased steadily during Count Alvise's narrative. To keep myself in countenance among the various idiotic commentaries on this cock-and-bull story of a vocal coxcomb and a vapouring great lady, I begin to unroll the engraving, and to examine stupidly the portrait of Zaffirino, once so renowned, now so forgotten. A ridiculous ass, this singer, under his triumphal arch, with his stuffed Cupids and the great fat winged kitchenmaid crowning him with laurels. How flat and vapid and vulgar it is, to be sure, all this odious eighteenth century!

But he, personally, is not so utterly vapid as I had thought. That effeminate, fat face of his is almost beautiful, with an odd smile, brazen and cruel. I have seen faces like this, if not in real life, at least in my boyish romantic dreams, when I read Swinburne and Baudelaire, the faces of wicked, vindictive women. Oh yes! he is decidedly a beautiful creature, this Zaffirino, and his voice must have had the same sort of beauty and the same expression of wickedness . . .

'Come on, Magnus,' sound the voices of my fellow-boarders, 'be a good fellow and sing us one of the old chap's songs; or at least something or other of that day, and we'll make believe it was the air with which he killed that poor lady.'

'Oh yes! the *Aria dei Mariti*, the "Husbands' Air",' mumbles old Alvise, between the puffs at his impossible black cigar. 'My poor grand-aunt, Pisana Vendramin; he went and killed her with those songs of his, with that *Aria dei Mariti.*'

I feel senseless rage overcoming me. Is it that horrible palpitation (by the way, there is a Norwegian doctor, my fellow-countryman, at Venice just now) which is sending the blood to my brain and making me mad? The people round the piano, the furniture, everything together seems to get mixed and to turn into moving blobs of colour. I set to singing; the only thing which remains distinct before my eyes being the portrait of Zaffirino, on the edge of that boarding-house piano; the sensual, effeminate face, with its wicked, cynical smile, keeps appearing and disappearing as the print wavers about in the draught that makes the candles smoke and gutter. And I set to singing madly, singing I don't know what. Yes; I begin to identify it: 'tis the *Biondina in Gondoleta*, the only song of the eighteenth century which is still remembered by the Venetian people. I sing it, mimicking every old-school grace; shakes, cadences, languishingly swelled and diminished notes, and adding all manner of buffooneries, until the audience, recovering from its surprise, begins to shake with laughing; until I begin to laugh myself, madly, frantically, between the phrases of the melody, my voice finally smothered in this dull, brutal laughter . . . And then, to crown it all, I shake my fist at this long-dead singer, looking at me with his wicked woman's face, with his mocking, fatuous smile.

'Ah! you would like to be revenged on me also!' I exclaim. 'You would like me to write you nice roulades and flourishes, another nice *Aria dei Mariti*, my fine Zaffirino!'

That night I dreamed a very strange dream. Even in the big half-furnished room the heat and closeness were stifling. The air seemed laden with the scent of all manner of white flowers, faint and heavy in their intolerable sweetness: tuberoses, gardenias, and jasmines drooping I know not where in neglected vases. The moonlight had transformed the marble floor around me into a shallow, shining pool. On account of the heat I had exchanged my bed for a big old-fashioned sofa of light wood, painted with little nosegays and sprigs, like an old silk; and I lay there, not attempting to sleep, and letting my thoughts go vaguely to my opera of *Ogier the Dane*, of which I had long finished writing the words, and for whose music I had hoped to find some inspiration in this strange Venice, floating, as it were, in the stagnant lagoon of the past. But Venice had merely put all my ideas into hopeless confusion; it was as if there arose out of its shallow waters a miasma of long-dead melodies, which sickened but intoxicated my soul. I lay on my sofa watching that pool of whitish light, which rose higher and higher, little trickles of light meeting it here and there, wherever the moon's rays struck upon some polished surface; while huge shadows waved to and fro in the draught of the open balcony.

I went over and over that old Norse story: how the Paladin Ogier, one of the knights of Charlemagne, was decoyed during his homeward wanderings from the Holy Land by the arts of an enchantress, the same who had once held in bondage the great Emperor Caesar and given him King Oberon for a son; how Ogier had tarried in that island only one day and one night, and yet, when he came home to his kingdom, he found all changed, his friends dead, his family dethroned, and not a man who knew his face; until at last, driven hither and thither like a beggar, a poor minstrel had taken compassion of his sufferings and given him all he could give – a song, the song of the prowess of a hero dead for hundreds of years, the Paladin Ogier the Dane.

The story of Ogier ran into a dream, as vivid as my waking thoughts had been vague. I was looking no longer at the pool of moonlight spreading round my couch, with its trickles of light and looming, waving shadows, but the frescoed walls of a great saloon. It was not, as I recognised in a second, the dining-room of that Venetian palace now turned into a boarding-house. It was a far larger room, a real ballroom, almost circular in its octagon shape, with eight huge white doors surrounded by stucco mouldings, and, high on the vault of the ceiling, eight little galleries or recesses like boxes at a theatre, intended no doubt for musicians and spectators. The place was imperfectly lighted by only one of the eight chandeliers, which revolved slowly, like huge spiders, each on its long cord. But the light struck upon the gilt stuccoes opposite me, and on a large expanse of fresco, the sacrifice of Iphigenia, with Agamemnon and Achilles in Roman helmets, lappets, and knee-breeches. It discovered also one of the oil panels let into the mouldings of the roof, a goddess in lemon and lilac draperies, foreshortened over a great green peacock. Round the room, where the light reached, I could make out big yellow satin sofas and heavy gilded consoles; in the shadow of a corner was what looked like a piano, and farther in the shade one of those big canopies which decorate the anterooms of Roman palaces. I looked about me, wondering where I was: a heavy, sweet smell, reminding me of the flavour of a peach, filled the place.

Little by little I began to perceive sounds; little, sharp, metallic, detached notes, like those of a mandoline; and there was united to them a voice, very low and sweet, almost a whisper, which grew and grew and grew, until the whole place was filled with that exquisite vibrating note, of a strange, exotic, unique quality. The note went on, swelling and swelling. Suddenly there was a horrible piercing shriek, and the thud of a body on the floor, and all manner of smothered exclamations. There, close by the canopy, a light suddenly appeared; and I could see, among the dark figures moving to and fro in the room, a woman lying on the ground, surrounded by other women. Her blond hair, tangled, full of diamond-sparkles which cut through the half-darkness, was hanging dishevelled; the laces of her bodice had been cut, and her white breast shone among the sheen of jewelled brocade; her face was bent forwards, and a thin white arm trailed, like a broken limb, across the knees of one of the women who were endeavouring to lift her. There was a sudden splash of water against the floor, more confused exclamations, a hoarse, broken moan, and a gurgling, dreadful sound . . . I awoke with a start and rushed to the window.

Outside, in the blue haze of the moon, the church and belfry of St George loomed blue and hazy, with the black hull and rigging, the red lights, of a large steamer moored before them. From the lagoon rose a damp sea-breeze. What was it all? Ah! I began to understand: that story of old Count Alvise's, the death of his grand-aunt, Pisana Vendramin. Yes, it was about that I had been dreaming.

I returned to my room; I struck a light, and sat down to my writing-table. Sleep had become impossible. I tried to work at my opera. Once or twice I thought I had got hold of what I had looked for so long . . . But as soon as I tried to lay hold of my theme, there arose in my mind the distant echo of that voice, of that long note swelled slowly by insensible degrees, that long note whose tone was so strong and so subtle.

There are in the life of an artist moments when, still unable to seize his own inspiration, or even clearly to discern it, he becomes aware of the approach of that long-invoked idea. A mingled joy and terror warn him that before another day, another hour have passed, the inspiration shall have crossed the threshold of his soul and flooded it with its rapture. All day I had felt the need of isolation and quiet, and at nightfall I went for a row on the most solitary part of the lagoon. All things seemed to tell that I was going to meet my inspiration, and I awaited its coming as a lover awaits his beloved.

I had stopped my gondola for a moment, and as I gently swayed to and fro on the water, all paved with moonbeams, it seemed to me that I was on the confines of an imaginary world. It lay close at hand, enveloped in luminous, pale blue mist, through which the moon had cut a wide and glistening path; out to sea, the little islands, like moored black boats, only accentuated the solitude of this region of moonbeams and wavelets; while the hum of the insects in orchards hard by merely added to the impression of untroubled silence. On some such seas, I thought, must the Paladin Ogier, have sailed when about to discover that during that sleep at the enchantress's knees centuries had elapsed and the heroic world had set, and the kingdom of prose had come.

While my gondola rocked stationary on that sea of moonbeams, I pondered over that twilight of the heroic world. In the soft rattle of the water on the hull I seemed to hear the rattle of all that armour, of all those swords swinging rusty on the walls, neglected by the degenerate sons of the great champions of old. I had long been in search of a theme which I called the theme of the 'Prowess of Ogier'; it was to appear from time to time in the course of my opera, to develop at last into that song of the Minstrel, which reveals to the hero that he is one of a long-dead world. And at this moment I seemed to feel the presence of that theme. Yet an instant, and my mind would be overwhelmed by that savage music, heroic, funereal.

Suddenly there came across the lagoon, cleaving, chequering, and fretting the silence with a lace-work of sound even as the moon was fretting and cleaving the water, a ripple of music, a voice breaking itself in a shower of little scales and cadences and trills.

I sank back upon my cushions. The vision of heroic days had vanished, and before my closed eyes there seemed to dance multitudes of little stars of light, chasing and interlacing like those sudden vocalisations.

'To shore! Quick!' I cried to the gondolier.

But the sounds had ceased; and there came from the orchards, with their mulberry-trees glistening in the moonlight, and their black swaying cypress-plumes, nothing save the confused hum, the monotonous chirp, of the crickets.

I looked around me: on one side empty dunes, orchards, and meadows, without house or steeple; on the other, the blue and misty sea, empty to where distant islets were profiled black on the horizon.

A faintness overcame me, and I felt myself dissolve. For all of a sudden a second ripple of voice swept over the lagoon, a shower of little notes, which seemed to form a little mocking laugh.

Then again all was still. This silence lasted so long that I fell once more to meditating on my opera. I lay in wait once more for the half-caught theme. But no. It was not that theme for which I was waiting and watching with bated breath. I realised my delusion when, on rounding the point of the Giudecca, the murmur of a voice arose from the midst of the waters, a thread of sound slender as a moonbeam, scarce audible, but exquisite, which expanded slowly, insensibly, taking volume and body, taking flesh almost and fire, an ineffable quality, full, passionate, but veiled, as it were, in a subtle, downy wrapper. The note grew stronger and stronger, and warmer and more passionate, until it burst through that strange and charming veil, and emerged beaming, to break itself in the luminous facets of a wonderful shake, long, superb, triumphant.

There was a dead silence.

'Row to St Mark's!' I exclaimed. 'Quick!'

The gondola glided through the long, glittering track of moonbeams, and rent the great band of yellow, reflected light, mirroring the cupolas of St Mark's, the lace-like pinnacles of the palace, and the slender pink belfry, which rose from the lit-up water to the pale and bluish evening sky.

In the larger of the two squares the military band was blaring through the last spirals of a *crescendo* of Rossini. The crowd was dispersing in this great open-air ballroom, and the sounds arose which invariably follow upon out-of-door music. A clatter of spoons and glasses, a rustle and grating of frocks and of chairs, and the click of scabbards on the pavement. I pushed my way among the fashionable youths contemplating the ladies while sucking the knob of their sticks; through the serried ranks of respectable families, marching arm in arm with their white frocked young ladies close in front. I took a seat before Florian's, among the customers stretching themselves before departing, and the waiters hurrying to and fro, clattering their empty cups and trays. Two imitation Neapolitans were slipping their guitar and violin under their arm, ready to leave the place.

'Stop!' I cried to them; 'don't go yet. Sing me something – sing *La Camesella* or *Funiculì, funiculà* – no matter what, provided you make a row'; and as they screamed and scraped their utmost, I added, 'But can't you sing louder, d—n you! – sing louder, do you understand?'

I felt the need of noise, of yells and false notes, of something vulgar and hideous to drive away that ghost-voice which was haunting me.

Again and again I told myself that it had been some silly prank of a romantic amateur, hidden in the gardens of the shore or gliding unperceived on the lagoon; and that the sorcery of moonlight and sea-mist had transfigured for my excited brain mere humdrum roulades out of exercises of Bordogni or Crescentini.

But all the same I continued to be haunted by that voice. My work was interrupted ever and anon by the attempt to catch its imaginary echo; and the heroic harmonies of my Scandinavian legend were strangely interwoven with voluptuous phrases and florid cadences in which I seemed to hear again that same accursed voice.

To be haunted by singing-exercises! It seemed too ridiculous for a man who professedly despised the art of singing. And still, I preferred to believe in that childish amateur, amusing himself with warbling to the moon.

One day, while making these reflections the hundredth time over, my eyes chanced to light upon the portrait of Zaffirino, which my friend had pinned against the wall. I pulled it down and tore it into half a dozen shreds. Then, already ashamed of my folly, I watched the torn pieces float down from the window, wafted hither and thither by the sea-breeze. One scrap got caught in a yellow blind below me; the others fell into the canal, and were speedily lost to sight in the dark water. I was overcome with shame. My heart beat like bursting. What a miserable, unnerved worm I had become in this cursed Venice, with its languishing moonlights, its atmosphere as of some stuffy boudoir, long unused, full of old stuffs and pot-pourri!

That night, however, things seemed to be going better. I was able to settle down to my opera, and even to work at it. In the intervals my thoughts returned, not without a certain pleasure, to those scattered fragments of the torn engraving fluttering down to the water. I was disturbed at my piano by the hoarse voices and the scraping of violins which rose from one of those music-boats that station at night under the hotels of the Grand Canal. The moon had set. Under my balcony the water stretched black into the distance, its darkness cut by the still darker outlines of the flotilla of gondolas in attendance on the music-boat, where the faces of the singers, and the guitars and violins, gleamed reddish under the unsteady light of the Chinese-lanterns.

'*Jammo, jammo; jammo, jammo jà,*' sang the loud, hoarse voices; then a tremendous scrape and twang, and the yelled-out burden, '*Funiculì, funiculà; funiculì, funiculà; jammo, jammo, jammo, jammo, jammo jà.*'

Then came a few cries of '*Bis, Bis!*' from a neighbouring hotel, a brief clapping of hands, the sound of a handful of coppers rattling into the boat, and the oar-stroke of some gondolier making ready to turn away.

'Sing the *Camesella,*' ordered some voice with a foreign accent.

'No, no! *Santa Lucia.*'

'I want the *Camesella.*'

'No! *Santa Lucia*. Hi! sing *Santa Lucia* – d'you hear?'

The musicians, under their green and yellow and red lamps, held a whispered consultation on the manner of conciliating these contradictory demands. Then, after a minute's hesitation, the violins began the prelude of that once famous air, which has remained popular in Venice – the words written, some hundred years ago, by the patrician Gritti, the music by an unknown composer – *La Biondina in Gondoleta*.

That cursed eighteenth century! It seemed a malignant fatality that made these brutes choose just this piece to interrupt me.

At last the long prelude came to an end; and above the cracked guitars and squeaking fiddles there arose, not the expected nasal chorus, but a single voice singing below its breath.

My arteries throbbed. How well I knew that voice! It was singing, as I have said, below its breath, yet none the less it sufficed to fill all that reach of the canal with its strange quality of tone, exquisite, far-fetched.

They were long-drawn-out notes, of intense but peculiar sweetness, a man's voice which had much of a woman's, but more even of a chorister's, but a chorister's voice without its limpidity and innocence; its youthfulness was veiled, muffled, as it were, in a sort of downy vagueness, as if a passion of tears withheld.

There was a burst of applause, and the old palaces re-echoed with the clapping. 'Bravo, bravo! Thank you, thank you! Sing again – please, sing again. Who can it be?'

And then a bumping of hulls, a splashing of oars, and the oaths of gondoliers trying to push each other away, as the red prow-lamps of the gondolas pressed round the gaily lit singing-boat.

But no one stirred on board. It was to none of them that this applause was due. And while everyone pressed on, and clapped and vociferated, one little red prow-lamp dropped away from the fleet; for a moment a single gondola stood forth black upon the black water, and then was lost in the night.

For several days the mysterious singer was the universal topic. The people of the music-boat swore that no one besides themselves had been on board, and that they knew as little as ourselves about the owner of that voice. The gondoliers, despite their descent from the spies of the old Republic, were equally unable to furnish any clue. No musical celebrity was known or suspected to be at Venice; and everyone agreed that such a singer must be a European celebrity. The strangest thing in this strange business was, that even among those learned in music there was no agreement on the subject of this voice: it was called by all sorts of names and described by all manner of incongruous adjectives; people went so far as to dispute whether the voice belonged to a man or to a woman: everyone had some new definition.

In all these musical discussions I, alone, brought forward no opinion. I felt a repugnance, an impossibility almost, of speaking about that voice; and the more or less commonplace conjectures of my friend had the invariable effect of sending me out of the room.

Meanwhile my work was becoming daily more difficult, and I soon passed from utter impotence to a state of inexplicable agitation. Every morning I arose with fine resolutions and grand projects of work; only to go to bed that night without having accomplished anything. I spent hours leaning on my balcony, or wandering through the network of lanes with their ribbon of blue sky, endeavouring vainly to expel the thought of that voice, or endeavouring in reality to reproduce it in my memory; for the more I tried to banish it from my thoughts, the more I grew to thirst for that extraordinary tone, for those mysteriously downy, veiled notes; and no sooner did I make an effort to work at my opera than my head was full of scraps of forgotten eighteenth-century airs, of frivolous or languishing little phrases; and I fell to wondering with a bitter-sweet longing how those songs would have sounded if sung by that voice.

At length it became necessary to see a doctor, from whom, however, I carefully hid away all the stranger symptoms of my malady. The air of the lagoons, the great heat, he answered cheerfully, had pulled me down a little; a tonic and a month in the country, with plenty of riding and no work, would make me myself again. That old idler, Count Alvise, who had insisted on accompanying me to the physician's, immediately suggested that I should go and stay with his son, who was boring himself to death superintending the maize harvest on the mainland: he could promise me excellent air, plenty of horses, and all the peaceful surroundings and the delightful occupations of a rural life – 'Be sensible, my dear Magnus, and just go quietly to Mistrà.'

Mistrà – the name sent a shiver all down me. I was about to decline the invitation, when a thought suddenly loomed vaguely in my mind.

'Yes, dear Count,' I answered; 'I accept your invitation with gratitude and pleasure. I will start to-morrow for Mistrà.'

The next day found me at Padua, on my way to the Villa of Mistrà. It seemed as if I had left an intolerable burden behind me. I was, for the first time since how long, quite light of heart. The tortuous, rough-paved streets, with their empty, gloomy porticoes; the ill-plastered palaces, with closed, discoloured shutters; the little rambling square, with meagre trees and stubborn grass; the Venetian garden-houses reflecting their crumbling graces in the muddy canal; the gardens without gates and the gates without gardens, the avenues leading nowhere; and the population of blind and legless beggars, of whining sacristans, which issued as by magic from between the flagstones and dust-heaps and weeds under the fierce August sun, all this dreariness merely amused and pleased me. My good spirits were heightened by a musical mass which I had the good fortune to hear at St Anthony's.

Never in all my days had I heard anything comparable, although Italy affords many strange things in the way of sacred music. Into the deep nasal chanting of the priests there had suddenly burst a chorus of children, singing absolutely independent of all time and tune; grunting of priests answered by squealing of boys, slow Gregorian modulation interrupted by jaunty barrel-organ pipings, an insane, insanely merry jumble of bellowing and barking, mewing and cackling and braying, such as would have enlivened a witches' meeting, or rather some mediaeval Feast of Fools. And, to make the grotesqueness of such music still more fantastic and Hoffmannlike, there was, besides, the magnificence of the piles of sculptured marbles and gilded bronzes, the tradition of the musical splendour for which St Anthony's had been famous in days gone by. I had read in old travellers, Lalande and Burney, that the Republic of St Mark had squandered immense sums not merely on the monuments and decoration, but on the musical establishment of its great cathedral of Terra Firma. In the midst of this ineffable concert of impossible voices and instruments, I tried to imagine the voice of Guadagni, the soprano for whom Gluck had written *Che farò senza Euridice*, and the fiddle of Tartini, that Tartini with whom the devil had once come and made music. And the delight in anything so absolutely, barbarously, grotesquely, fantastically incongruous as such a performance in such a place was heightened by a sense of profanation: such were the successors of those wonderful musicians of that hated eighteenth century!

The whole thing had delighted me so much, so very much more than the most faultless performance could have done, that I determined to enjoy it once more; and towards vesper-time, after a cheerful dinner with two bagmen at the inn of the Golden Star, and a pipe over the rough sketch of a possible cantata upon the music which the devil made for Tartini, I turned my steps once more towards St Anthony's.

The bells were ringing for sunset, and a muffled sound of organs seemed to issue from the huge, solitary church; I pushed my way under the heavy leathern curtain, expecting to be greeted by the grotesque performance of that morning.

I proved mistaken. Vespers must long have been over. A smell of stale incense, a crypt-like damp filled my mouth; it was already night in that vast cathedral. Out of the darkness glimmered the votive-lamps of the chapels, throwing wavering lights upon the red polished marble, the gilded railing, and chandeliers, and plaqueing with yellow the muscles of some sculptured figure. In a corner a burning taper put a halo about the head of a priest, burnishing his shining bald skull, his white surplice, and the open book before him. 'Amen,' he chanted; the book was closed with a snap, the light moved up the apse, some dark figures of women rose from their knees and passed quickly towards the door; a man saying his prayers before a chapel also got up, making a great clatter in dropping his stick.

The church was empty, and I expected every minute to be turned out by the sacristan making his evening round to close the doors. I was leaning against a pillar, looking into the greyness of the great arches, when the organ suddenly burst out into a series of chords, rolling through the echoes of the church: it seemed to be the conclusion of some service. And above the organ rose the notes of a voice; high, soft, enveloped in a kind of downiness, like a cloud of incense, and which ran through the mazes of a long cadence. The voice dropped into silence; with two thundering chords the organ closed in. All was silent. For a moment I stood leaning against one of the pillars of the nave: my hair was clammy, my knees sank beneath me, an enervating heat spread through my body; I tried to breathe more largely, to suck in the sounds with the incense-laden air. I was supremely happy, and yet as if I were dying; then suddenly a chill ran through me, and with it a vague panic. I turned away and hurried out into the open.

The evening sky lay pure and blue along the jagged line of roofs; the bats and swallows were wheeling about; and from the belfries all around, half-drowned by the deep bell of St Anthony's, jangled the peal of the *Ave Maria*.

'You really don't seem well,' young Count Alvise had said the previous evening, as he welcomed me, in the light of a lantern held up by a peasant, in the weedy back-garden of the Villa of Mistrà. Everything had seemed to me like a dream: the jingle of the horse's bells driving in the dark from Padua, as the lantern swept the acacia-hedges with their wide yellow light; the grating of the wheels on the gravel; the supper-table, illumined by a single petroleum lamp for fear of attracting mosquitoes, where a broken old lackey, in an old stable jacket, handed round the dishes among the fumes of onion; Alvise's fat mother gabbling dialect in a shrill, benevolent voice behind the bullfights on her fan; the unshaven village priest, perpetually fidgeting with his glass and foot, and sticking one shoulder up above the other. And now, in the afternoon, I felt as if I had been in this long, rambling, tumble-down Villa of Mistrà – a villa three-quarters of which was given up to the storage of grain and garden tools, or to the exercise of rats, mice, scorpions, and centipedes – all my life; as if I had always sat there, in Count Alvise's study, among the pile of undusted books on agriculture, the sheaves of accounts, the samples of grain and silkworm seed, the ink-stains and the cigar-ends; as if I had never heard of anything save the cereal basis of Italian agriculture, the diseases of maize, the peronospora of the vine, the breeds of bullocks, and the iniquities of farm labourers; with the blue cones of the Euganean hills closing in the green shimmer of plain outside the window.

After an early dinner, again with the screaming gabble of the fat old Countess, the fidgeting and shoulder-raising of the unshaven priest, the smell of fried oil and stewed onions, Count Alvise made me get into the cart beside him, and whirled me along among clouds of dust, between the endless glister of poplars, acacias, and maples, to one of his farms.

In the burning sun some twenty or thirty girls, in coloured skirts, laced bodices, and big straw-hats, were threshing the maize on the big red brick threshing-floor, while others were winnowing the grain in great sieves. Young Alvise III (the old one was Alvise II: everyone is Alvise, that is to say, Lewis, in that family; the name is on the house, the carts, the barrows, the very pails) picked up the maize, touched it, tasted it, said something to the girls that made them laugh, and something to the head farmer that made him look very glum; and then led me into a huge stable, where some twenty or thirty white bullocks were stamping, switching their tails, hitting their horns against the mangers in the dark. Alvise III patted each, called him by his name, gave him some salt or a turnip, and explained which was the Mantuan breed, which the Apulian, which the Romagnolo, and so on. Then he bade me jump into the trap, and off we went again through the dust, among the hedges and ditches, till we came to some more brick farm buildings with pinkish roofs smoking against the blue sky. Here there were more young women threshing and winnowing the maize, which made a great golden Danaë cloud; more bullocks stamping and lowing in the cool darkness; more joking, fault-finding, explaining; and thus through five farms, until I seemed to see the rhythmical rising and falling of the flails against the hot sky, the shower of golden grains, the yellow dust from the winnowing-sieves on to the bricks, the switching of innumerable tails and plunging of innumerable horns, the glistening of huge white flanks and foreheads, whenever I closed my eyes.

'A good day's work!' cried Count Alvise, stretching out his long legs with the tight trousers riding up over the Wellington boots. 'Mamma, give us some aniseed-syrup after dinner; it is an excellent restorative and precaution against the fevers of this country.'

'Oh! you've got fever in this part of the world, have you? Why, your father said the air was so good!'

'Nothing, nothing,' soothed the old Countess. 'The only thing to be dreaded are mosquitoes; take care to fasten your shutters before lighting the candle.'

'Well,' rejoined young Alvise, with an effort of conscience, 'of course there *are* fevers. But they needn't hurt you. Only, don't go out into the garden at night, if you don't want to catch them. Papa told me that you have fancies for moonlight rambles. It won't do in this climate, my dear fellow; it won't do. If you must stalk about at night, being a genius, take a turn inside the house; you can get quite exercise enough.'

After dinner the aniseed-syrup was produced, together with brandy and cigars, and they all sat in the long, narrow, half-furnished room on the first floor; the old Countess knitting a garment of uncertain shape and destination, the priest reading out the newspaper; Count Alvise puffing at his long, crooked cigar, and pulling the ears of a long, lean dog with a suspicion of mange and a stiff eye. From the dark garden outside rose the hum and whirr of countless insects, and the smell of the grapes which hung black against the starlit, blue sky, on the trellis. I went to the balcony. The garden lay dark beneath; against the twinkling horizon stood out the tall poplars. There was the sharp cry of an owl; the barking of a dog; a sudden whiff of warm, enervating perfume, a perfume that made me think of the taste of certain peaches, and suggested white, thick, wax-like petals. I seemed to have smelt that flower once before: it made me feel languid, almost faint.

'I am very tired,' I said to Count Alvise. 'See how feeble we city folk become!'

But, despite my fatigue, I found it quite impossible to sleep. The night seemed perfectly stifling. I had felt nothing like it at Venice. Despite the injunctions of the Countess I opened the solid wooden shutters, hermetically closed against mosquitoes, and looked out.

The moon had risen; and beneath it lay the big lawns, the rounded tree-tops, bathed in a blue, luminous mist, every leaf glistening and trembling in what seemed a heaving sea of light. Beneath the window was the long trellis, with the white shining piece of pavement under it. It was so bright that I could distinguish the green of the vine-leaves, the dull red of the catalpa-flowers. There was in the air a vague scent of cut grass, of ripe American grapes, of that white flower (it must be white) which made me think of the taste of peaches all melting into the delicious freshness of falling dew. From the village church came the stroke of one: Heaven knows how long I had been vainly attempting to sleep. A shiver ran through me, and my head suddenly filled as with the fumes of some subtle wine; I remembered all those weedy embankments, those canals full of stagnant water, the yellow faces of the peasants; the word malaria returned to my mind. No matter! I remained leaning on the window, with a thirsty longing to plunge myself into this blue moon-mist, this dew and perfume and silence, which seemed to vibrate and quiver like the stars that strewed the depths of heaven . . . What music, even Wagner's, or of that great singer of starry nights, the divine Schumann, what music could ever compare with this great silence, with this great concert of voiceless things that sing within one's soul?

As I made this reflection, a note, high, vibrating, and sweet, rent the silence, which immediately closed around it. I leaned out of the window, my heart beating as though it must burst. After a brief space the silence was cloven once more by that note, as the darkness is cloven by a falling star or a firefly rising slowly like a rocket. But this time it was plain that the voice did not come, as I had imagined, from the garden, but from the house itself, from some corner of this rambling old villa of Mistrà.

Mistrà – Mistrà! The name rang in my ears, and I began at length to grasp its significance, which seems to have escaped me till then. 'Yes,' I said to myself, 'it is quite natural.' And with this odd impression of naturalness was mixed a feverish, impatient pleasure. It was as if I had come to Mistrà on purpose, and that I was about to meet the object of my long and weary hopes.

Grasping the lamp with its singed green shade, I gently opened the door and made my way through a series of long passages and of big, empty rooms, in which my steps re-echoed as in a church, and my light disturbed whole swarms of bats. I wandered at random, farther and farther from the inhabited part of the buildings.

This silence made me feel sick; I gasped as under a sudden disappointment.

All of a sudden there came a sound – chords, metallic, sharp, rather like the tone of a mandoline – close to my ear. Yes, quite close: I was separated from the sounds only by a partition. I fumbled for a door; the unsteady light of my lamp was insufficient for my eyes, which were swimming like those of a drunkard. At last I found a latch, and, after a moment's hesitation, I lifted it and gently pushed open the door. At first I could not understand what manner of place I was in. It was dark all round me, but a brilliant light blinded me, a light coming from below and striking the opposite wall. It was as if I had entered a dark box in a half-lighted theatre. I was, in fact, in something of the kind, a sort of dark hole with a high balustrade, half-hidden by an up-drawn curtain. I remembered those little galleries or recesses for the use of musicians or lookers-on which exist under the ceiling of the ballrooms in certain old Italian palaces. Yes; it must have been one like that. Opposite me was a vaulted ceiling covered with gilt mouldings, which framed great time-blackened canvases; and lower down, in the light thrown up from below, stretched a wall covered with faded frescoes. Where had I seen that goddess in lilac and lemon draperies foreshortened over a big, green peacock? For she was familiar to me, and the stucco Tritons also who twisted their tails round her gilded frame. And that fresco, with warriors in Roman cuirasses and green and blue lappets, and knee-breeches – where could I have seen them before? I asked myself these questions without experiencing any surprise. Moreover, I was very calm, as one is calm sometimes in extraordinary dreams – could I be dreaming?

I advanced gently and leaned over the balustrade. My eyes were met at first by the darkness above me, where, like gigantic spiders, the big chandeliers rotated slowly, hanging from the ceiling. Only one of them was lit, and its Murano-glass pendants, its carnations and roses, shone opalescent in the light of the guttering wax. This chandelier lighted up the opposite wall and that piece of ceiling with the goddess and the green peacock; it illumined, but far less well, a corner of the huge room, where, in the shadow of a kind of canopy, a little group of people were crowding round a yellow satin sofa, of the same kind as those that lined the walls. On the sofa, half-screened from me by the surrounding persons, a woman was stretched out: the silver of her embroidered dress and the rays of her diamonds gleamed and shot forth as she moved uneasily. And immediately under the chandelier, in the full light, a man stooped over a harpsichord, his head bent slightly, as if collecting his thoughts before singing.

He struck a few chords and sang. Yes, sure enough, it was the voice, the voice that had so long been persecuting me! I recognised at once that delicate, voluptuous quality, strange, exquisite, sweet beyond words, but lacking all youth and clearness. That passion veiled in tears which had troubled my brain that night on the lagoon, and again on the Grand Canal singing the *Biondina*, and yet again, only two days since, in the deserted cathedral of Padua. But I recognised now what seemed to have been hidden from me till then, that this voice was what I cared most for in all the wide world.

The voice wound and unwound itself in long, languishing phrases, in rich, voluptuous *rifiorituras*, all fretted with tiny scales and exquisite, crisp shakes; it stopped ever and anon, swaying as if panting in languid delight. And I felt my body melt even as wax in the sunshine, and it seemed to me that I too was turning fluid and vaporous, in order to mingle with these sounds as the moonbeams mingle with the dew.

Suddenly, from the dimly lighted corner by the canopy, came a little piteous wail; then another followed, and was lost in the singer's voice. During a long phrase on the harpsichord, sharp and tinkling, the singer turned his head towards the dais, and there came a plaintive little sob. But he, instead of stopping, struck a sharp chord; and with a thread of voice so hushed as to be scarcely audible, slid softly into a long *cadenza*. At the same moment he threw his head backwards, and the light fell full upon the handsome, effeminate face, with its ashy pallor and big, black brows, of the singer Zaffirino. At the sight of that face, sensual and sullen, of that smile which was cruel and mocking like a bad woman's, I understood – I knew not why, by what process – that his singing *must* be cut short, that the accursed phrase *must* never be finished. I understood that I was before an assassin, that he was killing this woman, and killing me also, with his wicked voice.

I rushed down the narrow stair which led down from the box, pursued, as it were, by that exquisite voice, swelling, swelling by insensible degrees. I flung myself on the door which must be that of the big saloon. I could see its light between the panels. I bruised my hands in trying to wrench the latch. The door was fastened tight, and while I was struggling with that locked door I heard the voice swelling, swelling, rending asunder that downy veil which wrapped it, leaping forth clear, resplendent, like the sharp and glittering blade of a knife that seemed to enter deep into my breast. Then, once more, a wail, a death-groan, and that dreadful noise, that hideous gurgle of breath strangled by a rush of blood. And then a long shake, acute, brilliant, triumphant.

The door gave way beneath my weight, one half crashed in. I entered. I was blinded by a flood of blue moonlight. It poured in through four great windows, peaceful and diaphanous, a pale blue mist of moonlight, and turned the huge room into a kind of submarine cave, paved with moonbeams, full of shimmers, of pools of moonlight. It was as bright as at midday, but the brightness was cold, blue, vaporous, supernatural. The room was completely empty, like a great hay-loft. Only, there hung from the ceiling the ropes which had once supported a chandelier; and in a corner, among stacks of wood and heaps of Indian-corn, whence spread a sickly smell of damp and mildew, there stood a long, thin harpsichord, with spindle-legs, and its cover cracked from end to end.

I felt, all of a sudden, very calm. The one thing that mattered was the phrase that kept moving in my head, the phrase of that unfinished cadence which I had heard but an instant before. I opened the harpsichord, and my fingers came down boldly upon its keys. A jingle-jangle of broken strings, laughable and dreadful, was the only answer.

Then an extraordinary fear overtook me. I clambered out of one of the windows; I rushed up the garden and wandered through the fields, among the canals and the embankments, until the moon had set and the dawn began to shiver, followed, pursued for ever by that jangle of broken strings.

People expressed much satisfaction at my recovery. It seems that one dies of those fevers.

Recovery? But have I recovered? I walk, and eat and drink and talk; I can even sleep. I live the life of other living creatures. But I am wasted by a strange and deadly disease. I can never lay hold of my own inspiration. My head is filled with music which is certainly by me, since I have never heard it before, but which still is not my own, which I despise and abhor: little, tripping flourishes and languishing phrases, and long-drawn, echoing cadences.

O wicked, wicked voice, violin of flesh and blood made by the Evil One's hand, may I not even execrate thee in peace; but is it necessary that, at the moment when I curse, the longing to hear thee again should parch my soul like hell-thirst? And since I have satiated thy lust for revenge, since thou hast withered my life and withered my genius, is it not time for pity? May I not hear one note, only one note of thine, O singer, O wicked and contemptible wretch?

The Horror of the Heights

Arthur Conan Doyle

(WHICH INCLUDES THE MANUSCRIPT KNOWN AS THE JOYCE-ARMSTRONG FRAGMENT)

The idea that the extraordinary narrative which has been called the Joyce-Armstrong Fragment is an elaborate practical joke evolved by some unknown person, cursed by a perverted and sinister sense of humour, has now been abandoned by all who have examined the matter. The most *macabre* and imaginative of plotters would hesitate before linking his morbid fancies with the unquestioned and tragic facts which reinforce the statement. Though the assertions contained in it are amazing and even monstrous, it is none the less forcing itself upon the general intelligence that they are true, and that we must readjust our ideas to the new situation. This world of ours appears to be separated by a slight and precarious margin of safety from a most singular and unexpected danger. I will endeavour in this narrative, which reproduces the original document in its necessarily somewhat fragmentary form, to lay before the reader the whole of the facts up to date, prefacing my statement by saying that, if there be any who doubt the narrative of Joyce-Armstrong, there can be no question at all as to the facts concerning Lieutenant Myrtle, R.N., and Mr Hay Connor, who undoubtedly met their end in the manner described.

The Joyce-Armstrong Fragment was found in the field which is called Lower Haycock, lying one mile to the westward of the village of Withyham, upon the Kent and Sussex border. It was on the fifteenth of September last that an agricultural labourer, James Flynn, in the employment of Mathew Dodd, farmer, of the Chauntry Farm, Withyham, perceived a briar pipe lying near the footpath which skirts the hedge in Lower Haycock. A few paces farther on he picked up a pair of broken binocular glasses. Finally, among some nettles in the ditch, he caught sight of a flat, canvas-backed book, which proved to be a note-book with detachable leaves, some of which had come loose and were fluttering along the base of the hedge. These he collected, but some, including the first, were never recovered, and leave a deplorable hiatus in this all-important statement. The note-book was taken by the labourer to his master, who in turn showed it to Dr J. H. Atherton, of Hartfield. This gentleman at once recognised the need for an expert examination, and the manuscript was forwarded to the Aero Club in London, where it now lies.

The first two pages of the manuscript are missing. There is also one torn away at the end of the narrative, though none of these affect the general coherence of the story. It is conjectured that the missing opening is concerned with the record of Mr Joyce-Armstrong's qualifications as an aeronaut, which can be gathered from other sources and are admitted to be unsurpassed among the air-pilots of England. For many years he has been looked upon as among the most daring and the most intellectual of flying men, a combination which has enabled him to both invent and test several new devices, including the common gyroscopic attachment which is known by his name. The main body of the manuscript is written neatly in ink, but the last few lines are in pencil and are so ragged as to be hardly legible – exactly, in fact, as they might be expected to appear if they were scribbled off hurriedly from the seat of a moving aeroplane. There are, it may be added, several stains, both on the last page and on the outside cover, which have been pronounced by the Home Office experts to be blood – probably human and certainly mammalian. The fact that something closely resembling the organism of malaria was discovered in this blood, and that Joyce-Armstrong is known to have suffered from intermittent fever, is a remarkable example of the new weapons which modern science has placed in the hands of our detectives.

And now a word as to the personality of the author of this epoch-making statement. Joyce-Armstrong, according to the few friends who really knew something of the man, was a poet and a dreamer, as well as a mechanic and an inventor. He was a man of considerable wealth, much of which he had spent in the pursuit of his aeronautical hobby. He had four private aeroplanes in his hangars near Devizes, and is said to have made no fewer than one hundred and seventy ascents in the course of last year. He was a retiring man with dark moods, in which he would avoid the society of his fellows. Captain Dangerfield, who knew him better than anyone, says that there were times when his eccentricity threatened to develop into something more serious. His habit of carrying a shot-gun with him in his aeroplane was one manifestation of it.

Another was the morbid effect which the fall of Lieutenant Myrtle had upon his mind. Myrtle, who was attempting the height record, fell from an altitude of something over thirty thousand feet. Horrible to narrate, his head was entirely obliterated, though his body and limbs preserved their configuration. At every gathering of airmen, Joyce-Armstrong, according to Dangerfield, would ask, with an enigmatic smile: 'And where, pray, is Myrtle's head?'

On another occasion after dinner, at the mess of the Flying School on Salisbury Plain, he started a debate as to what will be the most permanent danger which airmen will have to encounter. Having listened to successive opinions as to air-pockets, faulty construction, and over-banking, he ended by shrugging his shoulders and refusing to put forward his own views, though he gave the impression that they differed from any advanced by his companions.

It is worth remarking that after his own complete disappearance it was found that his private affairs were arranged with a precision which may show that he had a strong premonition of disaster. With these essential explanations I will now give the narrative exactly as it stands, beginning at page three of the blood-soaked notebook: –

'Nevertheless, when I dined at Rheims with Coselli and Gustav Raymond I found that neither of them was aware of any particular danger in the higher layers of the atmosphere. I did not actually say what was in my thoughts, but I got so near to it that if they had any corresponding idea they could not have failed to express it. But then they are two empty, vainglorious fellows with no thought beyond seeing their silly names in the newspaper. It is interesting to note that neither of them had ever been much beyond the twenty-thousand-foot level. Of course, men have been higher than this both in balloons and in the ascent of mountains. It must be well above that point that the aeroplane enters the danger zone – always presuming that my premonitions are correct.

'Aeroplaning has been with us now for more than twenty years, and one might well ask: Why should this peril be only revealing itself in our day? The answer is obvious. In the old days of weak engines, when a hundred horse-power Gnome or Green was considered ample for every need, the flights were very restricted. Now that three hundred horse-power is the rule rather than the exception, visits to the upper layers have become easier and more common. Some of us can remember how, in our youth, Garros made a world-wide reputation by attaining nineteen thousand feet, and it was considered a remarkable achievement to fly over the Alps. Our standard now has been immeasurably raised, and there are twenty high flights for one in former years. Many of them have been undertaken with impunity. The thirty-thousand-foot level has been reached time after time with no discomfort beyond cold and asthma. What does this prove? A visitor might descend upon this planet a thousand times and never see a tiger. Yet tigers exist, and if he chanced to come down into a jungle he might be devoured. There are jungles of the upper air, and there are worse things than tigers which inhabit them. I believe in time they will map these jungles accurately out. Even at the present moment I could name two of them. One of them lies over the Pau-Biarritz district of France. Another is just over my head as I write here in my house in Wiltshire. I rather think there is a third in the Homburg-Wiesbaden district.

'It was the disappearance of the airmen that first set me thinking. Of course, everyone said that they had fallen into the sea, but that did not satisfy me at all. First, there was Verrier in France; his machine was found near Bayonne, but they never got his body. There was the case of Baxter also, who vanished, though his engine and some of the iron fixings were found in a wood in Leicestershire. In that case, Dr Middleton, of Amesbury, who was watching the flight with a telescope, declares that just before the clouds obscured the view he saw the machine, which was at an enormous height, suddenly rise perpendicularly upwards in a succession of jerks in a manner that he would have thought to be impossible. That was the last seen of Baxter. There was a correspondence in the papers, but it never led to anything. There were several other similar cases, and then there was the death of Hay Connor. What a cackle there was about an unsolved mystery of the air, and what columns in the halfpenny papers, and yet how little was ever done to get to the bottom of the business! He came down in a tremendous vol-plané from an unknown height. He never got off his machine and died in his pilot's seat. Died of what? "Heart disease," said the doctors. Rubbish! Hay Connor's heart was as sound as mine is. What did Venables say? Venables was the only man who was at his side when he died. He said that he was shivering and looked like a man who had been badly scared. "Died of fright," said Venables, but could not imagine what he was frightened about. Only said one word to Venables, which sounded like "Monstrous". They could make nothing of that at the inquest. But I could make something of it. Monsters! That was the last word of poor Harry Hay Connor. And he *did* die of fright, just as Venables thought.

'And then there was Myrtle's head. Do you really believe – does anybody really believe – that a man's head could be driven clean into his body by the force of a fall? Well, perhaps it may be possible, but I, for one, have never believed that it was so with Myrtle. And the grease upon his clothes – "all slimy with grease," said somebody at the inquest. Queer that nobody got thinking after that! I did – but, then, I had been thinking for a good long time. I've made three ascents – how Dangerfield used to chaff me about my shot-gun! – but I've never been high enough. Now, with this new light Paul Veroner machine and its one hundred and seventy-five Robur, I should easily touch the thirty thousand to-morrow. I'll have a shot at the record. Maybe I shall have a shot at something else as well. Of course, it's dangerous. If a fellow wants to avoid danger he had best keep out of flying altogether and subside finally into flannel slippers and a dressing-gown. But I'll visit the air-jungle to-morrow – and if there's anything there I shall know it. If I return, I'll find myself a bit of a celebrity. If I don't, this note-book may explain what I am trying to do, and how I lost my life in doing it. But no drivel about accidents or mysteries, if *you* please.

'I chose my Paul Veroner monoplane for the job. There's nothing like a monoplane when real work is to be done. Beaumont found that out in very early days. For one thing, it doesn't mind damp, and the weather looks as if we should be in the clouds all the time. It's a bonny little model and answers my hand like a tender-mouthed horse. The engine is a ten-cylinder rotary Robur working up to one hundred and seventy-five. It has all the modern improvements – enclosed fuselage, high-curved landing skids, brakes, gyroscopic steadiers, and three speeds, worked by an alteration of the angle of the planes upon the Venetian-blind principle. I took a shot-gun with me and a dozen cartridges filled with buck-shot. You should have seen the face of Perkins, my old mechanic, when I directed him to put them in. I was dressed like an Arctic explorer, with two jerseys under my overalls, thick socks inside my padded boots, a storm-cap with flaps, and my talc goggles. It was stifling outside the hangars, but I was going for the summit of the Himalayas, and had to dress for the part. Perkins knew there was something on and implored me to take him with me. Perhaps I should if I were using the biplane, but a monoplane is a one-man show – if you want to get the last foot of lift out of it. Of course, I took an oxygen bag; the man who goes for the altitude record without one will either be frozen or smothered – or both.

'I had a good look at the planes, the rudder-bar, and the elevating lever before I got in. Everything was in order so far as I could see. Then I switched on my engine and found that she was running sweetly. When they let her go she rose almost at once upon the lowest speed. I circled my home field once or twice just to warm her up, and then, with a wave to Perkins and the others, I flattened out my planes and put her on her highest. She skimmed like a swallow down wind for eight or ten miles until I turned her nose up a little and she began to climb in a great spiral for the cloud-bank above me. It's all-important to rise slowly and adapt yourself to the pressure as you go.

'It was a close, warm day for an English September, and there was the hush and heaviness of impending rain. Now and then there came sudden puffs of wind from the south-west – one of them so gusty and unexpected that it caught me napping and turned me half-round for an instant. I remember the time when gusts and whirls and air-pockets used to be things of danger – before we learned to put an overmastering power into our engines. Just as I reached the cloud-banks, with the altimeter marking three thousand, down came the rain. My word, how it poured! It drummed upon my wings and lashed against my face, blurring my glasses so that I could hardly see. I got down on to a low speed, for it was painful to travel against it. As I got higher it became hail, and I had to turn tail to it. One of my cylinders was out of action – a dirty plug, I should imagine, but still I was rising steadily with plenty of power. After a bit the trouble passed, whatever it was, and I heard the full, deep-throated purr – the ten singing as one. That's where the beauty of our modern silencers comes in. We can at last control our engines by ear. How they squeal and squeak and sob when they are in trouble! All those cries for help were wasted in the old days, when every sound was swallowed up by the monstrous racket of the machine. If only the early aviators could come back to see the beauty and perfection of the mechanism which have been bought at the cost of their lives!

'About nine-thirty I was nearing the clouds. Down below me, all blurred and shadowed with rain, lay the vast expanse of Salisbury Plain. Half-a-dozen flying machines were doing hackwork at the thousand-foot level, looking like little black swallows against the green background. I dare say they were wondering what I was doing up in cloud-land. Suddenly a grey curtain drew across beneath me and the wet folds of vapour were swirling round my face. It was clammily cold and miserable. But I was above the hail-storm, and that was something gained. The cloud was as dark and thick as a London fog. In my anxiety to get clear, I cocked her nose up until the automatic alarm-bell rang, and I actually began to slide backwards. My sopped and dripping wings had made me heavier than I thought, but presently I was in lighter cloud, and soon had cleared the first layer. There was a second – opal-coloured and fleecy – at a great height above my head, a white unbroken ceiling above, and a dark unbroken floor below, with the monoplane labouring upwards upon a vast spiral between them. It is deadly lonely in these cloud-spaces. Once a great flight of some small water-birds went past me, flying very fast to the westwards. The quick whirr of their wings and their musical cry were cheery to my ear. I fancy that they were teal, but I am a wretched zoologist. Now that we humans have become birds we must really learn to know our brethren by sight.

'The wind down beneath me whirled and swayed the broad cloud-plain. Once a great eddy formed in it, a whirlpool of vapour, and through it, as down a funnel, I caught sight of the distant world. A large white biplane was passing at a vast depth beneath me. I fancy it was the morning mail service betwixt Bristol and London. Then the drift swirled inwards again and the great solitude was unbroken.

'Just after ten I touched the lower edge of the upper cloud-stratum. It consisted of fine diaphanous vapour drifting swiftly from the westward. The wind had been steadily rising all this time and it was now blowing a sharp breeze – twenty-eight an hour by my gauge. Already it was very cold, though my altimeter only marked nine thousand. The engines were working beautifully, and we went droning steadily upwards. The cloud-bank was thicker than I had expected, but at last it thinned out into a golden mist before me, and then in an instant I had shot out from it, and there was an unclouded sky and a brilliant sun above my head – all blue and gold above, all shining silver below, one vast glimmering plain as far as my eyes could reach. It was a quarter past ten o'clock, and the barograph needle pointed to twelve thousand eight hundred. Up I went and up, my ears concentrated upon the deep purring of my motor, my eyes busy always with the watch, the revolution indicator, the petrol lever, and the oil pump. No wonder aviators are said to be a fearless race. With so many things to think of there is no time to trouble about oneself. About this time I noted how unreliable is the compass when above a certain height from earth. At fifteen thousand feet mine was pointing east and a point south. The sun and the wind gave me my true bearings.

'I had hoped to reach an eternal stillness in these high altitudes, but with every thousand feet of ascent the gale grew stronger.

My machine groaned and trembled in every joint and rivet as she faced it, and swept away like a sheet of paper when I banked her on the turn, skimming down wind at a greater pace, perhaps, than ever mortal man has moved. Yet I had always to turn again and tack up in the wind's eye, for it was not merely a height record that I was after. By all my calculations it was above little Wiltshire that my air-jungle lay, and all my labour might be lost if I struck the outer layers at some farther point.

'When I reached the nineteen-thousand-foot level, which was about midday, the wind was so severe that I looked with some anxiety to the stays of my wings, expecting momentarily to see them snap or slacken. I even cast loose the parachute behind me, and fastened its hook into the ring of my leathern belt, so as to be ready for the worst. Now was the time when a bit of scamped work by the mechanic is paid for by the life of the aeronaut. But she held together bravely. Every cord and strut was humming and vibrating like so many harp-strings, but it was glorious to see how, for all the beating and the buffeting, she was still the conqueror of Nature and the mistress of the sky. There is surely something divine in man himself that he should rise so superior to the limitations which Creation seemed to impose – rise, too, by such unselfish, heroic devotion as this air-conquest has shown. Talk of human degeneration! When has such a story as this been written in the annals of our race?

'These were the thoughts in my head as I climbed that monstrous inclined plane with the wind sometimes beating in my face and sometimes whistling behind my ears, while the cloud-land beneath me fell away to such a distance that the folds and hummocks of silver had all smoothed out into one flat, shining plain. But suddenly I had a horrible and unprecedented experience. I have known before what it is to be in what our neighbours have called a *tourbillon*, but never on such a scale as this. That huge, sweeping river of wind of which I have spoken had, as it appears, whirlpools within it which were as monstrous as itself.

Without a moment's warning I was dragged suddenly into the heart of one. I spun round for a minute or two with such velocity that I almost lost my senses, and then fell suddenly, left wing foremost, down the vacuum funnel in the centre. I dropped like a stone, and lost nearly a thousand feet. It was only my belt that kept me in my seat, and the shock and breathlessness left me hanging half-insensible over the side of the fuselage. But I am always capable of a supreme effort – it is my one great merit as an aviator. I was conscious that the descent was slower. The whirlpool was a cone rather than a funnel, and I had come to the apex. With a terrific wrench, throwing my weight all to one side, I levelled my planes and brought her head away from the wind. In an instant I had shot out of the eddies and was skimming down the sky. Then, shaken but victorious, I turned her nose up and began once more my steady grind on the upward spiral. I took a large sweep to avoid the danger-spot of the whirlpool, and soon I was safely above it. Just after one o'clock I was twenty-one thousand feet above the sea-level. To my great joy I had topped the gale, and with every hundred feet of ascent the air grew stiller. On the other hand, it was very cold, and I was conscious of that peculiar nausea which goes with rarefaction of the air. For the first time I unscrewed the mouth of my oxygen bag and took an occasional whiff of the glorious gas. I could feel it running like a cordial through my veins, and I was exhilarated almost to the point of drunkenness. I shouted and sang as I soared upwards into the cold, still outer world.

'It is very clear to me that the insensibility which came upon Glaisher, and in a lesser degree upon Coxwell, when, in 1862, they ascended in a balloon to the height of thirty thousand feet, was due to the extreme speed with which a perpendicular ascent is made. Doing it at an easy gradient and accustoming oneself to the lessened barometric pressure by slow degrees, there are no such dreadful symptoms. At the same great height I found that even without my oxygen inhaler I could breathe without undue distress. It was bitterly cold, however, and my thermometer was at zero Fahrenheit. At one-thirty I was nearly seven miles above the surface of the earth, and still ascending steadily. I found, however, that the rarefied air was giving markedly less support to my planes, and that my angle of ascent had to be considerably lowered in consequence. It was already clear that even with my light weight and strong engine-power there was a point in front of me where I should be held. To make matters worse, one of my sparking-plugs was in trouble again and there was intermittent misfiring in the engine. My heart was heavy with the fear of failure.

'It was about that time that I had a most extraordinary experience. Something whizzed past me in a trail of smoke and exploded with a loud, hissing sound, sending forth a cloud of steam. For the instant I could not imagine what had happened. Then I remembered that the earth is for ever being bombarded by meteor stones, and would be hardly inhabitable were they not in nearly every case turned to vapour in the outer layers of the atmosphere. Here is a new danger for the high-altitude man, for two others passed me when I was nearing the forty-thousand-foot mark. I cannot doubt that at the edge of the earth's envelope the risk would be a very real one.

'My barograph needle marked forty-one thousand three hundred when I became aware that I could go no farther. Physically, the strain was not as yet greater than I could bear, but my machine had reached its limit. The attenuated air gave no firm support to the wings, and the least tilt developed into side-slip, while she seemed sluggish on her controls. Possibly, had the engine been at its best, another thousand feet might have been within our capacity, but it was still misfiring, and two out of the ten cylinders appeared to be out of action. If I had not already reached the zone for which I was searching then I should never see it upon this journey. But was it not possible that I had attained it? Soaring in circles like a monstrous hawk upon the forty-thousand-foot level I let the monoplane guide herself, and with my Mannheim glass I made a careful observation of my surroundings. The heavens were perfectly clear; there was no indication of those dangers which I had imagined.

'I have said that I was soaring in circles. It struck me suddenly that I would do well to take a wider sweep and open up a new air-tract. If the hunter entered an earth-jungle he would drive through it if he wished to find his game. My reasoning had led me to believe that the air-jungle which I had imagined lay somewhere over Wiltshire. This should be to the south and west of me. I took my bearings from the sun, for the compass was hopeless and no trace of earth was to be seen – nothing but the distant silver cloud-plain. However, I got my direction as best I might and kept her head straight to the mark. I reckoned that my petrol supply would not last for more than another hour or so, but I could afford to use it to the last drop, since a single magnificent vol-plané could at any time take me to the earth.

'Suddenly I was aware of something new. The air in front of me had lost its crystal clearness. It was full of long, ragged wisps of something which I can only compare to very fine cigarette-smoke. It hung about in wreaths and coils, turning and twisting slowly in the sunlight. As the monoplane shot through it, I was aware of a faint taste of oil upon my lips, and there was a greasy scum upon the woodwork of the machine. Some infinitely fine organic matter appeared to be suspended in the atmosphere. There was no life there. It was inchoate and diffuse, extending for many square acres and then fringing off into the void. No, it was not life. But might it not be the remains of life? Above all, might it not be the food of life, of monstrous life, even as the humble grease of the ocean is the food for the mighty whale? The thought was in my mind when my eyes looked upwards and I saw the most wonderful vision that ever man has seen. Can I hope to convey it to you even as I saw it myself last Thursday?

'Conceive a jelly-fish such as sails in our summer seas,

bell-shaped and of enormous size – far larger, I should judge, than the dome of St Paul's. It was of a light pink colour veined with a delicate green, but the whole huge fabric so tenuous that it was but a fairy outline against the dark blue sky. It pulsated with a delicate and regular rhythm. From it there depended two long, drooping green tentacles, which swayed slowly backwards and forwards. This gorgeous vision passed gently with noiseless dignity over my head, as light and fragile as a soap-bubble, and drifted upon its stately way.

'I had half-turned my monoplane, that I might look after this beautiful creature, when, in a moment, I found myself amidst a perfect fleet of them, of all sizes, but none so large as the first. Some were quite small, but the majority about as big as an average balloon, and with much the same curvature at the top. There was in them a delicacy of texture and colouring which reminded me of the finest Venetian glass. Pale shades of pink and green were the prevailing tints, but all had a lovely iridescence where the sun shimmered through their dainty forms. Some hundreds of them drifted past me, a wonderful fairy squadron of strange, unknown argosies of the sky – creatures whose forms and substance were so attuned to these pure heights that one could not conceive anything so delicate within actual sight or sound of earth.

'But soon my attention was drawn to a new phenomenon – the serpents of the outer air. These were long, thin, fantastic coils of vapour-like material, which turned and twisted with great speed, flying round and round at such a pace that the eyes could hardly follow them. Some of these ghost-like creatures were twenty or thirty feet long, but it was difficult to tell their girth, for their outline was so hazy that it seemed to fade away into the air around them. These air-snakes were of a very light grey or smoke colour, with some darker lines within, which gave the impression of a definite organism. One of them whisked past my very face, and I was conscious of a cold, clammy contact, but their composition was so unsubstantial that I could not connect them with any thought of physical danger, any more than the beautiful bell-like creatures which had preceded them. There was no more solidity in their frames than in the floating spume from a broken wave.

'But a more terrible experience was in store for me. Floating downwards from a great height there came a purplish patch of vapour, small as I saw it first, but rapidly enlarging as it approached me, until it appeared to be hundreds of square feet in size. Though fashioned of some transparent, jelly-like substance, it was none the less of much more definite outline and solid consistence than anything which I had seen before. There were more traces, too, of a physical organisation, especially two vast shadowy, circular plates upon either side, which may have been eyes, and a perfectly solid white projection between them which was as curved and cruel as the beak of a vulture.

'The whole aspect of this monster was formidable and threatening, and it kept changing its colour from a very light mauve to a dark, angry purple so thick that it cast a shadow as it drifted between my monoplane and the sun. On the upper curve of its huge body there were three great projections which I can only describe as enormous bubbles, and I was convinced as I looked at them that they were charged with some extremely light gas which served to buoy up the misshapen and semi-solid mass in the rarefied air. The creature moved swiftly along, keeping pace easily with the monoplane, and for twenty miles or more it formed my horrible escort, hovering over me like a bird of prey which is waiting to pounce. Its method of progression – done so swiftly that it was not easy to follow – was to throw out a long, glutinous streamer in front of it, which in turn seemed to draw forward the rest of the writhing body. So elastic and gelatinous was it that never for two successive minutes was it the same shape, and yet each change made it more threatening and loathsome than the last.

'I knew that it meant mischief. Every purple flush of its hideous body told me so. The vague, goggling eyes which were turned always upon me were cold and merciless in their viscid hatred. I dipped the nose of my monoplane downwards to escape it. As I did so, as quick as a flash there shot out a long tentacle from this mass of floating blubber, and it fell as light and sinuous as a whiplash across the front of my machine. There was a loud hiss as it lay for a moment across the hot engine, and it whisked itself into the air again, while the huge flat body drew itself together as if in sudden pain. I dipped to a vol-piqué, but again a tentacle fell over the monoplane and was shorn off by the propeller as easily as it might have cut through a smoke wreath. A long, gliding, sticky, serpent-like coil came from behind and caught me round the waist, dragging me out of the fuselage. I tore at it, my fingers sinking into the smooth, glue-like surface, and for an instant I disengaged myself, but only to be caught round the boot by another coil, which gave me a jerk that tilted me almost on to my back.

'As I fell over I blazed off both barrels of my gun, though, indeed, it was like attacking an elephant with a pea-shooter to imagine that any human weapon could cripple that mighty bulk. And yet I aimed better than I knew, for, with a loud report, one of the great blisters upon the creature's back exploded with the puncture of the buck-shot. It was very clear that my conjecture was right, and that these vast clear bladders were distended with some lifting gas, for in an instant the huge cloud-like body turned sideways, writhing desperately to find its balance, while the white beak snapped and gaped in horrible fury. But already I had shot away on the steepest glide that I dared to attempt, my engine still full on, the flying propeller and the force of gravity shooting me downwards like an aerolite. Far behind me I saw a dull, purplish smudge growing swiftly smaller and merging into the blue sky behind it. I was safe out of the deadly jungle of the outer air.

'Once out of danger I throttled my engine, for nothing tears a machine to pieces quicker than running on full power from a height. It was a glorious spiral vol-plané from nearly eight miles of altitude – first, to the level of the silver cloud-bank, then to that of the storm-cloud beneath it, and finally, in beating rain, to the surface of the earth. I saw the Bristol Channel beneath me as I broke from the clouds, but, having still some petrol in my tank, I got twenty miles inland before I found myself stranded in a field half a mile from the village of Ashcombe. There I got three tins of petrol from a passing motor-car, and at ten minutes past six that evening I alighted gently in my own home meadow at Devizes, after such a journey as no mortal upon earth has ever yet taken and lived to tell the tale. I have seen the beauty and I have seen the horror of the heights – and greater beauty or greater horror than that is not within the ken of man.

'And now it is my plan to go once again before I give my results to the world. My reason for this is that I must surely have something to show by way of proof before I lay such a tale before my fellow-men. It is true that others will soon follow and will confirm what I have said, and yet I should wish to carry conviction from the first. Those lovely iridescent bubbles of the air should not be hard to capture. They drift slowly upon their way, and the swift monoplane could intercept their leisurely course. It is likely enough that they would dissolve in the heavier layers of the atmosphere, and that some small heap of amorphous jelly might be all that I should bring to earth with me. And yet something there would surely be by which I could substantiate my story. Yes, I will go, even if I run a risk by doing so. These purple horrors would not seem to be numerous. It is probable that I shall not see one. If I do I shall dive at once. At the worst there is always the shot-gun and my knowledge of . . .'

Here a page of the manuscript is unfortunately missing. On the next page is written, in large, straggling writing: –

'Forty-three thousand feet. I shall never see earth again. They are beneath me, three of them. God help me; it is a dreadful death to die!'

Such in its entirety is the Joyce-Armstrong Statement. Of the man nothing has since been seen. Pieces of his shattered monoplane have been picked up in the preserves of Mr Budd-Lushington upon the borders of Kent and Sussex, within a few miles of the spot where the notebook was discovered. If the unfortunate aviator's theory is correct that this air-jungle, as he called it, existed only over the south-west of England, then it would seem that he had fled from it at the full speed of his monoplane, but had been overtaken and devoured by these horrible creatures at some spot in the outer atmosphere above the place where the grim relics were found. The picture of that monoplane skimming down the sky, with the nameless terrors flying as swiftly beneath it and cutting it off always from the earth while they gradually closed in upon their victim, is one upon which a man who valued his sanity would prefer not to dwell. There are many, as I am aware, who still jeer at the facts which I have here set down, but even they must admit that Joyce-Armstrong has disappeared, and I would commend to them his own words: 'This note-book may explain what I am trying to do, and how I lost my life in doing it. But no drivel about accidents or mysteries, if *you* please.'

Kerfol

Edith Wharton

I

'You ought to buy it,' said my host; 'it's just the place for a solitary-minded devil like you. And it would be rather worthwhile to own the most romantic house in Brittany. The present people are dead broke, and it's going for a song – you ought to buy it.'

It was not with the least idea of living up to the character my friend Lanrivain ascribed to me (as a matter of fact, under my unsociable exterior I have always had secret yearnings for domesticity) that I took his hint one autumn afternoon and went to Kerfol. My friend was motoring over to Quimper on business: he dropped me on the way, at a cross-road on a heath, and said: 'First turn to the right and second to the left. Then straight ahead till you see an avenue. If you meet any peasants, don't ask your way. They don't understand French, and they would pretend they did and mix you up. I'll be back for you here by sunset – and don't forget the tombs in the chapel.'

I followed Lanrivain's directions with the hesitation occasioned by the usual difficulty of remembering whether he had said the first turn to the right and second to the left, or the contrary. If I had met a peasant I should certainly have asked, and probably been sent astray; but I had the desert landscape to myself, and so stumbled on the right turn and walked across the heath till I came to an avenue. It was so unlike any other avenue I have ever seen that I instantly knew it must be *the* avenue. The grey-trunked trees sprang up straight to a great height and then interwove their pale-grey branches in a long tunnel through which the autumn light fell faintly. I know most trees by name, but I haven't to this day been able to decide what those trees were. They had the tall curve of elms, the tenuity of poplars, the ashen colour of olives under a rainy sky; and they stretched ahead of me for half a mile or more without a break in their arch. If ever I saw an avenue that unmistakably led to something, it was the avenue at Kerfol. My heart beat a little as I began to walk down it.

Presently the trees ended and I came to a fortified gate in a long wall. Between me and the wall was an open space of grass, with other grey avenues radiating from it. Behind the wall were tall slate roofs mossed with silver, a chapel belfry, the top of a keep. A moat filled with wild shrubs and brambles surrounded the place; the drawbridge had been replaced by a stone arch, and the portcullis by an iron gate. I stood for a long time on the hither side of the moat, gazing about me, and letting the influence of the place sink in. I said to myself: 'If I wait long enough, the guardian will turn up and show me the tombs –' and I rather hoped he wouldn't turn up too soon.

I sat down on a stone and lit a cigarette. As soon as I had done it, it struck me as a puerile and portentous thing to do, with that great blind house looking down at me, and all the empty avenues converging on me. It may have been the depth of the silence that made me so conscious of my gesture. The squeak of my match sounded as loud as the scraping of a brake, and I almost fancied I heard it fall when I tossed it onto the grass. But there was more than that: a sense of irrelevance, of littleness, of futile bravado, in sitting there puffing my cigarette-smoke into the face of such a past.

I knew nothing of the history of Kerfol – I was new to Brittany, and Lanrivain had never mentioned the name to me till the day before – but one couldn't as much as glance at that pile without feeling in it a long accumulation of history. What kind of history I was not prepared to guess: perhaps only that sheer weight of many associated lives and deaths which gives a majesty to all old houses. But the aspect of Kerfol suggested something more – a perspective of stern and cruel memories stretching away, like its own grey avenues, into a blur of darkness.

Certainly no house had ever more completely and finally broken with the present. As it stood there, lifting its proud roofs and gables to the sky, it might have been its own funeral monument. 'Tombs in the chapel? The whole place is a tomb!' I reflected. I hoped more and more that the guardian would not come. The details of the place, however striking, would seem trivial compared with its collective impressiveness; and I wanted only to sit there and be penetrated by the weight of its silence.

'It's the very place for you!' Lanrivain had said; and I was overcome by the almost blasphemous frivolity of suggesting to any living being that Kerfol was the place for him. 'Is it possible that anyone could *not* see – ?' I wondered. I did not finish the thought: what I meant was undefinable. I stood up and wandered toward the gate. I was beginning to want to know more; not to *see* more – I was by now so sure it was not a question of seeing – but to feel more: feel all the place had to communicate. 'But to get in one will have to rout out the keeper,' I thought reluctantly, and hesitated. Finally I crossed the bridge and tried the iron gate. It yielded, and I walked through the tunnel formed by the thickness of the *chemin de ronde*. At the farther end, a wooden barricade had been laid across the entrance, and beyond it was a court enclosed in noble architecture. The main building faced me; and I now saw that one half was a mere ruined front, with gaping windows through which the wild growths of the moat and the trees of the park were visible. The rest of the house was still in its robust beauty. One end abutted on the round tower, the other on the small traceried chapel, and in an angle of the building stood a graceful well-head crowned with mossy urns. A few roses grew against the walls, and on an upper window-sill I remember noticing a pot of fuchsias.

My sense of the pressure of the invisible began to yield to my architectural interest. The building was so fine that I felt a desire to explore it for its own sake. I looked about the court, wondering in which corner the guardian lodged. Then I pushed open the barrier and went in. As I did so, a dog barred my way. He was such a remarkably beautiful little dog that for a moment he made me forget the splendid place he was defending. I was not sure of his breed at the time, but have since learned that it was Chinese, and that he was of a rare variety called the 'Sleeve-dog'. He was very small and golden brown, with large brown eyes and a ruffled throat: he looked like a large tawny chrysanthemum. I said to myself: 'These little beasts always snap and scream, and somebody will be out in a minute.'

The little animal stood before me, forbidding, almost menacing: there was anger in his large brown eyes. But he made no sound, he came no nearer. Instead, as I advanced, he gradually fell back, and I noticed that another dog, a vague rough brindled thing, had limped up on a lame leg. 'There'll be a hubbub now,' I thought; for at the same moment a third dog, a long-haired white mongrel, slipped out of a doorway and joined the others. All three stood looking at me with grave eyes; but not a sound came from them. As I advanced they continued to fall back on muffled paws, still watching me. 'At a given point, they'll all charge at my ankles: it's one of the jokes that dogs who live together put up on one,' I thought. I was not alarmed, for they were neither large nor formidable. But they let me wander about the court as I pleased, following me at a little distance – always the same distance – and always keeping their eyes on me. Presently I looked across at the ruined façade, and saw that in one of its empty window-frames another dog stood: a white pointer with one brown ear. He was an old grave dog, much more experienced than the others; and he seemed to be observing me with a deeper intentness.

'I'll hear from *him*,' I said to myself; but he stood in the window-frame, against the trees of the park, and continued to watch me without moving. I stared back at him for a time, to see if the sense that he was being watched would not rouse him. Half the width of the court lay between us, and we gazed at each other silently across it. But he did not stir, and at last I turned away. Behind me I found the rest of the pack, with a newcomer added: a small black greyhound with pale agate-coloured eyes. He was shivering a little, and his expression was more timid than that of the others. I noticed that he kept a little behind them. And still there was not a sound.

I stood there for fully five minutes, the circle about me – waiting, as they seemed to be waiting. At last I went up to the little golden-brown dog and stooped to pat him. As I did so, I heard myself give a nervous laugh. The little dog did not start, or growl, or take his eyes from me – he simply slipped back about a yard, and then paused and continued to look at me. 'Oh, hang it!' I exclaimed, and walked across the court toward the well.

As I advanced, the dogs separated and slid away into different corners of the court. I examined the urns on the well, tried a locked door or two, and looked up and down the dumb façade; then I faced about toward the chapel. When I turned I perceived that all the dogs had disappeared except the old pointer, who still watched me from the window. It was rather a relief to be rid of that cloud of witnesses; and I began to look about me for a way to the back of the house. 'Perhaps there'll be somebody in the garden,' I thought. I found a way across the moat, scrambled over a wall smothered in brambles, and got into the garden. A few lean hydrangeas and geraniums pined in the flower-beds, and the ancient house looked down on them indifferently. Its garden side was plainer and severer than the other: the long granite front, with its few windows and steep roof, looked like a fortress-prison. I walked around the farther wing, went up some disjointed steps, and entered the deep twilight of a narrow and incredibly old box-walk. The walk was just wide enough for one person to slip through, and its branches met overhead. It was like the ghost of a box-walk, its lustrous green all turning to the shadowy greyness of the avenues. I walked on and on, the branches hitting me in the face and springing back with a dry rattle; and at length I came out on the grassy top of the *chemin de ronde.* I walked along it to the gate-tower, looking down into the court, which was just below me. Not a human being was in sight; and neither were the dogs. I found a flight of steps in the thickness of the wall and went down them; and when I emerged again into the court, there stood the circle of dogs, the golden-brown one a little ahead of the others, the black greyhound shivering in the rear.

'Oh, hang it – you uncomfortable beasts, you!' I exclaimed, my voice startling me with a sudden echo. The dogs stood motionless, watching me. I knew by this time that they would not try to prevent my approaching the house, and the knowledge left me free to examine them. I had a feeling that they must be horribly cowed to be so silent and inert. Yet they did not look hungry or ill-treated. Their coats were smooth and they were not thin, except the shivering greyhound. It was more as if they had lived a long time with people who never spoke to them or looked at them: as though the silence of the place had gradually benumbed their busy inquisitive natures. And this strange passivity, this almost human lassitude, seemed to me sadder than the misery of starved and beaten animals. I should have liked to rouse them for a minute, to coax them into a game or a scamper; but the longer I looked into their fixed and weary eyes the more preposterous the idea became. With the windows of that house looking down on us, how could I have imagined such a thing? The dogs knew better: *they* knew what the house would tolerate and what it would not. I even fancied that they knew what was passing through my mind, and pitied me for my frivolity. But even that feeling probably reached them through a thick fog of listlessness. I had an idea that their distance from me was as nothing to my remoteness from them. The impression they produced was that of having in common one memory so deep and dark that nothing that had happened since was worth either a growl or a wag.

'I say,' I broke out abruptly, addressing myself to the dumb circle, 'do you know what you look like, the whole lot of you?

You look as if you'd seen a ghost – that's how you look! I wonder if there *is* a ghost here, and nobody but you left for it to appear to?' The dogs continued to gaze at me without moving . . .

It was dark when I saw Lanrivain's motor lamps at the cross-roads – and I wasn't exactly sorry to see them. I had the sense of having escaped from the loneliest place in the whole world, and of not liking loneliness – to that degree – as much as I had imagined I should. My friend had brought his solicitor back from Quimper for the night, and seated beside a fat and affable stranger I felt no inclination to talk of Kerfol . . .

But that evening, when Lanrivain and the solicitor were closeted in the study, Madame de Lanrivain began to question me in the drawing-room.

'Well – are you going to buy Kerfol?' she asked, tilting up her gay chin from her embroidery.

'I haven't decided yet. The fact is, I couldn't get into the house,' I said, as if I had simply postponed my decision, and meant to go back for another look.

'You couldn't get in? Why, what happened? The family are mad to sell the place, and the old guardian has orders –'

'Very likely. But the old guardian wasn't there.'

'What a pity! He must have gone to market. But his daughter – ?'

'There was nobody about. At least I saw no one.'

'How extraordinary! Literally nobody?'

'Nobody but a lot of dogs – a whole pack of them – who seemed to have the place to themselves.'

Madame de Lanrivain let the embroidery slip to her knee and folded her hands on it. For several minutes she looked at me thoughtfully.

'A pack of dogs – you *saw* them?'

'Saw them? I saw nothing else!'

'How many?' She dropped her voice a little. 'I've always wondered –'

I looked at her with surprise: I had supposed the place to be familiar to her. 'Have you never been to Kerfol?' I asked.

'Oh, yes: often. But never on that day.'

'What day?'

'I'd quite forgotten – and so had Hervé, I'm sure. If we'd remembered, we never should have sent you to-day – but then, after all, one doesn't half believe that sort of thing, does one?'

'What sort of thing?' I asked, involuntarily sinking my voice to the level of hers. Inwardly I was thinking: 'I *knew* there was something . . .'

Madame de Lanrivain cleared her throat and produced a reassuring smile. 'Didn't Hervé tell you the story of Kerfol? An ancestor of his was mixed up in it. You know every Breton house has its ghost-story; and some of them are rather unpleasant.'

'Yes – but those dogs?'

'Well, those dogs are the ghosts of Kerfol. At least, the peasants say there's one day in the year when a lot of dogs appear there; and that day the keeper and his daughter go off to Morlaix and get drunk. The women in Brittany drink dreadfully.' She stooped to match a silk; then she lifted her charming inquisitive Parisian face. 'Did you *really* see a lot of dogs? There isn't one at Kerfol,' she said.

II

Lanrivain, the next day, hunted out a shabby calf volume from the back of an upper shelf of his library.

'Yes – here it is. What does it call itself? *A History of the Assizes of the Duchy of Brittany. Quimper, 1702.* The book was written about a hundred years later than the Kerfol affair; but I believe the account is transcribed pretty literally from the judicial records. Anyhow, it's queer reading. And there's a Hervé de Lanrivain mixed up in it – not exactly *my* style, as you'll see. But then he's only a collateral. Here, take the book up to bed with you. I don't exactly remember the details; but after you've read it I'll bet anything you'll leave your light burning all night!'

I left my light burning all night, as he had predicted; but it was chiefly because, till near dawn, I was absorbed in my reading. The account of the trial of Anne de Cornault, wife of the lord of Kerfol, was long and closely printed. It was, as my friend had said, probably an almost literal transcription of what took place in the court-room; and the trial lasted nearly a month. Besides, the type of the book was very bad . . .

At first I thought of translating the old record. But it is full of wearisome repetitions, and the main lines of the story are forever straying off into side issues. So I have tried to disentangle it, and give it here in a simpler form. At times, however, I have reverted to the text because no other words could have conveyed so exactly the sense of what I felt at Kerfol; and nowhere have I added anything of my own.

III

It was in the year 16— that Yves de Cornault, lord of the domain of Kerfol, went to the *pardon* of Locronan to perform his religious duties. He was a rich and powerful noble, then in his sixty-second year, but hale and sturdy, a great horseman and hunter and a pious man. So all his neighbours attested. In appearance he was short and broad, with a swarthy face, legs slightly bowed from the saddle, a hanging nose and broad hands with black hairs on them. He had married young and lost his wife and son soon after, and since then had lived alone at Kerfol. Twice a year he went to Morlaix, where he had a handsome house by the river, and spent a week or ten days there; and occasionally he rode to Rennes on business. Witnesses were found to declare that during these absences he led a life different from the one he was known to lead at Kerfol, where he busied himself with his estate, attended mass daily, and found his only amusement in hunting the wild boar and water-fowl. But these rumours are not particularly relevant, and it is certain that among people of his own class in the neighbourhood he passed for a stern and even austere man, observant of his religious obligations, and keeping strictly to himself. There was no talk of any familiarity with the women on his estate, though at that time the nobility were very free with their peasants. Some people said he had never looked at a woman since his wife's death; but such things are hard to prove, and the evidence on this point was not worth much.

Well, in his sixty-second year, Yves de Cornault went to the *pardon* at Locronan, and saw there a young lady of Douarnenez, who had ridden over pillion behind her father to do her duty to the saint. Her name was Anne de Barrigan, and she came of good old Breton stock, but much less great and powerful than that of Yves de Cornault; and her father had squandered his fortune at cards, and lived almost like a peasant in his little granite manor on the moors . . . I have said I would add nothing of my own to this bald statement of a strange case; but I must interrupt myself here to describe the young lady who rode up to the lych-gate of Locronan at the very moment when the Baron de Cornault was also dismounting there. I take my description from a faded drawing in red crayon, sober and truthful enough to be by a late pupil of the Clouets, which hangs in Lanrivain's study, and is said to be a portrait of Anne de Barrigan. It is unsigned and has no mark of identity but the initials A. B., and the date 16—, the year after her marriage. It represents a young woman with a small oval face, almost pointed, yet wide enough for a full mouth with a tender depression at the corners. The nose is small, and the eyebrows are set rather high, far apart, and as lightly pencilled as the eyebrows in a Chinese painting. The forehead is high and serious, and the hair, which one feels to be fine and thick and fair, is drawn off it and lies close like a cap. The eyes are neither large nor small, hazel probably, with a look at once shy and steady. A pair of beautiful long hands are crossed below the lady's breast . . .

The chaplain of Kerfol, and other witnesses, averred that when the Baron came back from Locronan he jumped from his horse, ordered another to be instantly saddled, called to a young page to come with him, and rode away that same evening to the south. His steward followed the next morning with coffers laden on a pair of pack mules. The following week Yves de Cornault rode back to Kerfol, sent for his vassals and tenants, and told them he was to be married at All Saints to Anne de Barrigan of Douarnenez. And on All Saints' Day the marriage took place.

As to the next few years, the evidence on both sides seems to show that they passed happily for the couple. No one was found to say that Yves de Cornault had been unkind to his wife, and it was plain to all that he was content with his bargain. Indeed, it was admitted by the chaplain and other witnesses for the prosecution that the young lady had a softening influence on her husband, and that he became less exacting with his tenants, less harsh to peasants and dependents, and less subject to the fits of gloomy silence which had darkened his widowhood. As to his wife, the only grievance her champions could call up in her behalf was that Kerfol was a lonely place, and that when her husband was away on business at Rennes or Morlaix – whither she was never taken – she was not allowed so much as to walk in the park unaccompanied. But no one asserted that she was unhappy, though one servant-woman said she had surprised her crying, and had heard her say that she was a woman accursed to have no child, and nothing in life to call her own. But that was a natural enough feeling in a wife attached to her husband; and certainly it must have been a great grief to Yves de Cornault that she bore no son. Yet he never made her feel her childlessness as a reproach – she admits this in her evidence – but seemed to try to make her forget it by showering gifts and favours on her. Rich though he was, he had never been open-handed; but nothing was too fine for his wife, in the way of silks or gems or linen, or whatever else she fancied. Every wandering merchant was welcome at Kerfol, and when the master was called away he never came back without bringing his wife a handsome present – something curious and particular – from Morlaix or Rennes or Quimper. One of the waiting-women gave, in cross-examination, an interesting list of one year's gifts, which I copy. From Morlaix, a carved ivory junk, with Chinamen at the oars, that a strange sailor had brought back as a votive offering for Notre Dame de la Clarté, above Ploumanac'h; from Quimper, an embroidered gown, worked by the nuns of the Assumption; from Rennes, a silver rose that opened and showed an amber Virgin with a crown of garnets; from Morlaix, again, a length of Damascus velvet shot with gold, bought of a Jew from Syria; and for Michaelmas that same year, from Rennes, a necklet or bracelet of round stones – emeralds and pearls and rubies – strung like beads on a fine gold chain. This was the present that pleased the lady best, the woman said. Later on, as it happened, it was produced at the trial, and appears to have struck the Judges and the public as a curious and valuable jewel.

The very same winter, the Baron absented himself again, this time as far as Bordeaux, and on his return he brought his wife something even odder and prettier than the bracelet. It was a winter evening when he rode up to Kerfol and, walking into the hall, found her sitting by the hearth, her chin on her hand, looking into the fire. He carried a velvet box in his hand and, setting it down, lifted the lid and let out a little golden-brown dog.

Anne de Cornault exclaimed with pleasure as the little creature bounded toward her. 'Oh, it looks like a bird or a butterfly!' she cried as she picked it up; and the dog put its paws on her shoulders and looked at her with eyes 'like a Christian's'. After that she would never have it out of her sight, and petted and talked to it as if it had been a child – as indeed it was the nearest thing to a child she was to know. Yves de Cornault was much pleased with his purchase. The dog had been brought to him by a sailor from an East

India merchantman, and the sailor had bought it of a pilgrim in a bazaar at Jaffa, who had stolen it from a nobleman's wife in China: a perfectly permissible thing to do, since the pilgrim was a Christian and the nobleman a heathen doomed to hellfire. Yves de Cornault had paid a long price for the dog, for they were beginning to be in demand at the French court, and the sailor knew he had got hold of a good thing; but Anne's pleasure was so great that, to see her laugh and play with the little animal, her husband would doubtless have given twice the sum.

So far, all the evidence is at one, and the narrative plain sailing; but now the steering becomes difficult. I will try to keep as nearly as possible to Anne's own statements; though toward the end, poor thing . . .

Well, to go back. The very year after the little brown dog was brought to Kerfol, Yves de Cornault, one winter night, was found dead at the head of a narrow flight of stairs leading down from his wife's rooms to a door opening on the court. It was his wife who found him and gave the alarm, so distracted, poor wretch, with fear and horror – for his blood was all over her – that at first the roused household could not make out what she was saying, and thought she had suddenly gone mad. But there, sure enough, at the top of the stairs lay her husband, stone dead, and head foremost, the blood from his wounds dripping down to the steps below him. He had been dreadfully scratched and gashed about the face and throat, as if with curious pointed weapons; and one of his legs had a deep tear in it which had cut an artery, and probably caused his death. But how did he come there, and who had murdered him?

His wife declared that she had been asleep in her bed, and hearing his cry had rushed out to find him lying on the stairs; but this was immediately questioned. In the first place, it was proved that from her room she could not have heard the struggle on the stairs, owing to the thickness of the walls and the length of the intervening passage; then it was evident that she had not been in bed and asleep, since she was dressed when she roused the house, and her bed had not been slept in. Moreover, the door at the bottom of the stairs was ajar, and it was noticed by the chaplain (an observant man) that the dress she wore was stained with blood about the knees, and that there were traces of small blood-stained hands low down on the staircase walls, so that it was conjectured that she had really been at the postern-door when her husband fell and, feeling her way up to him in the darkness on her hands and knees, had been stained by his blood dripping down on her. Of course it was argued on the other side that the blood-marks on her dress might have been caused by her kneeling down by her husband when she rushed out of her room; but there was the open door below, and the fact that the finger-marks in the staircase all pointed upward.

The accused held to her statement for the first two days, in spite of its improbability; but on the third day word was brought to her that Hervé de Lanrivain, a young nobleman of the neighbourhood, had been arrested for complicity in the crime. Two or three witnesses thereupon came forward to say that it was known throughout the country that Lanrivain had formerly been on good terms with the lady of Cornault; but that he had been absent from Brittany for over a year, and people had ceased to associate their names. The witnesses who made this statement were not of a very reputable sort. One was an old herb-gatherer suspected of witchcraft, another a drunken clerk from a neighbouring parish, the third a half-witted shepherd who could be made to say anything; and it was clear that the prosecution was not satisfied with its case, and would have liked to find more definite proof of Lanrivain's complicity than the statement of the herb-gatherer, who swore to having seen him climbing the wall of the park on the night of the murder. One way of patching out incomplete proofs in those days was to put some sort of pressure, moral or physical, on the accused person. It is not clear what pressure was put on Anne de Cornault; but on the third day, when she was brought in court, she 'appeared weak and wandering', and after being encouraged to collect herself and speak the truth, on her honour and the wounds of her Blessed Redeemer, she confessed that she had in fact gone down the stairs to speak with Hervé de Lanrivain (who denied everything), and had been surprised there by the sound of her husband's fall. That was better; and the prosecution rubbed its hands with satisfaction. The satisfaction increased when various dependents living at Kerfol were induced to say – with apparent sincerity – that during the year or two preceding his death their master had once more grown uncertain and irascible, and subject to the fits of brooding silence which his household had learned to dread before his second marriage. This seemed to show that things had not been going well at Kerfol; though no one could be found to say that there had been any signs of open disagreement between husband and wife.

Anne de Cornault, when questioned as to her reason for going down at night to open the door to Hervé de Lanrivain, made an answer which must have sent a smile around the court. She said it was because she was lonely and wanted to talk with the young man. Was this the only reason? she was asked; and replied: 'Yes, by the Cross over your Lordships' heads.' 'But why at midnight?' the court asked. 'Because I could see him in no other way.' I can see the exchange of glances across the ermine collars under the Crucifix.

Anne de Cornault, further questioned, said that her married life had been extremely lonely: 'desolate' was the word she used. It was true that her husband seldom spoke harshly to her; but there were days when he did not speak at all. It was true that he had never struck or threatened her; but he kept her like a prisoner at Kerfol, and when he rode away to Morlaix or Quimper or Rennes he set so close a watch on her that she could not pick a flower in the garden without having a waiting-woman at her heels. 'I am no Queen, to need such honours,' she once said to him; and he had answered that a man who has a treasure does not leave the key in the lock when he goes out. 'Then take me with you,' she urged; but to this he said that towns were pernicious places, and young wives better off at their own firesides.

'But what did you want to say to Hervé de Lanrivain?' the court asked; and she answered: 'To ask him to take me away.'

'Ah – you confess that you went down to him with adulterous thoughts?'

'No.'

'Then why did you want him to take you away?'

'Because I was afraid for my life.'

'Of whom were you afraid?'

'Of my husband.'

'Why were you afraid of your husband?'

'Because he had strangled my little dog.'

Another smile must have passed around the court-room: in days when any nobleman had a right to hang his peasants – and most of them exercised it – pinching a pet animal's wind-pipe was nothing to make a fuss about.

At this point one of the Judges, who appears to have had a certain sympathy for the accused, suggested that she should be allowed to explain herself in her own way; and she thereupon made the following statement.

The first years of her marriage had been lonely; but her husband had not been unkind to her. If she had had a child she would not have been unhappy; but the days were long, and it rained too much.

It was true that her husband, whenever he went away and left her, brought her a handsome present on his return; but this did not make up for the loneliness. At least nothing had, till he brought her the little brown dog from the East: after that she was much less unhappy. Her husband seemed pleased that she was so fond of the dog; he gave her leave to put her jewelled bracelet around its neck, and to keep it always with her.

One day she had fallen asleep in her room, with the dog at her feet, as his habit was. Her feet were bare and resting on his back. Suddenly she was waked by her husband: he stood beside her, smiling not unkindly.

'You look like my great-grandmother, Juliane de Cornault, lying in the chapel with her feet on a little dog,' he said.

The analogy sent a chill through her, but she laughed and answered: 'Well, when I am dead you must put me beside her, carved in marble, with my dog at my feet.'

'Oho – we'll wait and see,' he said, laughing also, but with his black brows close together. 'The dog is the emblem of fidelity.'

'And do you doubt my right to lie with mine at my feet?'

'When I'm in doubt I find out,' he answered. 'I am an old man,' he added, 'and people say I make you lead a lonely life. But I swear you shall have your monument if you earn it.'

'And I swear to be faithful,' she returned, 'if only for the sake of having my little dog at my feet.'

Not long afterward he went on business to the Quimper Assizes; and while he was away his aunt, the widow of a great nobleman of the duchy, came to spend a night at Kerfol on her way to the *pardon* of Ste Barbe. She was a woman of piety and consequence, and much respected by Yves de Cornault, and when she proposed to Anne to go with her to Ste Barbe no one could object, and even the chaplain declared himself in favour of the pilgrimage. So Anne set out for Ste Barbe, and there for the first time she talked with Hervé de Lanrivain. He had come once or twice to Kerfol with his father, but she had never before exchanged a dozen words with him. They did not talk for more than five minutes now: it was under the chestnuts, as the procession was coming out of the chapel. He said: 'I pity you', and she was surprised, for she had not supposed that anyone thought her an object of pity. He added: 'Call for me when you need me', and she smiled a little, but was glad afterward, and thought often of the meeting.

She confessed to having seen him three times afterward: not more. How or where she would not say – one had the impression that she feared to implicate someone. Their meetings had been rare and brief; and at the last he had told her that he was starting the next day for a foreign country, on a mission which was not without peril and might keep him for many months absent. He asked her for a remembrance, and she had none to give him but the collar about the little dog's neck. She was sorry afterward that she had given it, but he was so unhappy at going that she had not had the courage to refuse.

Her husband was away at the time. When he returned a few days later he picked up the animal to pet it, and noticed that its collar was missing. His wife told him that the dog had lost it in the undergrowth of the park, and that she and her maids had hunted a whole day for it. It was true, she explained to the court, that she had made the maids search for the necklet – they all believed the dog had lost it in the park . . .

Her husband made no comment, and that evening at supper he was in his usual mood, between good and bad: you could never tell which. He talked a good deal, describing what he had seen and done at Rennes; but now and then he stopped and looked hard at her, and when she went to bed she found her little dog strangled on her pillow. The little thing was dead, but still warm; she stooped to lift it, and her distress turned to horror when she discovered that it had been strangled by twisting twice round its throat the necklet she had given to Lanrivain.

The next morning at dawn she buried the dog in the garden, and hid the necklet in her breast. She said nothing to her husband, then or later, and he said nothing to her; but that day he had a peasant hanged for stealing a faggot in the park, and the next day he nearly beat to death a young horse he was breaking.

Winter set in, and the short days passed, and the long nights, one by one; and she heard nothing of Hervé de Lanrivain. It might be that her husband had killed him; or merely that he had been robbed of the necklet. Day after day by the hearth among the spinning maids, night after night alone on her bed, she wondered and trembled. Sometimes at table her husband looked across at her and smiled; and then she felt sure that Lanrivain was dead. She dared not try to get news of him, for she was sure her husband would find out if she did: she had an idea that he could find out anything. Even when a witch-woman who was a noted seer, and could show you the whole world in her crystal, came to the castle for a night's shelter, and the maids flocked to her, Anne held back.

The winter was long and black and rainy. One day, in Yves de Cornault's absence, some gypsies came to Kerfol with a troop of performing dogs. Anne bought the smallest and cleverest, a white dog with a feathery coat and one blue and one brown eye. It seemed to have been ill-treated by the gypsies, and clung to her plaintively when she took it from them. That evening her husband came back, and when she went to bed she found the dog strangled on her pillow.

After that she said to herself that she would never have another dog; but one bitter cold evening a poor lean greyhound was found whining at the castle-gate, and she took him in and forbade the maids to speak of him to her husband. She hid him in a room that no one went to, smuggled food to him from her own plate, made him a warm bed to lie on and petted him like a child.

Yves de Cornault came home, and the next day she found the greyhound strangled on her pillow. She wept in secret, but said nothing, and resolved that even if she met a dog dying of hunger she would never bring him into the castle; but one day she found a young sheepdog, a brindled puppy with good blue eyes, lying with a broken leg in the snow of the park. Yves de Cornault was at Rennes, and she brought the dog in, warmed and fed it, tied up its leg and hid it in the castle till her husband's return. The day before, she gave it to a peasant woman who lived a long way off, and paid her handsomely to care for it and say nothing; but that night she heard a whining and scratching at her door, and when she opened it the lame puppy, drenched and shivering, jumped up on her with little sobbing barks. She hid him in her bed, and the next morning was about to have him taken back to the peasant woman when she heard her husband ride into the court. She shut the dog in a chest, and went down to receive him. An hour or two later, when she returned to her room, the puppy lay strangled on her pillow . . .

After that she dared not make a pet of any other dog; and her loneliness became almost unendurable. Sometimes, when she crossed the court of the castle, and thought no one was looking, she stopped to pat the old pointer at the gate. But one day as she was caressing him her husband came out of the chapel; and the next day the old dog was gone . . .

This curious narrative was not told in one sitting of the court, or received without impatience and incredulous comment. It was plain that the Judges were surprised by its puerility, and that it did not help the accused in the eyes of the public. It was an odd tale, certainly; but what did it prove? That Yves de Cornault disliked dogs, and that his wife, to gratify her own fancy, persistently ignored this dislike. As for pleading this trivial disagreement as an excuse for her relations – whatever their nature – with her supposed accomplice, the argument was so absurd that her own lawyer manifestly regretted having let her make use of it, and tried several times to cut short her story. But she went on to the end, with a kind of hypnotized insistence, as though the scenes she evoked were so real to her that she had forgotten where she was and imagined herself to be re-living them.

At length the Judge who had previously shown a certain kindness to her said (leaning forward a little, one may suppose, from his row of dozing colleagues): 'Then you would have us believe that you murdered your husband because he would not let you keep a pet dog?'

'I did not murder my husband.'

'Who did, then? Hervé de Lanrivain?'

'No.'

'Who then? Can you tell us?'

'Yes, I can tell you. The dogs –' At that point she was carried out of the court in a swoon.

It was evident that her lawyer tried to get her to abandon this line of defence. Possibly her explanation, whatever it was, had seemed convincing when she poured it out to him in the heat of their first private colloquy; but now that it was exposed to the cold daylight of judicial scrutiny, and the banter of the town, he was thoroughly ashamed of it, and would have sacrificed her without a scruple to save his professional reputation. But the obstinate Judge – who perhaps, after all, was more inquisitive than kindly – evidently wanted to hear the story out, and she was ordered, the next day, to continue her deposition.

She said that after the disappearance of the old watchdog nothing particular happened for a month or two. Her husband was much as usual: she did not remember any special incident. But one evening a pedlar woman came to the castle and was selling trinkets to the maids. She had no heart for trinkets, but she stood looking on while the women made their choice. And then, she did not know how, but the pedlar coaxed her into buying for herself a pear-shaped pomander with a strong scent in it – she had once seen something of the kind on a gypsy woman. She had no desire for the pomander, and did not know why she had bought it. The pedlar said that whoever wore it had the power to read the future; but she did not really believe that, or care much either. However, she bought the thing and took it up to her room, where she sat turning it about in her hand. Then the strange scent attracted her and she began to wonder what kind of spice was in the box. She opened it and found a grey bean rolled in a strip of paper; and on the paper she saw a sign she knew, and a message from Hervé de Lanrivain, saying that he was at home again and would be at the door in the court that night after the moon had set . . .

She burned the paper and sat down to think. It was nightfall, and her husband was at home . . . She had no way of warning Lanrivain, and there was nothing to do but to wait . . .

At this point I fancy the drowsy court-room beginning to wake up. Even to the oldest hand on the bench there must have been a certain relish in picturing the feelings of a woman on receiving such a message at nightfall from a man living twenty miles away, to whom she had no means of sending a warning . . .

She was not a clever woman, I imagine; and as the first result of her cogitation she appears to have made the mistake of being, that evening, too kind to her husband. She could not ply him with wine, according to the traditional expedient, for though he drank heavily at times he had a strong head; and when he drank beyond its strength it was because he chose to, and not because a woman coaxed him. Not his wife, at any rate – she was an old story by now. As I read the case, I fancy there was no feeling for her left in him but the hatred occasioned by his supposed dishonour.

At any rate, she tried to call up her old graces; but early in the evening he complained of pains and fever, and left the hall to go up to the closet where he sometimes slept. His servant carried him a cup of hot wine, and brought back word that he was sleeping and not to be disturbed; and an hour later, when Anne lifted the tapestry and listened at his door, she heard his loud regular breathing. She thought it might be a feint, and stayed a long time barefooted in the passage, her ear to the crack; but the breathing went on too steadily and naturally to be other than that of a man in a sound sleep. She crept back to her room reassured, and stood in the window watching the moon set through the trees of the park. The sky was misty and starless, and after the moon went down the night was black as pitch. She knew the time had come, and stole along the passage, past her husband's door – where she stopped again to listen to his breathing – to the top of the stairs. There she paused a moment, and assured herself that no one was following her; then she began to go down the stairs in the darkness. They were so steep and winding that she had to go very slowly, for fear of stumbling. Her one thought was to get the door unbolted, tell Lanrivain to make his escape, and hasten back to her room. She had tried the bolt earlier in the evening, and managed to put a little grease on it; but nevertheless, when she drew it, it gave a squeak . . . not loud, but it made her heart stop; and the next minute, overhead, she heard a noise . . .

'What noise?' the prosecution interposed.

'My husband's voice calling out my name and cursing me.'

'What did you hear after that?'

'A terrible scream and a fall.'

'Where was Hervé de Lanrivain at this time?'

'He was standing outside in the court. I just made him out in the darkness. I told him for God's sake to go, and then I pushed the door shut.'

'What did you do next?'

'I stood at the foot of the stairs and listened.'

'What did you hear?'

'I heard dogs snarling and panting.' (Visible discouragement of the bench, boredom of the public, and exasperation of the lawyer for the defence. Dogs again – ! But the inquisitive Judge insisted.)

'What dogs?'

She bent her head and spoke so low that she had to be told to repeat her answer: 'I don't know.'

'How do you mean – you don't know?'

'I don't know what dogs . . .'

The Judge again intervened: 'Try to tell us exactly what happened. How long did you remain at the foot of the stairs?'

'Only a few minutes.'

'And what was going on meanwhile overhead?'

'The dogs kept on snarling and panting. Once or twice he cried out. I think he moaned once. Then he was quiet.'

'Then what happened?'

'Then I heard a sound like the noise of a pack when the wolf is thrown to them – gulping and lapping.'

(There was a groan of disgust and repulsion through the court, and another attempted intervention by the distracted lawyer. But the inquisitive Judge was still inquisitive.)

'And all the while you did not go up?'

'Yes – I went up then – to drive them off.'

'The dogs?'

'Yes.'

'Well – ?'

'When I got there it was quite dark. I found my husband's flint and steel and struck a spark. I saw him lying there. He was dead.'

'And the dogs?'

'The dogs were gone.'

'Gone – where to?'

'I don't know. There was no way out – and there were no dogs at Kerfol.'

She straightened herself to her full height, threw her arms above her head, and fell down on the stone floor with a long scream. There was a moment of confusion in the court-room. Someone on the bench was heard to say: 'This is clearly a case for the ecclesiastical authorities' – and the prisoner's lawyer doubtless jumped at the suggestion.

After this, the trial loses itself in a maze of cross-questioning and squabbling. Every witness who was called corroborated Anne de Cornault's statement that there were no dogs at Kerfol: had been none for several months. The master of the house had taken a dislike to dogs, there was no denying it. But, on the other hand, at the inquest, there had been long and bitter discussions as to the nature of the dead man's wounds. One of the surgeons called in had spoken of marks that looked like bites. The suggestion of witchcraft was revived, and the opposing lawyers hurled tomes of necromancy at each other.

At last Anne de Cornault was brought back into court – at the instance of the same Judge – and asked if she knew where the dogs she spoke of could have come from. On the body of her

Redeemer she swore that she did not. Then the Judge put his final question: 'If the dogs you think you heard had been known to you, do you think you would have recognized them by their barking?'

'Yes.'

'Did you recognise them?'

'Yes.'

'What dogs do you take them to have been?'

'My dead dogs,' she said in a whisper . . . She was taken out of court, not to reappear there again. There was some kind of ecclesiastical investigation, and the end of the business was that the Judges disagreed with each other, and with the ecclesiastical committee, and that Anne de Cornault was finally handed over to the keeping of her husband's family, who shut her up in the keep of Kerfol, where she is said to have died many years later, a harmless mad-woman.

So ends her story. As for that of Hervé de Lanrivain, I had only to apply to his collateral descendant for its subsequent details. The evidence against the young man being insufficient, and his family influence in the duchy considerable, he was set free, and left soon afterward for Paris. He was probably in no mood for a worldly life, and he appears to have come almost immediately under the influence of the famous M. Arnauld d'Andilly and the gentlemen of Port Royal. A year or two later he was received into their Order, and without achieving any particular distinction he followed its good and evil fortunes till his death some twenty years later. Lanrivain showed me a portrait of him by a pupil of Philippe de Champaigne: sad eyes, an impulsive mouth and a narrow brow. Poor Hervé de Lanrivain: it was a grey ending. Yet as I looked at his stiff and sallow effigy, in the dark dress of the Jansenists, I almost found myself envying his fate. After all, in the course of his life two great things had happened to him: he had loved romantically, and he must have talked with Pascal . . .

Where Their Fire is Not Quenched

May Sinclair

There was nobody in the orchard. Harriott Leigh went out, carefully, through the iron gate into the field. She had made the latch slip into its notch without a sound.

The path slanted widely up the field from the orchard gate to the stile under the elder tree. George Waring waited for her there.

Years afterwards, when she thought of George Waring she smelt the sweet, hot, wine-scent of the elder flowers. Years afterwards, when she smelt elder flowers she saw George Waring, with his beautiful, gentle face, like a poet's or a musician's, his black-blue eyes, and sleek, olive-brown hair. He was a naval lieutenant.

Yesterday he had asked her to marry him and she had consented. But her father hadn't, and she had come to tell him that and say good-bye before he left her. His ship was to sail the next day.

He was eager and excited. He couldn't believe that anything could stop their happiness, that anything he didn't want to happen could happen.

'Well?' he said.

'He's a perfect beast, George. He won't let us. He says we're too young.'

'I was twenty last August,' he said, aggrieved.

'And I shall be seventeen in September.'

'And this is June. We're quite old, really. How long does he mean us to wait?'

'Three years.'

'Three years before we can be engaged even – why, we might be dead.'

She put her arms round him to make him feel safe. They kissed; and the sweet, hot, wine-scent of the elder flowers mixed with their kisses. They stood, pressed close together, under the elder tree.

Across the yellow fields of charlock they heard the village clock strike seven. Up in the house a gong clanged.

'Darling, I must go,' she said.

'Oh stay – stay *five* minutes.'

He pressed her close. It lasted five minutes, and five more. Then he was running fast down the road to the station, while Harriott went along the field-path, slowly, struggling with her tears.

'He'll be back in three months,' she said. 'I can live through three months.'

But he never came back. There was something wrong with the engines of his ship, the *Alexandra*. Three weeks later she went down in the Mediterranean, and George with her.

Harriott said she didn't care how soon she died now. She was quite sure it would be soon, because she couldn't live without him.

Five years passed.

The two lines of beech trees stretched on and on, the whole length of the Park, a broad green drive between. When you came to the middle they branched off right and left in the form of a cross, and at the end of the right arm there was a white stucco pavilion with pillars and a three-cornered pediment like a Greek temple. At the end of the left arm, the west entrance to the Park, double gates and a side door.

Harriott, on her stone seat at the back of the pavilion, could see Stephen Philpotts the very minute he came through the side door.

He had asked her to wait for him there. It was the place he always chose to read his poems aloud in. The poems were a pretext. She knew what he was going to say. And she knew what she would answer.

There were elder bushes in flower at the back of the pavilion, and Harriott thought of George Waring. She told herself that George was nearer to her now than he could ever have been, living. If she married Stephen she would not be unfaithful, because she loved him with another part of herself. It was not as though Stephen were taking George's place. She loved Stephen with her soul, in an unearthly way.

But her body quivered like a stretched wire when the door opened and the young man came towards her down the drive under the beech trees.

She loved him; she loved his slenderness, his darkness and sallow whiteness, his black eyes lighting up with the intellectual flame, the way his black hair swept back from his forehead, the way he walked, tiptoe, as if his feet were lifted with wings.

He sat down beside her. She could see his hands tremble. She felt that her moment was coming; it had come.

'I wanted to see you alone because there's something I must say to you. I don't quite know how to begin . . .'

Her lips parted. She panted lightly.

'You've heard me speak of Sybill Foster?'

Her voice came stammering, 'N-no, Stephen. Did you?'

'Well, I didn't mean to, till I knew it was all right. I only heard yesterday.'

'Heard what?'

'Why, that she'll have me. Oh, Harriott – do you know what it's like to be terribly happy?'

She knew. She had known just now, the moment before he told her. She sat there, stone-cold and stiff, listening to his raptures; listening to her own voice saying she was glad.

Ten years passed.

Harriott Leigh sat waiting in the drawing-room of a small house in Maida Vale. She had lived there ever since her father's death two years before.

She was restless. She kept on looking at the clock to see if it was four, the hour that Oscar Wade had appointed. She was not sure that he would come, after she had sent him away yesterday.

She now asked herself, why, when she had sent him away yesterday, she had let him come to-day. Her motives were not altogether clear. If she really meant what she had said then, she oughtn't to let him come to her again. Never again.

She had shown him plainly what she meant. She could see herself, sitting very straight in her chair, uplifted by a passionate integrity, while he stood before her, hanging his head, ashamed and beaten; she could feel again the throb in her voice as she kept on saying that she couldn't, she couldn't; he must see that she couldn't; that no, nothing would make her change her mind; she couldn't forget he had a wife; that he must think of Muriel.

To which he had answered savagely: 'I needn't. That's all over. We only live together for the look of the thing.'

And she, serenely, with great dignity: 'And for the look of the thing, Oscar, we must leave off seeing each other. Please go.'

'Do you mean it?'

'Yes. We must never see each other again.'

And he had gone then, ashamed and beaten.

She could see him, squaring his broad shoulders to meet the blow. And she was sorry for him. She told herself she had been unnecessarily hard. Why shouldn't they see each other again, now he understood where they must draw the line? Until yesterday the line had never been very clearly drawn. To-day she meant to ask him to forget what he had said to her. Once it was forgotten, they could go on being friends as if nothing had happened.

It was four o'clock. Half-past. Five. She had finished tea and given him up when, between the half-hour and six o'clock, he came.

He came as he had come a dozen times, with his measured, deliberate, thoughtful tread, carrying himself well braced, with a sort of held-in arrogance, his great shoulders heaving. He was a man of about forty, broad and tall, lean-flanked and short-necked, his straight, handsome features showing small and even in the big square face and in the flush that swamped it. The close-clipped, reddish-brown moustache bristled forwards from the pushed-out upper lip. His small, flat eyes shone, reddish-brown, eager and animal.

She liked to think of him when he was not there, but always at the first sight of him she felt a slight shock. Physically, he was very far from her admired ideal. So different from George Waring and Stephen Philpotts.

He sat down, facing her.

There was an embarrassed silence, broken by Oscar Wade.

'Well, Harriott, you said I could come.' He seemed to be throwing the responsibility on her.

'So I suppose you've forgiven me,' he said.

'Oh, yes, Oscar, I've forgiven you.'

He said she'd better show it by coming to dine with him somewhere that evening.

She could give no reason to herself for going. She simply went.

He took her to a restaurant in Soho. Oscar Wade dined well, even extravagantly, giving each dish its importance. She liked his extravagance. He had none of the mean virtues.

It was over. His flushed, embarrassed silence told her what he was thinking. But when he had seen her home he left her at her garden gate. He had thought better of it.

She was not sure whether she were glad or sorry. She had had her moment of righteous exaltation and she had enjoyed it. But there was no joy in the weeks that followed it. She had given up Oscar Wade because she didn't want him very much; and now she wanted him furiously, perversely, because she had given him up. Though he had no resemblance to her ideal, she couldn't live without him.

She dined with him again and again, till she knew Schnebler's Restaurant by heart, the white panelled walls picked out with gold; the white pillars, and the curling gold fronds of their capitals; the Turkey carpets, blue and crimson, soft under her feet;

the thick crimson velvet cushions, that clung to her skirts; the glitter of silver and glass on the innumerable white circles of the tables. And the faces of the diners, red, white, pink, brown, grey and sallow, distorted and excited; the curled mouths that twisted as they ate; the convoluted electric bulbs pointing, pointing down at them, under the red, crinkled shades. All shimmering in a thick air that the red light stained as wine stains water.

And Oscar's face, flushed with his dinner. Always, when he leaned back from the table and brooded in silence she knew what he was thinking. His heavy eyelids would lift; she would find his eyes fixed on hers, wondering, considering.

She knew now what the end would be. She thought of George Waring, and Stephen Philpotts, and of her life, cheated. She hadn't chosen Oscar, she hadn't really wanted him; but now he had forced himself on her she couldn't afford to let him go. Since George died no man had loved her, no other man ever would. And she was sorry for him when she thought of him going from her, beaten and ashamed.

She was certain, before he was, of the end. Only she didn't know when and where and how it would come. That was what Oscar knew.

It came at the close of one of their evenings when they had dined in a private sitting-room. He said he couldn't stand the heat and noise of the public restaurant.

She went before him, up a steep, red-carpeted stair to a white door on the second landing.

From time to time they repeated the furtive, hidden adventure. Sometimes she met him in the room above Schnebler's. Sometimes, when her maid was out, she received him at her house in Maida Vale. But that was dangerous, not to be risked too often.

Oscar declared himself unspeakably happy. Harriott was not quite sure. This was love, the thing she had never had, that she had dreamed of, hungered and thirsted for; but now she had it she was not satisfied. Always she looked for something just beyond it, some mystic, heavenly rapture, always beginning to come, that never came. There was something about Oscar that repelled her. But because she had taken him for her lover, she couldn't bring herself to admit that it was a certain coarseness. She looked another way and pretended it wasn't there. To justify herself, she fixed her mind on his good qualities, his generosity, his strength, the way he had built up his engineering business. She made him take her over his works and show her his great dynamos. She made him lend her the books he read. But always, when she tried to talk to him, he let her see that *that* wasn't what she was there for.

'My dear girl, we haven't time,' he said. 'It's a waste of our priceless moments.'

She persisted. 'There's something wrong about it all if we can't talk to each other.'

He was irritated. 'Women never seem to consider that a man can get all the talk he wants from other men. What's wrong is our meeting in this unsatisfactory way. We ought to live together. It's the only sane thing. I would, only I don't want to break up Muriel's home and make her miserable.'

'I thought you said she wouldn't care.'

'My dear, she cares for her home and her position and the children. You forget the children.'

Yes. She had forgotten the children. She had forgotten Muriel. She had left off thinking of Oscar as a man with a wife and children and a home.

He had a plan. His mother-in-law was coming to stay with Muriel in October and he would get away. He would go to Paris, and Harriott should come to him there. He could say he went on business. No need to lie about it; he *had* business in Paris.

He engaged rooms in an hotel in the rue de Rivoli. They spent two weeks there.

For three days Oscar was madly in love with Harriott and

Harriott with him. As she lay awake she would turn on the light and look at him as he slept at her side. Sleep made him beautiful and innocent; it laid a fine, smooth tissue over his coarseness; it made his mouth gentle; it entirely hid his eyes.

In six days reaction had set in. At the end of the tenth day, Harriott, returning with Oscar from Montmartre, burst into a fit of crying. When questioned, she answered wildly that the Hotel Saint Pierre was too hideously ugly; it was getting on her nerves. Mercifully Oscar explained her state as fatigue following excitement. She tried hard to believe that she was miserable because her love was purer and more spiritual than Oscar's; but all the time she knew perfectly well she had cried from pure boredom. She was in love with Oscar, and Oscar bored her. Oscar was in love with her, and she bored him. At close quarters, day in and day out, each was revealed to the other as an incredible bore.

At the end of the second week she began to doubt whether she had ever been really in love with him.

Her passion returned for a little while after they got back to London. Freed from the unnatural strain which Paris had put on them, they persuaded themselves that their romantic temperaments were better fitted to the old life of casual adventure.

Then, gradually, the sense of danger began to wake in them. They lived in perpetual fear, face to face with all the chances of discovery. They tormented themselves and each other by imagining possibilities that they would never have considered in their first fine moments. It was as though they were beginning to ask themselves if it were, after all, worthwhile running such awful risks, for all they got out of it. Oscar still swore that if he had been free he would have married her. He pointed out that his intentions at any rate were regular. But she asked herself: Would I marry *him*? Marriage would be the Hotel Saint Pierre all over again, without any possibility of escape. But, if she wouldn't marry him, was she in love with him? That was the test. Perhaps it was a good thing he wasn't free. Then she told herself that these doubts were morbid, and that the question wouldn't arise.

One evening Oscar called to see her. He had come to tell her that Muriel was ill.

'Seriously ill?'

'I'm afraid so. It's pleurisy. May turn to pneumonia. We shall know one way or another in the next few days.'

A terrible fear seized upon Harriott. Muriel might die of her pleurisy; and if Muriel died, she would have to marry Oscar. He was looking at her queerly, as if he knew what she was thinking, and she could see that the same thought had occurred to him and that he was frightened too.

Muriel got well again; but their danger had enlightened them. Muriel's life was now inconceivably precious to them both; she stood between them and that permanent union, which they dreaded and yet would not have the courage to refuse.

After enlightenment the rupture.

It came from Oscar, one evening when he sat with her in her drawing-room.

'Harriott,' he said, 'do you know I'm thinking seriously of settling down?'

'How do you mean, settling down?'

'Patching it up with Muriel, poor girl . . . Has it never occurred to you that this little affair of ours can't go on for ever?'

'You don't want it to go on?'

'I don't want to have any humbug about it. For God's sake, let's be straight. If it's done, it's done. Let's end it decently.'

'I see. You want to get rid of me.'

'That's a beastly way of putting it.'

'Is there any way that isn't beastly? The whole thing's beastly. I should have thought you'd have stuck to it now you've made it what you wanted. When I haven't an ideal, I haven't a single illusion, when you've destroyed everything you didn't want.'

'What didn't I want?'

'The clean, beautiful part of it. The part *I* wanted.'

'My part at least was real. It was cleaner and more beautiful than all that putrid stuff you wrapped it up in. You were a hypocrite, Harriott, and I wasn't. You're a hypocrite now if you say you weren't happy with me.'

'I was never really happy. Never for one moment. There was always something I missed. Something you didn't give me. Perhaps you couldn't.'

'No. I wasn't spiritual enough,' he sneered.

'You were not. And you made me what you were.'

'Oh, I noticed that you were always very spiritual *after* you'd got what you wanted.'

'What I wanted?' she cried. 'Oh, my God—'

'If you ever knew what you wanted.'

'What – I – wanted,' she repeated, drawing out her bitterness.

'Come,' he said, 'why not be honest? Face facts. I was awfully gone on you. You were awfully gone on me – once. We got tired of each other and it's over. But at least you might own we had a good time while it lasted.'

'A good time?'

'Good enough for me.'

'For you, because for you love only means one thing. Everything that's high and noble in it you dragged down to that, till there's nothing left for us but that. *That's* what you made of love.'

Twenty years passed.

It was Oscar who died first, three years after the rupture. He did it suddenly one evening, falling down in a fit of apoplexy.

His death was an immense relief to Harriott. Perfect security had been impossible as long as he was alive. But now there wasn't a living soul who knew her secret.

Still, in the first moment of shock Harriott told herself that Oscar dead would be nearer to her than ever. She forgot how little she had wanted him to be near her, alive. And long before the twenty years had passed she had contrived to persuade herself that he had never been near to her at all. It was incredible that she had ever known such a person as Oscar Wade. As for their affair, she couldn't think of Harriott Leigh as the sort of woman to whom such a thing could happen. Schnebler's and the Hotel Saint Pierre ceased to figure among prominent images of her past. Her memories, if she had allowed herself to remember, would have clashed disagreeably with the reputation for sanctity which she had now acquired.

For Harriott at fifty-two was the friend and helper of the Reverend Clement Farmer, Vicar of St Mary the Virgin, Maida Vale. She worked as a deaconess in his parish, wearing the uniform of a deaconess, the semi-religious gown, the cloak, the bonnet and veil, the cross and rosary, the holy smile. She was also secretary to the Maida Vale and Kilburn Home for Fallen Girls.

Her moments of excitement came when Clement Farmer, the lean, austere likeness of Stephen Philpotts, in his cassock and lace-bordered surplice, issued from the vestry, when he mounted the pulpit, when he stood before the altar rails and lifted up his arms in the Benediction; her moments of ecstasy when she received the Sacrament from his hands. And she had moments of calm happiness when his study door closed on their communion. All these moments were saturated with a solemn holiness.

And they were insignificant compared with the moment of her dying.

She lay dozing in her white bed under the black crucifix with the ivory Christ. The basins and medicine bottles had been cleared from the table by her pillow; it was spread for the last rites. The priest moved quietly about the room, arranging the candles, the Prayer Book and the Holy Sacrament. Then he drew a chair to her bedside and watched with her, waiting for her to come up out of her doze.

She woke suddenly. Her eyes were fixed upon him. She had a flash of lucidity. She was dying, and her dying made her supremely important to Clement Farmer.

'Are you ready?' he asked.

'Not yet. I think I'm afraid. Make me not afraid.'

He rose and lit the two candles on the altar. He took down the crucifix from the wall and stood it against the foot-rail of the bed.

She sighed. That was not what she had wanted.

'You will not be afraid now,' he said.

'I'm not afraid of the hereafter. I suppose you get used to it. Only it may be terrible just at first.'

'Our first state will depend very much on what we are thinking of at our last hour.'

'There'll be my – confession,' she said.

'And after it you will receive the Sacrament. Then you will have your mind fixed firmly upon God and your Redeemer . . . Do you feel able to make your confession now, Sister? Everything is ready.'

Her mind went back over her past and found Oscar Wade there. She wondered: Should she confess to him about Oscar Wade? One moment she thought it was possible; the next she knew that she couldn't. She could not. It wasn't necessary. For twenty years he had not been part of her life. No. She wouldn't confess about Oscar Wade. She had been guilty of other sins.

She made a careful selection.

'I have cared too much for the beauty of this world . . . I have failed in charity to my poor girls. Because of my intense repugnance to their sin . . . I have thought, often, about – people I love, when I should have been thinking about God.'

After that she received the Sacrament.

'Now,' he said, 'there is nothing to be afraid of.'

'I won't be afraid if – if you would hold my hand.'

He held it. And she lay still a long time, with her eyes shut. Then he heard her murmuring something. He stooped close.

'This – is – dying. I thought it would be horrible. And it's bliss . . . Bliss.'

The priest's hand slackened, as if at the bidding of some wonder. She gave a weak cry.

'Oh – don't let me go.'

His grasp tightened.

'Try,' he said, 'to think about God. Keep on looking at the crucifix.'

'If I look,' she whispered, 'you won't let go my hand?'

'I will not let you go.'

He held it till it was wrenched from him in the last agony.

She lingered for some hours in the room where these things had happened.

Its aspect was familiar and yet unfamiliar, and slightly repugnant to her. The altar, the crucifix, the lighted candles, suggested some tremendous and awful experience the details of which she was not able to recall. She seemed to remember that they had been connected in some way with the sheeted body on the bed; but the nature of the connection was not clear; and she did not associate the dead body with herself. When the nurse came in and laid it out, she saw that it was the body of a middle-aged woman. Her own living body was that of a young woman of about thirty-two.

Her mind had no past and no future, no sharp-edged, coherent memories, and no idea of anything to be done next.

Then, suddenly, the room began to come apart before her eyes, to split into shafts of floor and furniture and ceiling that shifted and were thrown by their commotion into different planes. They leaned slanting at every possible angle; they crossed and overlaid each other with a transparent mingling of dislocated perspectives, like reflections fallen on an interior seen behind glass.

The bed and the sheeted body slid away somewhere out of

sight. She was standing by the door that still remained in position.

She opened it and found herself in the street, outside a building of yellowish-grey brick and freestone, with a tall slated spire. Her mind came together with a palpable click of recognition. This object was the Church of St Mary the Virgin, Maida Vale. She could hear the droning of the organ. She opened the door and slipped in.

She had gone back into a definite space and time, and recovered a certain limited section of coherent memory. She remembered the rows of pitch-pine benches, with their Gothic peaks and mouldings; the stone-coloured walls and pillars with their chocolate stencilling; the hanging rings of lights along the aisles of the nave; the high altar with its lighted candles, and the polished brass cross, twinkling. These things were somehow permanent and real, adjusted to the image that now took possession of her.

She knew what she had come there for. The service was over. The choir had gone from the chancel; the sacristan moved before the altar, putting out the candles. She walked up the middle aisle to a seat that she knew under the pulpit. She knelt down and covered her face with her hands. Peeping sideways through her fingers, she could see the door of the vestry on her left at the end of the north aisle. She watched it steadily.

Up in the organ loft the organist drew out the Recessional, slowly and softly, to its end in the two solemn, vibrating chords.

The vestry door opened and Clement Farmer came out, dressed in his black cassock. He passed before her, close, close outside the bench where she knelt. He paused at the opening. He was waiting for her. There was something he had to say.

She stood up and went towards him. He still waited. He didn't move to make way for her. She came close, closer than she had ever come to him, so close that his features grew indistinct. She bent her head back, peering, short-sightedly, and found herself looking into Oscar Wade's face.

He stood still, horribly still, and close, barring her passage.

She drew back; his heaving shoulders followed her. He leaned forward, covering her with his eyes. She opened her mouth to scream and no sound came.

She was afraid to move lest he should move with her. The heaving of his shoulders terrified her.

One by one the lights in the side aisles were going out. The lights in the middle aisle would go next. They had gone. If she didn't get away she would be shut up with him there, in the appalling darkness.

She turned and moved towards the north aisle, groping, steadying herself by the book ledge.

When she looked back, Oscar Wade was not there.

Then she remembered that Oscar Wade was dead. Therefore, what she had seen was not Oscar; it was his ghost. He was dead; dead seventeen years ago. She was safe from him for ever.

When she came out on to the steps of the church she saw that the road it stood in had changed. It was not the road she remembered. The pavement on this side was raised slightly and covered in. It ran under a succession of arches. It was a long gallery walled with glittering shop windows on one side; on the other a line of tall grey columns divided it from the street.

She was going along the arcades of the rue de Rivoli. Ahead of her she could see the edge of an immense grey pillar jutting out. That was the porch of the Hotel Saint Pierre. The revolving glass doors swung forward to receive her; she crossed the grey, sultry vestibule under the pillared arches. She knew it. She knew the porter's shining, wine-coloured mahogany pen on her left, and the shining, wine-coloured mahogany barrier on the clerk's bureau on her right; she made straight for the great grey carpeted staircase; she climbed the endless flights that turned round and round the caged-in shaft of the well, past the latticed doors of the lift, and came up on to a landing that she knew, and into the long, ash-grey, foreign corridor lit by a dull window at one end.

It was there that the horror of the place came on her. She had no longer any memory of St Mary's Church, so that she was unaware of her backward course through time. All space and time were here.

She remembered she had to go to the left, the left.

But there was something there; where the corridor turned by the window; at the end of all the corridors. If she went the other way she would escape it.

The corridor stopped there. A blank wall. She was driven back past the stairhead to the left.

At the corner, by the window, she turned down another long ash-grey corridor on her right, and to the right again where the night-light sputtered on the table-flap at the turn.

This third corridor was dark and secret and depraved. She knew the soiled walls and the warped door at the end. There was a sharp-pointed streak of light at the top. She could see the number on it now, 107.

Something had happened there. If she went in it would happen again.

Oscar Wade was in the room waiting for her behind the closed door. She felt him moving about in there. She leaned forward, her ear to the key-hole, and listened. She could hear the measured, deliberate, thoughtful footsteps. They were coming from the bed to the door.

She turned and ran; her knees gave way under her; she sank and ran on, down the long grey corridors and the stairs, quick and blind, a hunted beast seeking for cover, hearing his feet coming after her.

The revolving doors caught her and pushed her out into the street.

The strange quality of her state was this, that it had no time. She remembered dimly that there had once been a thing called time;

but she had forgotten altogether what it was like. She was aware of things happening and about to happen; she fixed them by the place they occupied, and measured their duration by the space she went through.

So now she thought: If I could only go back and get to the place where it hadn't happened.

To get back farther—

She was walking now on a white road that went between broad grass borders. To the right and left were the long raking lines of the hills, curve after curve, shimmering in a thin mist.

The road dropped to the green valley. It mounted the humped bridge over the river. Beyond it she saw the twin gables of the grey house pricked up over the high, grey garden wall. The tall iron gate stood in front of it between the ball-topped stone pillars.

And now she was in a large, low-ceilinged room with drawn blinds. She was standing before the wide double bed. It was her father's bed. The dead body, stretched out in the middle under the drawn white sheet, was her father's body.

The outline of the sheet sank from the peak of the upturned toes to the shin bone, and from the high bridge of the nose to the chin.

She lifted the sheet and folded it back across the breast of the dead man. The face she saw then was Oscar Wade's face, stilled and smoothed in the innocence of sleep, the supreme innocence of death. She stared at it, fascinated, in a cold, pitiless joy.

Oscar was dead.

She remembered how he used to lie like that beside her in the room in the Hotel Saint Pierre, on his back with his hands folded on his waist, his mouth half open, his big chest rising and falling. If he was dead, it would never happen again. She would be safe.

The dead face frightened her, and she was about to cover it up again when she was aware of a light heaving, a rhythmical rise and fall. As she drew the sheet up tighter, the hands under it began to struggle convulsively, the broad ends of the fingers appeared above the edge, clutching it to keep it down. The mouth opened; the eyes opened; the whole face stared back at her in a look of agony and horror.

Then the body drew itself forwards from the hips and sat up, its eyes peering into her eyes; he and she remained for an instant motionless, each held there by the other's fear.

Suddenly she broke away, turned and ran, out of the room, out of the house.

She stood at the gate, looking up and down the road, not knowing by which way she must go to escape Oscar. To the right, over the bridge and up the hill and across the downs she would come to the arcades of the rue de Rivoli and the dreadful grey corridors of the hotel. To the left the road went through the village.

If she could get further back she would be safe, out of Oscar's reach. Standing by her father's death-bed she had been young, but not young enough. She must get back to the place where she was younger still, to the Park and the green drive under the beech trees and the white pavilion at the cross. She knew how to find it. At the end of the village the high road ran right and left, east and west, under the Park walls; the south gate stood there at the top, looking down the narrow street.

She ran towards it through the village, past the long grey barns of Goodyer's farm, past the grocer's shop, past the yellow front and blue sign of the 'Queen's Head', past the post office, with its one black window blinking under its vine, past the church and the yew-trees in the churchyard, to where the south gate made a delicate black pattern on the green grass.

These things appeared insubstantial, drawn back behind a sheet of air that shimmered over them like thin glass. They opened out, floated past and away from her; and instead of the high road and park walls she saw a London street of dingy white façades, and instead of the south gate the swinging glass doors of Schnebler's Restaurant.

The glass doors swung open and she passed into the restaurant. The scene beat on her with the hard impact of reality: the white and gold panels, the white pillars and their curling gold capitals, the white circles of the tables, glittering, the flushed faces of the diners, moving mechanically.

She was driven forward by some irresistible compulsion to a table in the corner, where a man sat alone. The table napkin he was using hid his mouth, and jaw, and chest; and she was not sure of the upper part of the face above the straight, drawn edge. It dropped; and she saw Oscar Wade's face. She came to him, dragged, without power to resist; she sat down beside him, and he leaned to her over the table; she could feel the warmth of his red, congested face; the smell of wine floated towards her on his thick whisper.

'I knew you would come.'

She ate and drank with him in silence, nibbling and sipping slowly, staving off the abominable moment it would end in.

At last they got up and faced each other. His long bulk stood before her, above her; she could almost feel the vibration of its power.

'Come,' he said. 'Come.'

And she went before him, slowly, slipping out through the maze of the tables, hearing behind her Oscar's measured, deliberate, thoughtful tread. The steep, red-carpeted staircase rose up before her.

She swerved from it, but he turned her back.

'You know the way,' he said.

At the top of the flight she found the white door of the room she knew. She knew the long windows guarded by drawn muslin blinds; the gilt looking-glass over the chimney-piece that reflected Oscar's head and shoulders grotesquely between two white porcelain babies with bulbous limbs and garlanded loins, she knew the sprawling stain on the drab carpet by the table, the shabby, infamous couch behind the screen.

They moved about the room, turning and turning in it like beasts in a cage, uneasy, inimical, avoiding each other.

At last they stood still, he at the window, she at the door, the length of the room between.

'It's no good your getting away like that,' he said. 'There couldn't be any other end to it – to what we did.'

'But that *was* ended.'

'Ended there, but not here.'

'Ended for ever. We've done with it for ever.'

'We haven't. We've got to begin again. And go on. And go on.'

'Oh, no. No. Anything but that.'

'There isn't anything else.'

'We can't. We can't. Don't you remember how it bored us?'

'Remember? Do you suppose I'd touch you if I could help it? . . . That's what we're here for. We must. We must.'

'No. No. I shall get away – now.'

She turned to the door to open it.

'You can't,' he said. 'The door's locked.'

'Oscar – what did you do that for?'

'We always did it. Don't you remember?'

She turned to the door again and shook it; she beat on it with her hands.

'It's no use, Harriott. If you got out now you'd only have to come back again. You might stave it off for an hour or so, but what's that in an immortality?'

'Immortality?'

'That's what we're in for.'

'Time enough to talk about immortality when we're dead . . . Ah—'

They were being drawn towards each other across the room, moving slowly, like figures in some monstrous and appalling dance, their heads thrown back over their shoulders, their faces turned from the horrible approach. Their arms rose slowly, heavy with intolerable reluctance; they stretched them out towards each other, aching, as if they held up an overpowering weight. Their feet dragged and were drawn.

Suddenly her knees sank under her; she shut her eyes; all her being went down before him in darkness and terror.

It was over. She had got away, she was going back, back, to the green drive of the Park, between the beech trees, where Oscar had never been, where he would never find her. When she passed through the south gate her memory became suddenly young and clean. She forgot the rue de Rivoli and the Hotel Saint Pierre; she forgot Schnebler's Restaurant and the room at the top of the stairs. She was back in her youth. She was Harriott Leigh going to wait for Stephen Philpotts in the pavilion opposite the west gate. She could feel herself, a slender figure moving fast over the grass between the lines of the great beech trees. The freshness of her youth was upon her.

She came to the heart of the drive where it branched right and left in the form of a cross. At the end of the right arm the white Greek temple, with its pediment and pillars, gleamed against the wood.

She was sitting on their seat at the back of the pavilion, watching the side door that Stephen would come in by.

The door was pushed open; he came towards her, light and young, skimming between the beech trees with his eager, tiptoeing stride. She rose up to meet him. She gave a cry.

'Stephen!'

It had been Stephen. She had seen him coming. But the man who stood before her between the pillars of the pavilion was Oscar Wade.

And now she was walking along the field-path that slanted from the orchard door to the stile; further and further back, to where young George Waring waited for her under the elder tree. The smell of the elder flowers came to her over the field. She could feel on her lips and in all her body the sweet, innocent excitement of her youth.

'George, oh, George!'

As she went along the field-path she had seen him. But the man who stood waiting for her under the elder tree was Oscar Wade.

'I told you it's no use getting away, Harriott. Every path brings you back to me. You'll find me at every turn.'

'But how did you get *here*?'

'As I got into the pavilion. As I got into your father's room, on to his death bed. Because I *was* there. I am in all your memories.'

'My memories are innocent. How could you take my father's place, and Stephen's, and George Waring's? You?'

'Because I did take them.'

'Never. My love for *them* was innocent.'

'Your love for me was part of it. You think the past affects the future. Has it never struck you that the future may affect the past? In your innocence there was the beginning of your sin. You *were* what you *were to be*.'

'I shall get away,' she said.

'And, this time, I shall go with you.'

The stile, the elder tree, and the field floated away from her. She was going under the beech trees down the Park drive towards the south gate and the village, slinking close to the right-hand row of trees. She was aware that Oscar Wade was going with her under the left-hand row, keeping even with her, step by step, and tree by tree. And presently there was grey pavement under her feet and a row of grey pillars on her right hand. They were walking side by side down the rue de Rivoli towards the hotel.

They were sitting together now on the edge of the dingy white bed. Their arms hung by their sides, heavy and limp, their heads drooped, averted. Their passion weighed on them with the unbearable, unescapable boredom of immortality.

'Oscar – how long will it last?'

'I can't tell you. I don't know whether *this* is one moment of eternity, or the eternity of one moment.'

'It must end some time,' she said. 'Life doesn't go on for ever. We shall die.'

'Die? We *have* died. Don't you know what this is? Don't you know where you are? This is death. We're dead, Harriott. We're in hell.'

'Yes. There can't be anything worse than this.'

'This isn't the worst. We're not quite dead yet, as long as we've life in us to turn and run and get away from each other; as long as we can escape into our memories. But when you've got back to the farthest memory of all and there's nothing beyond it – When there's no memory but this—

'In the last hell we shall not run away any longer; we shall find no more roads, no more passages, no more open doors. We shall have no need to look for each other.

'In the last death we shall be shut up in this room, behind that locked door, together. We shall lie here together, for ever and ever, joined so fast that even God can't put us asunder. We shall be one flesh and one spirit, one sin repeated for ever, and ever; spirit loathing flesh, flesh loathing spirit; you and I loathing each other.'

'Why? Why?' she cried.

'Because that's all that's left us. That's what you made of love.'

The darkness came down swamping, it blotted out the room. She was walking along a garden path between high borders of phlox and larkspur and lupin. They were taller than she was, their flowers swayed and nodded above her head. She tugged at the tall stems and had no strength to break them. She was a little thing.

She said to herself then that she was safe. She had gone back so far that she was a child again; she had the blank innocence of childhood. To be a child, to go small under the heads of the lupins, to be blank and innocent, without memory, was to be safe.

The walk led her out through a yew hedge on to a bright green lawn. In the middle of the lawn there was a shallow round pond in a ring of rockery cushioned with small flowers, yellow and white and purple. Gold-fish swam in the olive brown water. She would be safe when she saw the gold-fish swimming towards her. The old one with the white scales would come up first, pushing up his nose, making bubbles in the water.

At the bottom of the lawn there was a privet hedge cut by a broad path that went through the orchard. She knew what she would find there; her mother was in the orchard. She would lift her up in her arms to play with the hard red balls of the apples that hung from the tree. She had got back to the farthest memory of all; there was nothing beyond it.

There would be an iron gate in the wall of the orchard. It would lead into a field.

Something was different here, something that frightened her. An ash-grey door instead of an iron gate.

She pushed it open and came into the last corridor of the Hotel Saint Pierre.

The Call of Cthulhu

H. P. Lovecraft

(Found Among the Papers of the Late Francis Wayland Thurston, of Boston)

'Of such great powers or beings there may be conceivably a survival . . . a survival of a hugely remote period when . . . consciousness was manifested, perhaps, in shapes and forms long since withdrawn before the tide of advancing humanity . . . forms of which poetry and legend alone have caught a flying memory and called them gods, monsters, mythical beings of all sorts and kinds . . .'

– *Algernon Blackwood*

I

The Horror in Clay

The most merciful thing in the world, I think, is the inability of the human mind to correlate all its contents. We live on a placid island of ignorance in the midst of black seas of infinity, and it was not meant that we should voyage far. The sciences, each straining in its own direction, have hitherto harmed us little; but some day the piecing together of dissociated knowledge will open up such terrifying vistas of reality, and of our frightful position therein, that we shall either go mad from the revelation or flee from the deadly light into the peace and safety of a new dark age.

Theosophists have guessed at the awesome grandeur of the cosmic cycle wherein our world and human race form transient incidents. They have hinted at strange survivals in terms which would freeze the blood if not masked by a bland optimism. But it is not from them that there came the single glimpse of forbidden aeons which chills me when I think of it and maddens me when I dream of it. That glimpse, like all dread glimpses of truth, flashed out from an accidental piecing together of separated things – in this case an old newspaper item and the notes of a dead professor. I hope that no one else will accomplish this piecing out; certainly, if I live, I shall never knowingly supply a link in so hideous a chain. I think that the professor, too, intended to keep silent regarding the part he knew, and that he would have destroyed his notes had not sudden death seized him.

My knowledge of the thing began in the winter of 1926–27 with the death of my grand-uncle George Gammell Angell, Professor Emeritus of Semitic Languages in Brown University, Providence, Rhode Island. Professor Angell was widely known as an authority on ancient inscriptions, and had frequently been resorted to by the heads of prominent museums; so that his passing at the age of ninety-two may be recalled by many. Locally, interest was intensified by the obscurity of the cause of death. The professor had been stricken whilst returning from the Newport boat; falling suddenly, as witnesses said, after having been jostled by a nautical-looking negro who had come from one of the queer dark courts on the precipitous hillside which formed a short cut from the waterfront to the deceased's home in Williams Street. Physicians were unable to find any visible disorder, but concluded after perplexed debate that some obscure lesion of the heart, induced by the brisk ascent of so steep a hill by so elderly a man, was responsible for the end. At the time I saw no reason to dissent from this dictum, but latterly I am inclined to wonder – and more than wonder.

As my grand-uncle's heir and executor, for he died a childless widower, I was expected to go over his papers with some thoroughness; and for that purpose moved his entire set of files and boxes to my quarters in Boston. Much of the material which I correlated will be later published by the American Archaeological Society, but there was one box which I found exceedingly puzzling, and which I felt much averse from shewing to other eyes. It had been locked, and I did not find the key till it occurred to me to examine the personal ring which the professor carried always in his pocket. Then indeed I succeeded in opening it, but when I did so seemed only to be confronted by a greater and more closely locked barrier. For what could be the meaning of the queer clay bas-relief and the disjointed jottings, ramblings, and cuttings which I found? Had my uncle, in his latter years, become credulous of the most superficial impostures? I resolved to search out the eccentric sculptor responsible for this apparent disturbance of an old man's peace of mind.

The bas-relief was a rough rectangle less than an inch thick and about five by six inches in area; obviously of modern origin. Its designs, however, were far from modern in atmosphere and suggestion; for although the vagaries of cubism and futurism are many and wild, they do not often reproduce that cryptic regularity which lurks in prehistoric writing. And writing of some kind the bulk of these designs seemed certainly to be; though my memory, despite much familiarity with the papers and collections of my uncle, failed in any way to identify this particular species, or even to hint at its remotest affiliations.

Above these apparent hieroglyphics was a figure of evidently pictorial intent, though its impressionistic execution forbade a very clear idea of its nature. It seemed to be a sort of monster, or symbol representing a monster, of a form which only a diseased fancy could conceive. If I say that my somewhat extravagant imagination yielded simultaneous pictures of an octopus, a dragon, and a human caricature, I shall not be unfaithful to the spirit of the thing. A pulpy, tentacled head surmounted a grotesque and scaly body with rudimentary wings; but it was the *general outline* of the whole which made it most shockingly frightful. Behind the figure was a vague suggestion of a Cyclopean architectural background.

The writing accompanying this oddity was, aside from a stack of press cuttings, in Professor Angell's most recent hand; and made no pretence to literary style. What seemed to be the main document was headed 'CTHULHU CULT' in characters painstakingly printed to avoid the erroneous reading of a word so unheard-of. The manuscript was divided into two sections, the first of which was headed '1925 – Dream and Dream Work of H. A. Wilcox, 7 Thomas St, Providence, R.I.', and the second, 'Narrative of Inspector John R. Legrasse, 121 Bienville St, New Orleans, La., at 1908 A. A. S. Mtg. – Notes on Same, & Prof. Webb's Acct.' The other manuscript papers were all brief notes, some of them accounts of the queer dreams of different persons, some of them citations from theosophical books and magazines (notably W. Scott-Elliot's *Atlantis and the Lost Lemuria*), and the rest comments on long-surviving secret societies and hidden cults, with references to passages in such mythological and anthropological source-books as Frazer's *Golden Bough* and Miss Murray's *Witch-Cult in Western Europe*. The cuttings largely alluded to outré mental illnesses and outbreaks of group folly or mania in the spring of 1925.

The first half of the principal manuscript told a very peculiar tale. It appears that on March 1st, 1925, a thin, dark young man of neurotic and excited aspect had called upon Professor Angell bearing the singular clay bas-relief, which was then exceedingly damp and fresh. His card bore the name of Henry Anthony Wilcox, and my uncle had recognised him as the youngest son of an excellent family slightly known to him, who had latterly been studying sculpture at the Rhode Island School of Design and living alone at the Fleur-de-Lys Building near that institution. Wilcox was a precocious youth of known genius but great eccentricity, and had from childhood excited attention through the strange stories and odd dreams he was in the habit of relating. He called himself 'psychically hypersensitive', but the staid folk of the ancient commercial city dismissed him as merely 'queer'. Never mingling much with his kind, he had dropped gradually from social visibility, and was now known only to a small group of aesthetes from other towns. Even the Providence Art Club, anxious to preserve its conservatism, had found him quite hopeless.

On the occasion of the visit, ran the professor's manuscript, the sculptor abruptly asked for the benefit of his host's archaeological knowledge in identifying the hieroglyphics on the bas-relief. He spoke in a dreamy, stilted manner which suggested pose and alienated sympathy; and my uncle shewed some sharpness in replying, for the conspicuous freshness of the tablet implied kinship with anything but archaeology. Young Wilcox's rejoinder, which impressed my uncle enough to make him recall and record it verbatim, was of a fantastically poetic cast which must have typified his whole conversation, and which I have since found highly characteristic of him. He said, 'It is new, indeed, for I made it last night in a dream of strange cities; and dreams are older than brooding Tyre, or the contemplative Sphinx, or garden-girdled Babylon.'

It was then that he began that rambling tale which suddenly played upon a sleeping memory and won the fevered interest of my uncle. There had been a slight earthquake tremor the night before, the most considerable felt in New England for some years; and Wilcox's imagination had been keenly affected. Upon retiring, he had had an unprecedented dream of great Cyclopean cities of titan blocks and sky-flung monoliths, all dripping with green ooze and sinister with latent horror. Hieroglyphics had covered the walls and pillars, and from some undetermined point below had come a voice that was not a voice; a chaotic sensation which only fancy would transmute into sound, but which he attempted to render by the almost unpronounceable jumble of letters, '*Cthulhu fhtagn*'.

This verbal jumble was the key to the recollection which excited and disturbed Professor Angell. He questioned the sculptor with scientific minuteness; and studied with almost frantic intensity the bas-relief on which the youth had found himself working, chilled and clad only in his night-clothes, when waking had stolen bewilderingly over him. My uncle blamed his old age, Wilcox afterward said, for his slowness in recognising both hieroglyphics and pictorial design. Many of his questions seemed highly out-of-place to his visitor, especially those which tried to connect the latter with strange cults or societies; and Wilcox could not understand the repeated promises of silence which he was offered in exchange for an admission of membership in some widespread mystical or paganly religious body. When Professor Angell became convinced that the sculptor was indeed ignorant of any cult or system of cryptic lore, he besieged his visitor with demands for future reports of dreams. This bore regular fruit, for after the first interview the manuscript records daily calls of the young man, during which he related startling fragments of nocturnal imagery whose burden was always some terrible Cyclopean vista of dark and dripping stone, with a subterrene voice or intelligence shouting monotonously in enigmatical sense-impacts uninscribable save as gibberish. The two sounds most frequently repeated are those rendered by the letters '*Cthulhu*' and '*R'lyeh*'.

On March 23d, the manuscript continued, Wilcox failed to appear; and inquiries at his quarters revealed that he had been stricken with an obscure sort of fever and taken to the home of his family in Waterman Street. He had cried out in the night, arousing several other artists in the building, and had manifested since then only alternations of unconsciousness and delirium. My uncle at once telephoned the family, and from that time forward kept close watch of the case; calling often at the Thayer Street office of Dr Tobey, whom he learned to be in charge. The youth's febrile mind, apparently, was dwelling on strange things; and the doctor shuddered now and then as he spoke of them. They included not only a repetition of what he had formerly dreamed, but touched wildly on a gigantic thing 'miles high' which walked or lumbered about. He at no time fully described this object, but occasional frantic words, as repeated by Dr Tobey, convinced the professor that it must be identical with the nameless monstrosity he had sought to depict in his dream-sculpture. Reference to this object, the doctor added, was invariably a prelude to the young man's subsidence into lethargy. His temperature, oddly enough, was not greatly above normal; but his whole condition was otherwise such as to suggest true fever rather than mental disorder.

On April 2nd at about 3 p.m. every trace of Wilcox's malady suddenly ceased. He sat upright in bed, astonished to find himself at home and completely ignorant of what had happened in dream or reality since the night of March 22nd. Pronounced well by his physician, he returned to his quarters in three days; but to Professor Angell he was of no further assistance. All traces of strange dreaming had vanished with his recovery, and my uncle kept no record of his night-thoughts after a week of pointless and irrelevant accounts of thoroughly usual visions.

Here the first part of the manuscript ended, but references to certain of the scattered notes gave me much material for thought – so much, in fact, that only the ingrained scepticism then forming my philosophy can account for my continued distrust of the artist. The notes in question were those descriptive of the dreams of various persons covering the same period as that in which young Wilcox had had his strange visitations. My uncle, it seems, had quickly instituted a prodigiously far-flung body of inquiries amongst nearly all the friends whom he could question without impertinence, asking for nightly reports of their dreams, and the dates of any notable visions for some time past. The reception of his request seems to have been varied; but he must, at the very least, have received more responses than any ordinary man could have handled without a secretary. This original correspondence was not preserved, but his notes formed a thorough and really significant digest. Average people in society and business – New England's traditional 'salt of the earth' – gave an almost completely negative result, though scattered cases of uneasy but formless nocturnal impressions appear here and there, always between March 23rd and April 2nd – the period of young Wilcox's delirium. Scientific men were little more affected, though four cases of vague description suggest fugitive glimpses of strange landscapes, and in one case there is mentioned a dread of something abnormal.

It was from the artists and poets that the pertinent answers came, and I know that panic would have broken loose had they been able to compare notes. As it was, lacking their original letters, I half suspected the compiler of having asked leading questions, or of having edited the correspondence in corroboration of what he had latently resolved to see. That is why I continued to feel that Wilcox, somehow cognisant of the old data which my uncle had possessed, had been imposing on the veteran scientist. These responses from aesthetes told a disturbing tale. From February 28th to April 2nd a large proportion of them had dreamed very bizarre things, the intensity of the dreams being immeasurably the stronger during the period of the sculptor's delirium. Over a fourth of those who reported anything, reported scenes and half-sounds not unlike those which Wilcox had described; and some of the dreamers confessed acute fear of the gigantic nameless thing visible toward the last. One case, which the note describes with emphasis, was very sad. The subject, a widely known architect with leanings toward theosophy and occultism, went violently insane on the date of young Wilcox's seizure, and expired several months later after incessant screamings to be saved from some escaped denizen of hell. Had my uncle referred to these cases by name instead of merely by number, I should have attempted some corroboration and personal investigation; but as it was, I succeeded in tracing down only a few. All of these, however, bore out the notes in full. I have often wondered if all the objects of the professor's questioning felt as puzzled as did this fraction. It is well that no explanation shall ever reach them.

The press cuttings, as I have intimated, touched on cases of panic, mania, and eccentricity during the given period. Professor Angell must have employed a cutting bureau, for the number of extracts was tremendous and the sources scattered throughout the globe. Here was a nocturnal suicide in London, where a lone sleeper had leaped from a window after a shocking cry. Here likewise a rambling letter to the editor of a paper in South America, where a fanatic deduces a dire future from visions he has seen. A despatch from California describes a theosophist colony as donning white robes en masse for some 'glorious fulfilment' which never arrives, whilst items from India speak guardedly of serious native unrest toward the end of March. Voodoo orgies multiply in Hayti, and African outposts report ominous mutterings. American officers in the Philippines find certain tribes bothersome about this time, and New York policemen are mobbed by hysterical Levantines on the night of March 22–23. The west of Ireland, too, is full of wild rumour and legendry, and a fantastic painter named Ardois-Bonnot hangs a blasphemous 'Dream Landscape' in the Paris spring salon of 1926. And so numerous are the recorded troubles in insane asylums, that only a miracle can have stopped the medical fraternity from noting strange parallelisms and drawing mystified conclusions. A weird bunch of cuttings, all told; and I can at this date scarcely envisage the callous rationalism with which I set them aside. But I was then convinced that young Wilcox had known of the older matters mentioned by the professor.

II

The Tale of Inspector Legrasse

The older matters which had made the sculptor's dream and bas-relief so significant to my uncle formed the subject of the second half of his long manuscript. Once before, it appears, Professor Angell had seen the hellish outlines of the nameless monstrosity, puzzled over the unknown hieroglyphics, and heard the ominous syllables which can be rendered only as '*Cthulhu*'; and all this in so stirring and horrible a connexion that it is small wonder he pursued young Wilcox with queries and demands for data.

The earlier experience had come in 1908, seventeen years before, when the American Archaeological Society held its annual meeting in St Louis. Professor Angell, as befitted one of his authority and attainments, had had a prominent part in all the deliberations; and was one of the first to be approached by the several outsiders who took advantage of the convocation to offer questions for correct answering and problems for expert solution.

The chief of these outsiders, and in a short time the focus of interest for the entire meeting, was a commonplace-looking middle-aged man who had travelled all the way from New Orleans for certain special information unobtainable from any local source. His name was John Raymond Legrasse, and he was by profession an Inspector of Police. With him he bore the subject of his visit, a grotesque, repulsive, and apparently very ancient stone statuette whose origin he was at a loss to determine. It must not be fancied that Inspector Legrasse had the least interest in archaeology. On the contrary, his wish for enlightenment was prompted by purely professional considerations. The statuette, idol, fetish, or whatever it was, had been captured some months before in the wooded swamps south of New Orleans during a raid on a supposed voodoo meeting; and so singular and hideous were the rites connected with it, that the police could not but realise that they had stumbled on a dark cult totally unknown to them, and infinitely more diabolic than even the blackest of the African voodoo circles. Of its origin, apart from the erratic and unbelievable tales extorted from the captured members, absolutely nothing was to be discovered; hence the anxiety of the police for any antiquarian lore which might help them to place the frightful symbol, and through it track down the cult to its fountain-head.

Inspector Legrasse was scarcely prepared for the sensation which his offering created. One sight of the thing had been enough to throw the assembled men of science into a state of tense excitement, and they lost no time in crowding around him to gaze at the diminutive figure whose utter strangeness and air of genuinely abysmal antiquity hinted so potently at unopened and archaic vistas. No recognised school of sculpture had animated this terrible object, yet centuries and even thousands of years seemed recorded in its dim and greenish surface of unplaceable stone.

The figure, which was finally passed slowly from man to man for close and careful study, was between seven and eight inches in height, and of exquisitely artistic workmanship. It represented a monster of vaguely anthropoid outline, but with an octopus-like head whose face was a mass of feelers, a scaly, rubbery-looking body, prodigious claws on hind and fore feet, and long, narrow wings behind. This thing, which seemed instinct with a fearsome and unnatural malignancy, was of a somewhat bloated corpulence, and squatted evilly on a rectangular block or pedestal covered with undecipherable characters. The tips of the wings touched the back edge of the block, the seat occupied the centre, whilst the long, curved claws of the doubled-up, crouching hind legs gripped the front edge and extended a quarter of the way down toward the bottom of the pedestal. The cephalopod head was bent forward, so that the ends of the facial feelers brushed the backs of huge fore paws which clasped the croucher's elevated knees. The aspect of the whole was abnormally life-like, and the more subtly fearful because its source was so totally unknown. Its vast, awesome, and incalculable age was unmistakable; yet not one link did it shew with any known type of art belonging to civilisation's youth – or indeed to any other time. Totally separate and apart, its very material was a mystery; for the soapy, greenish-black stone with its golden or iridescent flecks and striations resembled nothing familiar to geology or mineralogy. The characters along the base were equally baffling; and no member present, despite a representation of half the world's expert learning in this field, could form the least notion of even the remotest linguistic kinship. They, like the subject and material, belonged to something horribly remote and distinct from mankind as we know it; something frightfully suggestive of old and unhallowed cycles of life in which our world and our conceptions have no part.

And yet, as the members severally shook their heads and confessed defeat at the Inspector's problem, there was one man in that gathering who suspected a touch of bizarre familiarity in the monstrous shape and writing, and who presently told with some diffidence of the odd trifle he knew. This person was the late William Channing Webb, Professor of Anthropology in Princeton University, and an explorer of no slight note. Professor Webb had been engaged, forty-eight years before, in a tour of Greenland and Iceland in search of some Runic inscriptions which he failed to unearth; and whilst high up on the West Greenland coast had encountered a singular tribe or cult of degenerate Esquimaux whose religion, a curious form of devil-worship, chilled him with its deliberate bloodthirstiness and repulsiveness. It was a faith of which other Esquimaux knew little, and which they mentioned only with shudders, saying that it had come down from horribly ancient aeons before ever the world was made. Besides nameless rites and human sacrifices there were certain queer hereditary rituals addressed to a supreme elder devil or *tornasuk*; and of this Professor Webb had taken a careful phonetic copy from an aged *angekok* or wizard-priest, expressing the sounds in Roman letters as best he knew how. But just now of prime significance was the fetish which this cult had cherished, and around which they danced when the aurora leaped high over the ice cliffs. It was, the professor stated, a very crude bas-relief of stone, comprising a hideous picture and some cryptic writing. And so far as he could tell, it was a rough parallel in all essential features of the bestial thing now lying before the meeting.

This data, received with suspense and astonishment by the assembled members, proved doubly exciting to Inspector Legrasse; and he began at once to ply his informant with questions. Having noted and copied an oral ritual among the swamp cult-worshippers his men had arrested, he besought the professor to remember as best he might the syllables taken down amongst the diabolist Esquimaux. There then followed an exhaustive comparison of details, and a moment of really awed silence when both detective and scientist agreed on the virtual identity of the phrase common to two hellish rituals so many worlds of distance apart. What, in substance, both the Esquimau wizards and the Louisiana swamp-priests had chanted to their kindred idols was something very like this – the word-divisions being guessed at from traditional breaks in the phrase as chanted aloud:

'Ph'nglui mglw'nafh Cthulhu R'lyeh wgah'nagl fhtagn.'

Legrasse had one point in advance of Professor Webb, for several among his mongrel prisoners had repeated to him what older celebrants had told them the words meant. This text, as given, ran something like this:

'In his house at R'lyeh dead Cthulhu waits dreaming.'

And now, in response to a general and urgent demand, Inspector Legrasse related as fully as possible his experience with the swamp worshippers; telling a story to which I could see my uncle attached profound significance. It savoured of the wildest dreams of myth-maker and theosophist, and disclosed an astonishing degree of cosmic imagination among such half-castes and pariahs as might be expected to possess it.

On November 1st, 1907, there had come to the New Orleans police a frantic summons from the swamp and lagoon country to the south. The squatters there, mostly primitive but good-natured descendants of Lafitte's men, were in the grip of stark terror from an unknown thing which had stolen upon them in the night. It was voodoo, apparently, but voodoo of a more terrible sort than they had ever known; and some of their women and children had disappeared since the malevolent tom-tom had begun its incessant beating far within the black haunted woods where no dweller ventured. There were insane shouts and harrowing screams, soul-chilling chants and dancing devil-flames; and, the frightened messenger added, the people could stand it no more.

So a body of twenty police, filling two carriages and an automobile, had set out in the late afternoon with the shivering squatter as a guide. At the end of the passable road they alighted, and for miles splashed on in silence through the terrible cypress woods where day never came. Ugly roots and malignant hanging nooses of Spanish moss beset them, and now and then a pile of dank stones or fragment of a rotting wall intensified by its hint of morbid habitation a depression which every malformed tree and every fungous islet combined to create. At length the squatter settlement, a miserable huddle of huts, hove in sight;

and hysterical dwellers ran out to cluster around the group of bobbing lanterns. The muffled beat of tom-toms was now faintly audible far, far ahead; and a curdling shriek came at infrequent intervals when the wind shifted. A reddish glare, too, seemed to filter through the pale undergrowth beyond endless avenues of forest night. Reluctant even to be left alone again, each one of the cowed squatters refused point-blank to advance another inch toward the scene of unholy worship, so Inspector Legrasse and his nineteen colleagues plunged on unguided into black arcades of horror that none of them had ever trod before.

The region now entered by the police was one of traditionally evil repute, substantially unknown and untraversed by white men. There were legends of a hidden lake unglimpsed by mortal sight, in which dwelt a huge, formless white polypous thing with luminous eyes; and squatters whispered that bat-winged devils flew up out of caverns in inner earth to worship it at midnight. They said it had been there before D'Iberville, before La Salle, before the Indians, and before even the wholesome beasts and birds of the woods. It was nightmare itself, and to see it was to die. But it made men dream, and so they knew enough to keep away. The present voodoo orgy was, indeed, on the merest fringe of this abhorred area, but that location was bad enough; hence perhaps the very place of the worship had terrified the squatters more than the shocking sounds and incidents.

Only poetry or madness could do justice to the noises heard by Legrasse's men as they ploughed on through the black morass toward the red glare and the muffled tom-toms. There are vocal qualities peculiar to men, and vocal qualities peculiar to beasts; and it is terrible to hear the one when the source should yield the other. Animal fury and orgiastic licence here whipped themselves to daemoniac heights by howls and squawking ecstasies that tore and reverberated through those nighted woods like pestilential tempests from the gulfs of hell. Now and then the less organised ululation would cease, and from what seemed a well-drilled chorus of hoarse voices would rise in sing-song chant that hideous phrase or ritual:

'Ph'nglui mglw'nafh Cthulhu R'lyeh wgah'nagl fhtagn.'

Then the men, having reached a spot where the trees were thinner, came suddenly in sight of the spectacle itself. Four of them reeled, one fainted, and two were shaken into a frantic cry which the mad cacophony of the orgy fortunately deadened. Legrasse dashed swamp water on the face of the fainting man, and all stood trembling and nearly hypnotised with horror.

In a natural glade of the swamp stood a grassy island of perhaps an acre's extent, clear of trees and tolerably dry. On this now leaped and twisted a more indescribable horde of human abnormality than any but a Sime or an Angarola could paint. Void of clothing, this hybrid spawn were braying, bellowing, and writhing about a monstrous ring-shaped bonfire; in the centre of which, revealed by occasional rifts in the curtain of flame, stood a great granite monolith some eight feet in height; on top of which, incongruous with its diminutiveness, rested the noxious carven statuette. From a wide circle of ten scaffolds set up at regular intervals with the flame-girt monolith as a centre hung, head downward, the oddly marred bodies of the helpless squatters who had disappeared. It was inside this circle that the ring of worshippers jumped and roared, the general direction of the mass motion being from left to right in endless Bacchanal between the ring of bodies and the ring of fire.

It may have been only imagination and it may have been only echoes which induced one of the men, an excitable Spaniard, to fancy he heard antiphonal responses to the ritual from some far and unillumined spot deeper within the wood of ancient legendry and horror. This man, Joseph D. Galvez, I later met and questioned; and he proved distractingly imaginative. He indeed went so far as to hint of the faint beating of great wings, and of a glimpse of shining eyes and a mountainous white bulk beyond the remotest trees – but I suppose he had been hearing too much native superstition.

Actually, the horrified pause of the men was of comparatively brief duration. Duty came first; and although there must have been nearly a hundred mongrel celebrants in the throng, the police relied on their firearms and plunged determinedly into the nauseous rout. For five minutes the resultant din and chaos were beyond description. Wild blows were struck, shots were fired, and escapes were made; but in the end Legrasse was able to count some forty-seven sullen prisoners, whom he forced to dress in haste and fall into line between two rows of policemen. Five of the worshippers lay dead, and two severely wounded ones were carried away on improvised stretchers by their fellow-prisoners. The image on the monolith, of course, was carefully removed and carried back by Legrasse.

Examined at headquarters after a trip of intense strain and weariness, the prisoners all proved to be men of a very low, mixed-blooded, and mentally aberrant type. Most were seamen, and a sprinkling of negroes and mulattoes, largely West Indians or Brava Portuguese from the Cape Verde Islands, gave a colouring of voodooism to the heterogeneous cult. But before many questions were asked, it became manifest that something far deeper and older than negro fetichism was involved. Degraded and ignorant as they were, the creatures held with surprising consistency to the central idea of their loathsome faith.

They worshipped, so they said, the Great Old Ones who lived ages before there were any men, and who came to the young world out of the sky. Those Old Ones were gone now, inside the earth and under the sea; but their dead bodies had told their secrets in dreams to the first men, who formed a cult which had never died. This was that cult, and the prisoners said it had always existed and always would exist, hidden in distant wastes and dark places all over the world until the time when the great priest Cthulhu, from his dark house in the mighty city of R'lyeh under the waters, should rise and bring the earth again beneath his sway. Some day he would call, when the stars were ready, and the secret cult would always be waiting to liberate him.

Meanwhile no more must be told. There was a secret which even torture could not extract. Mankind was not absolutely alone among the conscious things of earth, for shapes came out of the dark to visit the faithful few. But these were not the Great Old Ones. No man had ever seen the Old Ones. The carven idol was great Cthulhu, but none might say whether or not the others were precisely like him. No one could read the old writing now, but things were told by word of mouth. The chanted ritual was not the secret – that was never spoken aloud, only whispered. The chant meant only this: 'In his house at R'lyeh dead Cthulhu waits dreaming.'

Only two of the prisoners were found sane enough to be hanged, and the rest were committed to various institutions. All denied a part in the ritual murders, and averred that the killing had been done by Black Winged Ones which had come to them from their immemorial meeting-place in the haunted wood. But of those mysterious allies no coherent account could ever be gained. What the police did extract, came mainly from an immensely aged mestizo named Castro, who claimed to have sailed to strange ports and talked with undying leaders of the cult in the mountains of China.

Old Castro remembered bits of hideous legend that paled the speculations of theosophists and made man and the world seem recent and transient indeed. There had been aeons when other Things ruled on the earth, and They had had great cities. Remains of Them, he said the deathless Chinamen had told him, were still to be found as Cyclopean stones on islands in the Pacific. They all died vast epochs of time before men came, but there were arts which could revive Them when the stars had come round again to the right positions in the cycle of eternity. They had, indeed, come themselves from the stars, and brought Their images with Them.

These Great Old Ones, Castro continued, were not composed altogether of flesh and blood. They had shape – for did not this star-fashioned image prove it? – but that shape was not made of matter. When the stars were right, They could plunge from world to world through the sky; but when the stars were wrong, they could not live. But although They no longer lived, They would never really die. They all lay in stone houses in Their great city of R'lyeh, preserved by the spells of mighty Cthulhu for a glorious resurrection when the stars and the earth might once more be ready for Them. But at that time some force from outside must serve to liberate Their bodies. The spells that preserved Them intact likewise prevented Them from making an initial move, and They could only lie awake in the dark and think whilst uncounted millions of years rolled by. They knew all that was occurring in the universe, but Their mode of speech was transmitted thought. Even now They talked in Their tombs. When, after infinities of chaos, the first men came, the Great Old Ones spoke to the sensitive among them by moulding their dreams; for only thus could Their language reach the fleshly minds of mammals.

Then, whispered Castro, those first men formed the cult around small idols which the Great Ones shewed them; idols brought in dim aeras from dark stars. That cult would never die till the stars came right again, and the secret priests would take great Cthulhu from His tomb to revive His subjects and resume His rule of earth. The time would be easy to know, for then mankind would have become as the Great Old Ones; free and wild and beyond good and evil, with laws and morals thrown aside and all men shouting and killing and revelling in joy. Then the liberated Old Ones would teach them new ways to shout and kill and revel and enjoy themselves, and all the earth would flame with a holocaust of ecstasy and freedom. Meanwhile the cult, by appropriate rites, must keep alive the memory of those ancient ways and shadow forth the prophecy of their return.

In the elder time chosen men had talked with the entombed Old Ones in dreams, but then something had happened. The great stone city R'lyeh, with its monoliths and sepulchres, had sunk beneath the waves; and the deep waters, full of the one primal mystery through which not even thought can pass, had cut off the spectral intercourse. But memory never died, and high-priests said that the city would rise again when the stars were right. Then came out of the earth the black spirits of earth, mouldy and shadowy, and full of dim rumours picked up in caverns beneath forgotten sea-bottoms. But of them old Castro dared not speak much. He cut himself off hurriedly, and no amount of persuasion or subtlety could elicit more in this direction. The *size* of the Old Ones, too, he curiously declined to mention. Of the cult, he said that he thought the centre lay amid the pathless deserts of Arabia, where Irem, the City of Pillars, dreams hidden and untouched. It was not allied to the European witch-cult, and was virtually unknown beyond its members. No book had ever really hinted of it, though the deathless Chinamen said that there were double meanings in the *Necronomicon* of the mad Arab Abdul Alhazred which the initiated might read as they chose, especially the much-discussed couplet:

'That is not dead which can eternal lie,
And with strange aeons even death may die.'

Legrasse, deeply impressed and not a little bewildered, had inquired in vain concerning the historic affiliations of the cult. Castro, apparently, had told the truth when he said that it was wholly secret. The authorities at Tulane University could shed no light upon either cult or image, and now the detective had come to the highest authorities in the country and met with no more than the Greenland tale of Professor Webb.

The feverish interest aroused at the meeting by Legrasse's tale, corroborated as it was by the statuette, is echoed in the subsequent correspondence of those who attended; although scant mention occurs in the formal publications of the society. Caution is the first care of those accustomed to face occasional charlatanry and imposture. Legrasse for some time lent the image to Professor Webb, but at the latter's death it was returned to him and remains in his possession, where I viewed it not long ago. It is truly a terrible thing, and unmistakably akin to the dream-sculpture of young Wilcox.

That my uncle was excited by the tale of the sculptor I did not wonder, for what thoughts must arise upon hearing, after a knowledge of what Legrasse had learned of the cult, of a sensitive young man who had *dreamed* not only the figure and exact hieroglyphics of the swamp-found image and the Greenland devil tablet, but had come *in his dreams* upon at least three of the precise words of the formula uttered alike by Esquimau diabolists and mongrel Louisianans? Professor Angell's instant start on an investigation of the utmost thoroughness was eminently natural; though privately I suspected young Wilcox of having heard of the cult in some indirect way, and of having invented a series of dreams to heighten and continue the mystery at my uncle's expense. The dream-narratives and cuttings collected by the professor were, of course, strong corroboration; but the rationalism of my mind and the extravagance of the whole subject led me to adopt what I thought the most sensible conclusions. So, after thoroughly studying the manuscript again and correlating the theosophical and anthropological notes with the cult narrative of Legrasse, I made a trip to Providence to see the sculptor and give him the rebuke I thought proper for so boldly imposing upon a learned and aged man.

Wilcox still lived alone in the Fleur-de-Lys Building in Thomas Street, a hideous Victorian imitation of seventeenth-century Breton architecture which flaunts its stuccoed front amidst the lovely colonial houses on the ancient hill, and under the very shadow of the finest Georgian steeple in America. I found him at work in his rooms, and at once conceded from the specimens scattered about that his genius is indeed profound and authentic. He will, I believe, some time be heard from as one of the great decadents; for he has crystallised in clay and will one day mirror in marble those nightmares and phantasies which Arthur Machen evokes in prose, and Clark Ashton Smith makes visible in verse and in painting.

Dark, frail, and somewhat unkempt in aspect, he turned languidly at my knock and asked me my business without rising. When I told him who I was, he displayed some interest; for my uncle had excited his curiosity in probing his strange dreams, yet had never explained the reason for the study. I did not enlarge his knowledge in this regard, but sought with some subtlety to draw him out. In a short time I became convinced of his absolute sincerity, for he spoke of the dreams in a manner none could mistake. They and their subconscious residuum had influenced his art profoundly, and he shewed me a morbid statue whose contours almost made me shake with the potency of its black suggestion. He could not recall having seen the original of this thing except in his own dream bas-relief, but the outlines had formed themselves insensibly under his hands. It was, no doubt, the giant shape he had raved of in delirium. That he really knew nothing of the hidden cult, save from what my uncle's relentless catechism had let fall, he soon made clear; and again I strove to think of some way in which he could possibly have received the weird impressions.

He talked of his dreams in a strangely poetic fashion; making me see with terrible vividness the damp Cyclopean city of slimy green stone – whose *geometry*, he oddly said, was *all wrong* – and hear with frightened expectancy the ceaseless, half-mental calling from underground: *'Cthulhu fhtagn'*, *'Cthulhu fhtagn'*. These words had formed part of that dread ritual which told of dead Cthulhu's dream-vigil in his stone vault at R'lyeh, and I felt deeply moved despite my rational beliefs. Wilcox, I was sure, had heard of the cult in some casual way, and had soon forgotten it amidst the mass of his equally weird reading and imagining. Later, by virtue of its sheer impressiveness, it had found subconscious expression in dreams, in the bas-relief, and in the terrible statue I now beheld; so that his imposture upon my uncle had been a very innocent one. The youth was of a type, at once slightly affected and slightly ill-mannered, which I could never like; but I was willing enough now to admit both his genius and his honesty. I took leave of him amicably, and wish him all the success his talent promises.

The matter of the cult still remained to fascinate me, and at times I had visions of personal fame from researches into its origin and connexions. I visited New Orleans, talked with Legrasse and others of that old-time raiding-party, saw the frightful image, and even questioned such of the mongrel prisoners as still survived. Old Castro, unfortunately, had been dead for some years. What I now heard so graphically at first-hand, though it was really no more than a detailed confirmation of what my uncle had written, excited me afresh; for I felt sure that I was on the track of a very real, very secret, and very ancient religion whose discovery would make me an anthropologist of note. My attitude was still one of absolute materialism, *as I wish it still were*, and I discounted with almost inexplicable perversity the coincidence of the dream notes and odd cuttings collected by Professor Angell.

One thing I began to suspect, and which I now fear I *know*, is that my uncle's death was far from natural. He fell on a narrow hill street leading up from an ancient waterfront swarming with foreign mongrels, after a careless push from a negro sailor. I did not forget the mixed blood and marine pursuits of the cult-members in Louisiana, and would not be surprised to learn of secret methods and poison needles as ruthless and as anciently known as the cryptic rites and beliefs. Legrasse and his men, it is true, have been let alone; but in Norway a certain seaman who saw things is dead. Might not the deeper inquiries of my uncle after encountering the sculptor's data have come to sinister ears? I think Professor Angell died because he knew too much, or because he was likely to learn too much. Whether I shall go as he did remains to be seen, for I have learned much now.

III

The Madness from the Sea

If heaven ever wishes to grant me a boon, it will be a total effacing of the results of a mere chance which fixed my eye on a certain stray piece of shelf-paper. It was nothing on which I would naturally have stumbled in the course of my daily round, for it was an old number of an Australian journal, the *Sydney Bulletin* for April 18, 1925. It had escaped even the cutting bureau which had at the time of its issuance been avidly collecting material for my uncle's research.

I had largely given over my inquiries into what Professor Angell called the 'Cthulhu Cult', and was visiting a learned friend in Paterson, New Jersey; the curator of a local museum and a mineralogist of note. Examining one day the reserve specimens roughly set on the storage shelves in a rear room of the museum, my eye was caught by an odd picture in one of the old papers spread beneath the stones. It was the *Sydney Bulletin* I have mentioned, for my friend has wide affiliations in all conceivable foreign parts; and the picture was a half-tone cut of a hideous stone image almost identical with that which Legrasse had found in the swamp.

Eagerly clearing the sheet of its precious contents, I scanned the item in detail; and was disappointed to find it of only moderate length. What it suggested, however, was of portentous significance to my flagging quest; and I carefully tore it out for immediate action. It read as follows:

MYSTERY DERELICT FOUND AT SEA

Vigilant Arrives With Helpless Armed New Zealand Yacht in Tow.
One Survivor and Dead Man Found Aboard. Tale of
Desperate Battle and Deaths at Sea.
Rescued Seaman Refuses
Particulars of Strange Experience.
Odd Idol Found in His Possession. Inquiry
to Follow.

The Morrison Co.'s freighter *Vigilant*, bound from Valparaiso, arrived this morning at its wharf in Darling Harbour, having in tow the battled and disabled but heavily armed steam yacht *Alert* of Dunedin, N. Z., which was sighted April 12th in S. Latitude 34° 21′, W. Longitude 152° 17′ with one living and one dead man aboard.

The *Vigilant* left Valparaiso March 25th, and on April 2nd was driven considerably south of her course by exceptionally heavy storms and monster waves. On April 12th the derelict was sighted; and though apparently deserted, was found upon boarding to contain one survivor in a half-delirious condition and one man who had evidently been dead for more than a week. The living man was clutching a horrible stone idol of unknown origin, about a foot in height, regarding whose nature authorities at Sydney University, the Royal Society, and the Museum in College Street all profess complete bafflement, and which the survivor says he found in the cabin of the yacht, in a small carved shrine of common pattern.

This man, after recovering his senses, told an exceedingly strange story of piracy and slaughter. He is Gustaf Johansen, a Norwegian of some intelligence, and had been second mate of the two-masted schooner *Emma* of Auckland, which sailed for Callao February 20th with a complement of eleven men. The *Emma*, he says, was delayed and thrown widely south of her course by the great storm of March 1st, and on March 22nd, in S. Latitude 49° 51′, W. Longitude 128° 34′, encountered the *Alert*, manned by a queer and evil-looking crew of Kanakas and half-castes. Being ordered peremptorily to turn back, Capt. Collins refused; whereupon the strange crew began to fire savagely and without warning upon the schooner with a peculiarly heavy battery of brass cannon forming part of the yacht's equipment. The *Emma's* men shewed fight, says the survivor, and though the schooner began to sink from shots beneath the waterline they managed to heave alongside their enemy and board her, grappling with the savage crew on the yacht's deck, and being forced to kill them all, the number being slightly superior, because of their particularly abhorrent and desperate though rather clumsy mode of fighting.

Three of the *Emma's* men, including Capt. Collins and First Mate Green, were killed; and the remaining eight under Second Mate Johansen proceeded to navigate the captured yacht, going ahead in their original direction to see if any reason for their ordering back had existed. The next day, it appears, they raised and landed on a small island, although none is known to exist in that part of the ocean; and six of the men somehow died ashore, though Johansen is queerly reticent about this part of his story, and speaks only of their falling into a rock chasm. Later, it seems, he and one companion boarded the yacht and tried to manage her, but were beaten about by the storm of April 2nd. From that time till his rescue on the 12th the man remembers little, and he does not even recall when William Briden, his companion, died. Briden's death reveals no apparent cause, and was probably due to excitement or exposure. Cable advices from Dunedin report that the *Alert* was well known there as an island trader, and bore an evil reputation along the waterfront. It was owned by a curious group of half-castes whose frequent meetings and night trips to the woods attracted no little curiosity; and it had set sail in great haste just after the storm and earth tremors of March 1st. Our Auckland correspondent gives the *Emma* and her crew an excellent reputation, and Johansen is described as a sober and worthy man. The admiralty will institute an inquiry on the whole matter beginning tomorrow, at which every effort will be made to induce Johansen to speak more freely than he has done hitherto.

This was all, together with the picture of the hellish image; but what a train of ideas it started in my mind! Here were new treasuries of data on the Cthulhu Cult, and evidence that it had strange interests at sea as well as on land. What motive prompted the hybrid crew to order back the *Emma* as they sailed about with their hideous idol? What was the unknown island on which six of the *Emma's* crew had died, and about which the mate Johansen was so secretive? What had the vice-admiralty's investigation brought out, and what was known of the noxious cult in Dunedin? And most marvellous of all, what deep and more than natural linkage of dates was this which gave a malign and now undeniable significance to the various turns of events so carefully noted by my uncle?

March 1st – our February 28th according to the International Date Line – the earthquake and storm had come. From Dunedin the *Alert* and her noisome crew had darted eagerly forth as if imperiously summoned, and on the other side of the earth poets and artists had begun to dream of a strange, dank Cyclopean city whilst a young sculptor had moulded in his sleep the form of the dreaded Cthulhu. March 23rd the crew of the *Emma* landed on an unknown island and left six men dead; and on that date the dreams of sensitive men assumed a heightened vividness and darkened with dread of a giant monster's malign pursuit, whilst an architect had gone mad and a sculptor had lapsed suddenly into delirium! And what of this storm of April 2nd – the date on which all dreams of the dank city ceased, and Wilcox emerged unharmed from the bondage of strange fever? What of all this – and of those hints of old Castro about the sunken, star-born Old Ones and their coming reign; their faithful cult *and their mastery of dreams*? Was I tottering on the brink of cosmic horrors beyond man's power to bear? If so, they must be horrors of the mind alone, for in some way the second of April had put a stop to whatever monstrous menace had begun its siege of mankind's soul.

That evening, after a day of hurried cabling and arranging, I bade my host adieu and took a train for San Francisco. In less than a month I was in Dunedin; where, however, I found that little was known of the strange cult-members who had lingered in the old sea-taverns. Waterfront scum was far too common for special mention; though there was vague talk about one inland trip these mongrels had made, during which faint drumming and red flame were noted on the distant hills. In Auckland I learned that Johansen had returned *with yellow hair turned white* after a perfunctory and inconclusive questioning at Sydney, and had thereafter sold his cottage in West Street and sailed with his wife to his old home in Oslo. Of his stirring experience he would tell his friends no more than he had told the admiralty officials, and all they could do was to give me his Oslo address.

After that I went to Sydney and talked profitlessly with seamen and members of the vice-admiralty court. I saw the *Alert*, now sold and in commercial use, at Circular Quay in Sydney Cove, but gained nothing from its non-committal bulk. The crouching image with its cuttlefish head, dragon body, scaly wings, and hieroglyphed pedestal, was preserved in the Museum at Hyde Park; and I studied it long and well, finding it a thing of balefully exquisite workmanship, and with the same utter mystery, terrible antiquity, and unearthly strangeness of material which I had noted in Legrasse's smaller specimen. Geologists, the curator told me, had found it a monstrous puzzle; for they vowed that the world held no rock like it. Then I thought with a shudder of what old Castro had told Legrasse about the primal Great Ones: 'They had come from the stars, and had brought Their images with Them.'

Shaken with such a mental revolution as I had never before known, I now resolved to visit Mate Johansen in Oslo. Sailing for London, I reëmbarked at once for the Norwegian capital; and one autumn day landed at the trim wharves in the shadow of the Egeberg. Johansen's address, I discovered, lay in the Old Town of King Harold Haardrada, which kept alive the name of Oslo during all the centuries that the greater city masqueraded as 'Christiana'. I made the brief trip by taxicab, and knocked with palpitant heart at the door of a neat and ancient building with plastered front. A sad-faced woman in black answered my summons, and I was stung with disappointment when she told me in halting English that Gustaf Johansen was no more.

He had not survived his return, said his wife, for the doings at sea in 1925 had broken him. He had told her no more than he had told the public, but had left a long manuscript – of 'technical matters' as he said – written in English, evidently in order to safeguard her from the peril of casual perusal. During a walk through a narrow lane near the Gothenburg dock, a bundle of papers falling from an attic window had knocked him down. Two Lascar sailors at once helped him to his feet, but before the ambulance could reach him he was dead. Physicians found no adequate cause for the end, and laid it to heart trouble and a weakened constitution.

I now felt gnawing at my vitals that dark terror which will never leave me till I, too, am at rest; 'accidentally' or otherwise. Persuading the widow that my connexion with her husband's 'technical matters' was sufficient to entitle me to his manuscript, I bore the document away and began to read it on the London boat. It was a simple, rambling thing – a naive sailor's effort at a post-facto diary – and strove to recall day by day that last awful voyage. I cannot attempt to transcribe it verbatim in all its cloudiness and redundance, but I will tell its gist enough to shew why the sound of the water against the vessel's sides became so unendurable to me that I stopped my ears with cotton.

Johansen, thank God, did not know quite all, even though he saw the city and the Thing, but I shall never sleep calmly again when I think of the horrors that lurk ceaselessly behind life in time and in space, and of those unhallowed blasphemies from elder stars which dream beneath the sea, known and favoured by a nightmare cult ready and eager to loose them on the world whenever another earthquake shall heave their monstrous stone city again to the sun and air.

Johansen's voyage had begun just as he told it to the vice-admiralty. The *Emma*, in ballast, had cleared Auckland on February 20th, and had felt the full force of that earthquake-born tempest which must have heaved up from the sea-bottom the horrors that filled men's dreams. Once more under control, the ship was making good progress when held up by the *Alert* on March 22nd, and I could feel the mate's regret as he wrote of her bombardment and sinking. Of the swarthy cult-fiends on the *Alert* he speaks with significant horror. There was some peculiarly abominable quality about them which made their destruction seem almost a duty, and Johansen shews ingenuous wonder at the charge of ruthlessness brought against his party during the proceedings of the court of inquiry. Then, driven ahead by curiosity in their captured yacht under Johansen's command, the men sight a great stone pillar sticking out of the sea, and in S. Latitude 47° 9′, W. Longitude 126° 43′ come upon a coastline of mingled mud, ooze, and weedy Cyclopean masonry which can be nothing less than the tangible substance of earth's supreme terror – the nightmare corpse-city of R'lyeh, that was built in measureless aeons behind history by the vast, loathsome shapes that seeped down from the dark stars. There lay great Cthulhu and his hordes, hidden in green slimy vaults and sending out at last, after cycles incalculable, the thoughts that spread fear to the dreams of the sensitive and called imperiously to the faithful to come on a pilgrimage of liberation and restoration. All this Johansen did not suspect, but God knows he soon saw enough!

I suppose that only a single mountain-top, the hideous monolith-crowned citadel whereon great Cthulhu was buried, actually emerged from the waters. When I think of the *extent* of all that may be brooding down there I almost wish to kill myself forthwith. Johansen and his men were awed by the cosmic majesty of this dripping Babylon of elder daemons, and must have guessed without guidance that it was nothing of this or of any sane planet. Awe at the unbelievable size of the greenish stone blocks, at the dizzying height of the great carven monolith, and at the stupefying identity of the colossal statues and bas-reliefs with the queer image found in the shrine on the *Alert*, is poignantly visible in every line of the mate's frightened description.

Without knowing what futurism is like, Johansen achieved something very close to it when he spoke of the city; for instead of describing any definite structure or building, he dwells only on broad impressions of vast angles and stone surfaces – surfaces too great to belong to anything right or proper for this earth, and impious with horrible images and hieroglyphs. I mention his talk about *angles* because it suggests something Wilcox had told me of his awful dreams. He has said that the *geometry* of the dream-place he saw was abnormal, non-Euclidean, and loathsomely redolent of spheres and dimensions apart from ours. Now an unlettered seaman felt the same thing whilst gazing at the terrible reality.

Johansen and his men landed at a sloping mud-bank on this monstrous Acropolis, and clambered slipperily up over titan oozy blocks which could have been no mortal staircase. The very sun of heaven seemed distorted when viewed through the polarising miasma welling out from this sea-soaked perversion, and twisted menace and suspense lurked leeringly in those crazily elusive angles of carven rock where a second glance shewed concavity after the first shewed convexity.

Something very like fright had come over all the explorers before anything more definite than rock and ooze and weed was seen. Each would have fled had he not feared the scorn of the others, and it was only half-heartedly that they searched – vainly, as it proved – for some portable souvenir to bear away.

It was Rodriguez the Portuguese who climbed up the foot of the monolith and shouted of what he had found. The rest followed him, and looked curiously at the immense carved door with the now familiar squid-dragon bas-relief. It was, Johansen said, like a great barn-door; and they all felt that it was a door because of the ornate lintel, threshold, and jambs around it, though they could not decide whether it lay flat like a trap-door or slantwise like an outside cellar-door. As Wilcox would have said, the geometry of the place was all wrong. One could not be sure that the sea and the ground were horizontal, hence the relative position of everything else seemed phantasmally variable.

Briden pushed at the stone in several places without result. Then Donovan felt over it delicately around the edge, pressing each point separately as he went. He climbed interminably along the grotesque stone moulding – that is, one would call it climbing if the thing was not after all horizontal – and the men wondered how any door in the universe could be so vast. Then, very softly and slowly, the acre-great panel began to give inward at the top; and they saw that it was balanced. Donovan slid or somehow propelled himself down or along the jamb and re-joined his fellows, and everyone watched the queer recession of the monstrously carven portal. In this phantasy of prismatic distortion it moved anomalously in a diagonal way, so that all the rules of matter and perspective seemed upset.

The aperture was black with a darkness almost material. That tenebrousness was indeed a *positive quality*; for it obscured such parts of the inner walls as ought to have been revealed, and actually burst forth like smoke from its aeon-long imprisonment, visibly darkening the sun as it slunk away into the shrunken and gibbous sky on flapping membraneous wings. The odour arising from the newly opened depths was intolerable, and at length the quick-eared Hawkins thought he heard a nasty, slopping sound down there. Everyone listened, and everyone was listening still when It lumbered slobberingly into sight and gropingly squeezed Its gelatinous green immensity through the black doorway into the tainted outside air of that poison city of madness.

Poor Johansen's handwriting almost gave out when he wrote of this. Of the six men who never reached the ship, he thinks two perished of pure fright in that accursed instant. The Thing cannot be described – there is no language for such abysms of shrieking and immemorial lunacy, such eldritch contradictions of all matter, force, and cosmic order. A mountain walked or stumbled. God! What wonder that across the earth a great architect went mad, and poor Wilcox raved with fever in that telepathic instant? The Thing of the idols, the green, sticky spawn of the stars, had awaked to claim his own. The stars were right again, and what an age-old cult had failed to do by design, a band of innocent sailors had done by accident. After vigintillions of years great Cthulhu was loose again, and ravening for delight.

Three men were swept up by the flabby claws before anybody turned. God rest them, if there be any rest in the universe. They were Donovan, Guerrera, and Ångstrom. Parker slipped as the other three were plunging frenziedly over endless vistas of green-crusted rock to the boat, and Johansen swears he was swallowed up by an angle of masonry which shouldn't have been there; an angle which was acute, but behaved as if it were obtuse. So only Briden and Johansen reached the boat, and pulled desperately for the *Alert* as the mountainous monstrosity flopped down the slimy stones and hesitated floundering at the edge of the water.

Steam had not been suffered to go down entirely, despite the departure of all hands for the shore; and it was the work of only a few moments of feverish rushing up and down between wheel and engines to get the *Alert* under way. Slowly, amidst the distorted horrors of that indescribable scene, she began to churn the lethal waters; whilst on the masonry of that charnel shore that was not of earth the titan Thing from the stars slavered and gibbered like Polypheme cursing the fleeing ship of Odysseus. Then, bolder than the storied Cyclops, great Cthulhu slid greasily into the water and began to pursue with vast wave-raising strokes of cosmic potency. Briden looked back and went mad, laughing shrilly as he kept on laughing at intervals till death found him one night in the cabin whilst Johansen was wandering deliriously.

But Johansen had not given out yet. Knowing that the Thing could surely overtake the *Alert* until steam was fully up, he resolved on a desperate chance; and, setting the engine for full speed, ran lightning-like on deck and reversed the wheel. There was a mighty eddying and foaming in the noisome brine, and as the steam mounted higher and higher the brave Norwegian drove his vessel head on against the pursuing jelly which rose above the unclean froth like the stern of a daemon galleon. The awful squid-head with writhing feelers came nearly up to the bowsprit of the sturdy yacht, but Johansen drove on relentlessly. There was a bursting as of an exploding bladder, a slushy nastiness as of a cloven sunfish, a stench as of a thousand opened graves, and a sound that the chronicler would not put on paper. For an instant the ship was befouled by an acrid and blinding green cloud, and then there was only a venomous seething astern; where – God in heaven! – the scattered plasticity of that nameless sky-spawn was nebulously *recombining* in its hateful original form, whilst its distance widened every second as the *Alert* gained impetus from its mounting steam.

That was all. After that Johansen only brooded over the idol in the cabin and attended to a few matters of food for himself and the laughing maniac by his side. He did not try to navigate after the first bold flight, for the reaction had taken something out of his soul. Then came the storm of April 2nd, and a gathering of the clouds about his consciousness. There is a sense of spectral whirling through liquid gulfs of infinity, of dizzying rides through reeling universes on a comet's tail, and of hysterical plunges from the pit to the moon and from the moon back again to the pit, all livened by a cachinnating chorus of the distorted, hilarious elder gods and the green, bat-winged mocking imps of Tartarus.

Out of that dream came rescue – the *Vigilant*, the vice-admiralty court, the streets of Dunedin, and the long voyage back home to the old house by the Egeberg. He could not tell – they would think him mad. He would write of what he knew before death came, but his wife must not guess. Death would be a boon if only it could blot out the memories.

That was the document I read, and now I have placed it in the tin box beside the bas-relief and the papers of Professor Angell. With it shall go this record of mine – this test of my own sanity, wherein is pieced together that which I hope may never be pieced together again. I have looked upon all that the universe has to hold of horror, and even the skies of spring and the flowers of summer must ever afterward be poison to me. But I do not think my life will be long. As my uncle went, as poor Johansen went, so I shall go. I know too much, and the cult still lives.

Cthulhu still lives, too, I suppose, again in that chasm of stone which has shielded him since the sun was young. His accursed city is sunken once more, for the *Vigilant* sailed over the spot after the April storm; but his ministers on earth still bellow and prance and slay around idol-capped monoliths in lonely places. He must have been trapped by the sinking whilst within his black abyss, or the world would by now be screaming with fright and frenzy. Who knows the end? What has risen may sink, and what has sunk may rise. Loathsomeness waits and dreams in the deep, and decay spreads over the tottering cities of men. A time will come – but I must not and cannot think! Let me pray that, if I do not survive this manuscript, my executors may put caution before audacity and see that it meets no other eye.

Couching at the Door

D. K. Broster

I

The first inkling which Augustine Marchant had of the matter was on one fine summer morning about three weeks after his visit to Prague – that is to say, in June, 1898. He was reclining, as his custom was when writing his poetry, on the very comfortable sofa in his library at Abbot's Medding, near the French windows, one of which was open to the garden. Pausing for inspiration – he was nearly at the end of his poem, *Salutation to All Unbeliefs* – he let his eyes wander round the beautifully appointed room, with its cloisonné and Satsuma, Buhl and first editions, and then allowed them to stray towards the sunlight outside. And so, between the edge of the costly Herat carpet and the sill of the open window, across the strip of polished oak flooring, he observed what he took to be a small piece of dark fluff blowing in the draught; and instantly made a note to speak to his housekeeper about it. There was slackness somewhere; and in Augustine Marchant's house no one was allowed to be slack but himself.

There had been a time when the poet would not for a moment have been received, as he was now, in country and even county society – those days, even before the advent of *The Yellow Book* and *The Savoy*, when he had lived in London, writing the plays and poems which had so startled and shocked all but the 'decadent' and the 'advanced', *Pomegranates of Sin, Queen Theodora and Queen Marozia, The Nights of the Tour de Nesle, Amor Cypriacus* and the rest. But when, as the 'nineties began to wane, he inherited

Abbot's Medding from a distant cousin and came to live there, being then at the height of an almost international reputation, Wiltshire society at first tolerated him for his kinship with the late Lord Medding, and then, placated by the excellence of his dinners and further mollified by the patent staidness of his private life, decided that, in his personal conduct at any rate, he must have turned over a new leaf. Perhaps indeed he had never been as bad as he was painted, and if his writings continued to be no less scandalously free and free-thinking than before, and needed to be just as rigidly kept out of the hands of daughters, well, no country gentleman in the neighbourhood was obliged to read them!

And indeed Augustine Marchant in his fifty-first year was too keenly alive to the value of the good opinion of county society to risk shocking it by any overt doings of his. He kept his licence for his pen. When he went abroad, as he did at least twice a year – but that was another matter altogether. The nose of Mrs Grundy was not sharp enough to smell out his occupations in Warsaw or Berlin or Naples, her eyes long-sighted enough to discern what kind of society he frequented even so near home as Paris. At Abbot's Medding his reputation for being 'wicked' was fast declining into just enough of a sensation to titillate a croquet party. He had charming manners, could be witty at moments (though he could not keep it up), still retained his hyacinthine locks (by means of hair restorers), wore his excellently cut velvet coats and flowing ties with just the right air – half poet, half man of the world – and really had, at Abbot's Medding, no dark secret to hide beyond the fact, sedulously concealed by him for five-and-twenty years, that he had never been christened Augustine. Between Augustus and Augustine, what a gulf! But he had crossed it, and his French poems (which had to be smuggled into his native land) were signed Augustin – Augustin Lemarchant.

Removing his gaze from the objectionable evidence of domestic carelessness upon the floor, Mr Marchant now fixed it meditatively upon the ruby-set end of the gold pencil which he was using. Rossell & Ward, his publishers, were about to bring out an édition de luxe of *Queen Theodora and Queen Marozia* with illustrations by a hitherto unknown young artist – if they were not too daring. It would be a sumptuous affair in a limited edition. And, as he thought of this, the remembrance of his recent stay in Prague returned to the poet. He smiled to himself, as a man smiles when he looks at a rare wine, and thought: 'Yes, if these blunt-witted Pharisees round Abbott's Medding only knew!' It was a good thing that the upholders of British petty morality were seldom great travellers; a dispensation of . . . ahem, Providence!

Twiddling his gold pencil between plump fingers, Augustine Marchant returned to his ode, weighing one epithet against another. Except in summer he was no advocate of open windows, and even in summer he considered that to get the most out of that delicate and precious instrument, his brain, his feet must always be kept thoroughly warm; he had therefore cast over them, before settling into his semi reclining position, a beautiful rose-coloured Indian *sari* of the purest and thickest silk, leaving the ends trailing on the floor. And he became aware, with surprise and annoyance, that the piece of brown fluff or whatever it was down there, travelling in the draught from the window, had reached the nearest end of the *sari* and was now, impelled by the same current, travelling up it.

The master of Abbot's Medding reached out for the silver hand-bell on the table by his side. There must be more breeze coming in than he had realized, and he might take cold, a catastrophe against which he guarded himself as against the plague. Then he saw that the upward progress of the dark blot – it was about the size of a farthing – could not by any possibility be assigned to any other agency than its own. It was *climbing* up – some horrible insect, plainly, some disgusting kind of almost legless and very hairy spider, round and vague in outline. The poet sat up and shook the *sari* violently. When he looked again the invader was gone. He had obviously shaken it on to the floor, and on the floor somewhere it must still be. The idea perturbed him, and he decided to take his writing out to the summer-house, and give orders later that the library was to be thoroughly swept.

Ah! it was good to be out of doors, and in a pleasance so delightfully laid out, so exquisitely kept, as his! In the basin of the fountain the sea-nymphs of rosy-veined marble clustered round a Thetis as beautiful as Aphrodite herself; the lightest and featheriest of acacia trees swayed near. And as the owner of all this went past over the weedless turf he repeated snatches of Verlaine to himself about 'sveltes jets d'eau' and 'sanglots d'exstase.'

Then, turning his head to look back at the fountain, he became aware of a little dark-brown object about the size of a halfpenny running towards him over the velvet-smooth sward . . .

He believed afterwards that he must first have had a glimpse of the truth at that instant in the garden, or he would not have acted so instinctively as he did, and so promptly. For a moment later he was standing at the edge of the basin of Thetis, his face blanched in the sunshine, his hand firmly clenched. Inside that closed hand something feather-soft pulsated . . . Holding back as best he could the disgust and the something more which clutched at him, Augustine Marchant stooped and plunged his whole fist into the bubbling water, and let the stream of the fountain whirl away what he had picked up. Then with uncertain steps he went and sat down on the nearest seat and shut his eyes. After a while he took out his lawn handkerchief and carefully dried his hand with the intaglio ring, dried it and then looked curiously at the palm. 'I did not know I had so much courage,' he was thinking; 'so much courage and good sense!' . . . It would doubtless drown very quickly.

Burrows, his butler, was coming over the lawn. 'Mr and Mrs Morrison have arrived, sir.'

'Ah, yes; I had forgotten for the moment.' Augustine Marchant got up and walked towards the house and his guests, throwing back his shoulders and practising his famous enigmatic smile, for Mrs Morrison was a woman worth impressing.

(But what had it been exactly? Why, just what it had looked – a tuft of fur blowing over the grass, a tuft of fur! Sheer imagination that it had moved in his closed hand with a life of its own . . . Then why had he shut his eyes as he stooped and made a grab at it? Thank God, thank God, it was nothing now but a drenched smear swirling round the nymphs of Thetis!)

'Ah, dear lady, you must forgive me! Unpardonable of me not to be in to receive you!' He was in the drawing-room now, fragrant with its bank of hothouse flowers, bending over the hand of the fashionably attired guest on the sofa, in her tight bodice and voluminous sleeves, with a fly-away hat perched at a rakish angle on her gold-brown hair.

'Your man told us that you were writing in the garden,' said her goggle-eyed husband reverentially.

'*Cher maître*, it is we who ought not to be interrupting your rendezvous with the Muse,' returned Mrs Morrison in her sweet, high voice. 'Terrible to bring you from such company into that of mere visitors!'

Running his hand through his carefully tended locks the *cher maître* replied: 'Between a visit from the Muse and one from Beauty's self no true poet would hesitate! – Moreover, luncheon awaits us, and I trust it is a good one.'

He liked faintly to shock fair admirers by admitting that he cared for the pleasures of the table; it was quite safe to do so, since none of them had sufficient acumen to see that it was true.

The luncheon was excellent, for Augustine kept an admirable cook. Afterwards he showed his guests over the library – yes, even though it had not received the sweeping which would now be unnecessary – and round the garden; and in the summer-house was prevailed upon to read some of *Amor Cypriacus* aloud. And Mrs Frances (nowadays Francesca) Morrison was thereafter able to recount to envious friends how the Poet himself had read her stanza after stanza from that most *daring* poem of his; and how poor Fred, fanning himself meanwhile with his straw hat – not from the torridity of the verse but because of the afternoon heat – said afterwards that he had not understood a single word. A good thing, perhaps . . .

When they had gone Augustine Marchant reflected rather cynically: 'All that was just so much bunkum when I wrote it.' For ten years ago, in spite of those audacious, glowing verses, he was an ignorant neophyte. Of course, since then . . . He smiled, a private, sly, self-satisfied smile. It was certainly pleasant to know oneself no longer a fraud!

Returning to the summer-house to fetch his poems he saw what he took to be Mrs Morrison's fur boa lying on the floor just by the basket chair which she had occupied. Odd of her not to have missed it on departure – a tribute to his verses perhaps. His housekeeper must send it after her by post. But just at that moment his head gardener approached, desiring some instructions, and when the matter was settled, and Augustine Marchant turned once more to enter the summer-house, he found that he had been mistaken about the dropped boa, for there was nothing on the floor.

Besides, he remembered now that Mrs Morrison's boa had been a rope of grey feathers, not of dark fur. As he took up *Amor Cypriacus* he asked himself lazily what could have led him to imagine a woman's boa there at all, much less a fur one.

Suddenly he knew why. A lattice in the house of memory had opened, and he remained rigid, staring out at the jets of the fountain rising and falling in the afternoon sun. Yes; of that glamorous, wonderful, abominable night in Prague the part he least wished to recall was connected – incidentally but undeniably – with a fur boa . . . a long boa of dark fur . . .

He had to go up to town next day to a dinner in his honour. There and then he decided to go up that same night, by a late train, a most unusual proceeding, and most disturbing to his valet, who knew that it was doubtful whether he could at such short notice procure him a first-class carriage to himself. However, Augustine Marchant went, and even, to the man's amazement, deliberately chose a compartment with another occupant when he might, after all, have had an empty one.

The dinner was brilliant; Augustine had never spoken better. Next day he went round to the little street not far from the British Museum where he found Lawrence Storey, his new illustrator, working feverishly at his drawings for *Queen Theodora and Queen Marozia*, and quite overwhelmed at the honour of a personal visit. Augustine was very kind to him, and, while offering a few criticisms, highly praised his delineation of those two Messalinas of tenth-century Rome, their long supple hands, their heavy eyes, their full, almost repellent mouths. Storey had followed the same type for mother and daughter, but with a subtle difference.

'They were certainly two most evil women, especially the younger,' he observed ingenuously. 'But I suppose that, from an artistic point of view, that doesn't matter nowadays!'

Augustine, smoking one of his special cigarettes, made a delicate little gesture. 'My dear fellow, Art has nothing whatever to do with what is called "morality"; happily we know that at last! Show me how you thought of depicting the scene where Marozia orders the execution of her mother's papal paramour. Good, very good! Yes, the lines there, even the fall of that loose sleeve from the extended arm, express with clarity what I had in mind. You have great gifts!'

'I have tried to make her look wicked,' said the young man, reddening with pleasure. 'But,' he added deprecatingly, 'it is very hard for a ridiculously inexperienced person like myself to have the right artistic vision. For to you, Mr Marchant, who have penetrated into such wonderful arcana of the forbidden, it would be foolish to pretend to be other than I am.'

'How do you know that I have penetrated into any such

arcana?' enquired the poet, half-shutting his eyes and looking (though not to the almost worshipping gaze of young Storey) like a great cat being stroked.

'Why, one has only to read you!'

'You must come down and stay with me soon,' were Augustine Marchant's parting words. (He would give the boy a few days' good living, for which he would be none the worse; let him drink some decent wine.) 'How soon do you think you will be able to finish the rough sketches for the rest, and the designs for the *culs de lampe*? A fortnight or three weeks? Good; I shall look to see you then. Good-bye, my dear fellow; I am very, very much pleased with what you have shown me!'

The worst of going up to London from the country was that one was apt to catch a cold in town. When he got back, Augustine Marchant was almost sure that this misfortune had befallen him, so he ordered a fire in his bedroom, despite the season, and consumed a recherché little supper in seclusion.

And, as the cold turned out to have been imaginary, he was very comfortable, sitting there in his silken dressing-gown, toasting his toes and holding up a glass of golden Tokay to the flames. Really *Theodora and Marozia* would make as much sensation when it came out with these illustrations as when it first appeared!

All at once he set down his glass. Not far away on his left stood a big cheval mirror, like a woman's, in which a good portion of the bed behind him was reflected. And, in this mirror, he had just seen the valance of the bed move. There could be no draught to speak of in this warm room, he never allowed a cat in the house, and it was quite impossible that there should be a rat about. If after all some stray cat should have got in it must be ejected at once. Augustine hitched round in his chair to look at the actual bed-hanging.

Yes, the topaz-hued silk valance again swung very slightly outwards as though it were being pushed. Augustine bent forward to the bell-pull to summon his valet. Then the flask of Tokay rolled over on the table as he leapt from his chair instead. Something like a huge, dark caterpillar was emerging very slowly from under his bed, moving as a caterpillar moves, with undulations running over it. Where its head should have been was merely a tapering end smaller than the rest of it, but of like substance. It was a dark fur boa.

Augustine Marchant felt that he screamed, but he could not have done so, for his tongue clave to the roof of his mouth. He merely stood staring, staring, all the blood gone from his heart. Still very slowly, the thing continued to creep out from under the valance, waving that eyeless, tapering end to and fro, as though uncertain where to proceed. 'I am going mad, mad, mad!' thought Augustine, and then, with a revulsion: 'No, it can't be! It's a real snake of some kind!'

That could be dealt with. He snatched up the poker as the boa-thing, still swaying the head which was no head, kept pouring steadily out from under the lifted yellow frill, until quite three feet were clear of the bed. Then he fell upon it furiously, with blow after blow.

But they had no effect on the furry, spineless thing; it merely gave under them and rippled up in another place. Augustine hit the bed, the floor; at last, really screaming, he threw down his weapon and fell upon the thick, hairy rope with both hands, crushing it together into a mass – there was little if any resistance in it – hurled it into the fire and, panting, kept it down with shovel and tongs. The flames licked up instantly and, with a roar, made short work of it, though there seemed to be some slight effort to escape, which was perhaps only the effect of the heat. A moment later there was a very strong smell of burnt hair, and that was all.

Augustine Marchant seized the fallen flask of Tokay and drained from its mouth what little was left in the bottom ere, staggering to the bed, he flung himself upon it and buried his face in the pillows, even heaping them over his head as if he could thus stifle the memory of what he had seen.

He kept his bed next morning; the supposed cold afforded a good pretext. Long before the maid came in to re-lay the fire he had crawled out to make sure that there were no traces left of . . . what he had burnt there. There were none. A nightmare could not have left a trace, he told himself. But well he knew that it was not a nightmare.

And now he could think of nothing but that room in Prague and the long fur boa of the woman. Some department of his mind (he supposed) must have projected that thing, scarcely noticed at the time, scarcely remembered, into the present and the here. It was terrible to think that one's mind possessed such dark, unknown powers. But not so terrible as if the . . . apparition . . . had been endowed with an entirely separate objective existence. In a day or two he would consult his doctor and ask him to give him a tonic.

But, expostulated an uncomfortably lucid part of his brain, you are trying to run with the hare and hunt with the hounds. Is it not better to believe that the thing *had* an objective existence, for you have burnt it to nothing? Well and good! But if it is merely a projection from your own mind, what is to prevent it from reappearing, like the phoenix, from ashes?

There seemed no answer to that, save in an attempt to persuade himself that he had been feverish last night. Work was the best antidote. So Augustine Marchant rose, and was surprised and delighted to find the atmosphere of his study unusually soothing and inspiring; and that day, against all expectation, *Salutation to All Unbeliefs* was completed by some stanzas with which he was not too ill-pleased. Realizing nevertheless that he should be glad of company that evening, he had earlier sent round a note to the local solicitor, a good fellow, to come and dine with him; played a game of billiards with the lawyer afterwards, and retired to bed after some vintage port and a good stiff whisky and soda with scarcely a thought of the visitant of the previous night.

He woke at that hour when the thrushes in early summer punctually greet the new day – three o'clock. They were greeting it even vociferously, and Augustine Marchant was annoyed with their enthusiasm. His golden damask window curtains kept out all but a glimmer of the new day, yet as, lying upon his back, the poet opened his eyes for a moment, his only half-awakened sense of vision reported something swinging to and fro in the dimness like a pendulum of rope. It was indistinct, but seemed to be hanging from the tester of the bed. And, wide awake in an instant, with an unspeakable anguish of premonition tearing through him, he felt, next moment, a light thud on the coverlet about the level of his knees. Something had arrived on the bed . . .

And Augustine Marchant neither shrieked nor leapt from his bed; he could not. Yet, now that his eyes were grown used to the twilight of the room, he saw it clearly, the fur rope which he had burnt to extinction two nights ago, dark and shining as before, rippling with a gentle movement as it coiled itself neatly together in the place where it had struck the bed, and subsided there in a symmetrical round, with only that tapering end a little raised, and, as it were, looking at him – only, eyeless and featureless, it could not look. One thought of disgusted relief, that it was not at any rate going to attack him, and Augustine Marchant fainted.

Yet his swoon must have merged into sleep, for he woke in a more or less ordinary fashion to find his man placing his early tea-tray beside him and enquiring when he should draw his bath. There was nothing on the bed.

'I shall change my bedroom,' thought Augustine to himself, looking at the haggard, fallen-eyed man who faced him in the mirror as he shaved. No, better still, I will go away for a change. Then I shall not have these . . . dreams. I'll go to old Edgar Fortescue for a few days; he begged me again not long ago to come any time.'

So to the house of that old Maecenas he went. He was much too great a man now to be in need of Sir Edgar's patronage. It was homage which he received there, both from host and guests. The stay did much to soothe his scarified nerves. Unfortunately the last day undid the good of all the foregoing ones.

Sir Edgar possessed a pretty young wife – his third – and, among other charms in his place in Somerset, an apple orchard underplanted with flowers. And in the cool of the evening Augustine walked there with his host and hostess almost as if he were the Almighty with the dwellers in Eden. Presently they sat down upon a rustic seat (but a very comfortable one) under the shade of the apple boughs, amid the incongruous but pleasant parterres.

'You have come at the wrong season for these apple-trees, Marchant,' observed Sir Edgar after a while, taking out his cigar. 'Blossom-time or apple-time – they are showy at either, in spite of the underplanting. – What is attracting you on that tree – a tit? We have all kinds here, pretty, destructive little beggars!'

'I did not know that I was looking . . . It's nothing . . . thinking of something else,' stammered the poet. Surely, surely he had been mistaken in thinking that he had seen a sinuous, dark, furry thing undulating like a caterpillar down the stem of that particular apple-tree at a few yards' distance?

Talk went on, even his own; there was safety in it. It was only the breeze which faintly rustled that bed of heliotrope behind the seat. Augustine wanted desperately to get up and leave the orchard, but neither Sir Edgar nor his wife seemed disposed to move, and so the poet remained at his end of the seat, his left hand playing nervously with a long bent of grass which had escaped the scythe.

All at once he felt a tickling sensation on the back of his hand, looked down and saw that featureless snout of fur protruding upwards from underneath the rustic bench, and sweeping itself backwards and forwards against his hand with a movement which was almost caressing. He was on his feet in a flash.

'Do you mind if I go in?' he asked abruptly. 'I'm not . . . feeling very well.'

If the thing could follow him it was of no use to go away. He returned to Abbot's Medding looking so much the worse for his change of air that Burrows expressed a respectful hope that he was not indisposed. And almost the first thing that occurred, when Augustine sat down at his writing-table to attend to his correspondence, was the unwinding of itself from one of its curved legs of a soft, brown, oscillating serpent which slowly waved an end at him as if in welcome . . .

In welcome, yes, that was it! The creature, incredible though it was, the creature seemed glad to see him! Standing at the other end of the room, his hands pressed over his eyes – for what was the use of attempting to hurt or destroy it? – Augustine Marchant thought shudderingly that, like a witch's cat, a 'familiar' would not, presumably, be ill disposed towards its master. Its master! Oh God!

The hysteria which he had been trying to keep down began to mount uncontrollably when, removing his hands, Augustine glanced again towards his writing-table, and saw that the boa had coiled itself in his chair and was sweeping its end to and fro over the back, somewhat in the way that a cat, purring meanwhile, rubs itself against furniture or a human leg in real or simulated affection.

'Oh, go, go away from there!' he suddenly screamed at it, advancing with outstretched hand. 'In the Devil's name, get out!'

To his utter amazement, he was obeyed. The rhythmic movements ceased, the fur snake poured itself down out of the chair and writhed towards the door. Venturing back to his writing-table after a moment Augustine saw it coiled on the threshold, the blind end turned towards him as usual, as though watching. And he began to laugh. What would happen if he rang and someone came; would the opening door scrape it aside . . . would it vanish? Had it, in short, an existence for anyone else but himself?

But he dared not make the experiment. He left the room by the French window, feeling that he could never enter the house again. And perhaps, had it not been for the horrible knowledge just acquired that it could follow him, he might easily have gone away for good from Abbot's Medding and all his treasures and comforts. But of what use would that be – and how should he account for so extraordinary an action? No; he must think and plan while he yet remained sane.

To what, then, could he have recourse? The black magic in which he had dabbled with such disastrous consequences might possibly help him. Left to himself he was but an amateur, but he had a number of books . . . There was also that other realm whose boundaries sometimes marched side by side with magic – religion. But how could he pray to a Deity in whom he did not believe? Rather pray to the Evil which had sent this curse upon him to show him how to banish it. Yet since he had deliberately followed what religion stigmatised as sin, what even the world would label as lust and necromancy, supplication to the dark powers was not likely to deliver him from them. They must somehow be outwitted, circumvented.

He kept his *grimoires* and books of the kind in a locked bookcase in another room, not in his study; in that room he sat up till midnight. But the spells which he read were useless; moreover, he did not really believe in them. The irony of the situation was that, in a sense, he had only played at sorcery; it had but lent a spice to sensuality. He wandered wretchedly about the room dreading at any moment to see his 'familiar' wreathed round some object in it. At last he stopped at a small bookcase which held some old forgotten books of his mother's – Longfellow and Mrs Hemans, *John Halifax, Gentleman*, and a good many volumes of sermons and mild essays. And when he looked at that blameless assembly a cloud seemed to pass over Augustine Marchant's vision, and he saw his mother, gentle and lace-capped, as years and years ago she used to sit, hearing his lessons, in an antimacassared chair. She had been everything to him then, the little boy whose soul was not smirched. He called silently to her now: 'Mamma, Mamma, can't you help me? Can't you send this thing away?'

When the cloud had passed he found that he had stretched out his hand and removed a big book. Looking at it he saw that it was her Bible, with 'Sarah Amelia Marchant' on the faded yellow flyleaf. Her spirit *was* going to help him! He turned over a page or two, and out of the largish print there sprang instantly at him: *Now the serpent was more subtle than any beast of the field*. Augustine shuddered and almost put the Bible back, but the conviction that there was help there urged him to go on. He turned a few more pages of Genesis and his eyes were caught by this verse, which he had never seen before in his life.

'And if thou doest well, shalt thou not be accepted? And if thou doest not well, sin lieth at the door. And unto thee shall be his desire, and thou shalt rule over him.'

What strange words! What could they possibly mean? Was there light for him in them? 'Unto thee shall be his desire.' That Thing, the loathsome semblance of affection which hung about it . . . 'Thou shalt rule over him.' It *had* obeyed him, up to a point . . . Was this Book, of all others, showing him the way to be free? But the meaning of the verse was so obscure! He had not, naturally, such a thing as a commentary in the house. Yet, when he came to think of it, he remembered that some pious and anonymous person, soon after the publication of *Pomegranates of Sin*, had sent him a Bible in the Revised Version, with an inscription recommending him to read it. He had it somewhere, though he had always meant to get rid of it.

After twenty minutes' search through the sleeping house he found it in one of the spare bedrooms. But it gave him little enlightenment, for there was scant difference in the rendering, save that for, 'lieth at the door', this version had, 'coucheth', and that the margin held an alternative translation for the end of the verse: 'And unto thee is its desire, but thou shouldest rule over it.'

Nevertheless, Augustine Marchant stood after midnight in this silent, sheeted guest-chamber repeating: *'But thou shouldest rule over it.'*

And all at once he thought of a way of escape.

II

It was going to be a marvellous experience, staying with Augustine Marchant. Sometimes Lawrence Storey hoped there would be no other guests at Abbot's Medding; at other times he hoped there would be. A *tête-à-tête* of four days with the great poet – could he sustain his share worthily? For Lawrence, despite the remarkable artistic gifts which were finding their first real flowering in these illustrations to Augustine's poem, was still unspoilt, still capable of wonder and admiration, still humble and almost naïf. It was still astonishing to him that he, an architect's assistant, should have been snatched away, as Ganymede by the eagle, from the lower world of elevations and drains to serve on Olympus. It was not, indeed, Augustine Marchant who had first discovered him; but it was Augustine Marchant who was going to make him famous.

The telegraph-poles flitted past the second-class carriage window and more than one traveller glanced with a certain envy and admiration at the fair, good-looking young man who diffused such an impression of happiness and candour, and had such a charming smile on his boyish lips. He carried with him a portfolio which he never let out of reach of his hand; the oldish couple opposite, speculating upon its contents, might have changed their opinion of him had they seen them.

But no shadow of the dark weariness of things unlawful rested on Lawrence Storey; to know Augustine Marchant, to be illustrating his great poem, to have learnt from him that art and morality had no kinship, this was to plunge into a new realm of freedom and enlarging experience. Augustine Marchant's poetry, he felt, had already taught his hand what his brain and heart knew nothing of.

There was a dog-cart to meet him at the station, and in the scented June evening he was driven with a beating heart past meadows and hayfields to his destination.

Mr Marchant, awaiting him in the hall, was at his most charming. 'My dear fellow, are those the drawings? Come, let us lock them away at once in my safe! If you had brought me diamonds I should not be one quarter so concerned about thieves. And did you have a comfortable journey? I have had you put in the orange room; it is next to mine. There is no one else staying here, but there are a few people coming to dinner to meet you.'

There was only just time to dress for dinner, so that Lawrence did not get an opportunity to study his host until he saw him seated at the head of the table. Then he was immediately struck by the fact that he looked curiously ill. His face – ordinarily by no means attenuated – seemed to have fallen in, there were dark circles under his eyes, and the perturbed Lawrence, observing him as the meal progressed, thought that his manner, too, seemed strange and once or twice quite absent-minded. And there was one moment when, though the lady on his right was addressing him, he sharply turned his head away and looked down at the side of his chair just as if he saw something on the floor. Then he apologised, saying that he had a horror of cats, and that sometimes the tiresome animal from the stables . . . But after that he continued to entertain his guests in his own inimitable way, and, even to the shy Lawrence, the evening proved very pleasant.

The three ensuing days were wonderful and exciting to the young artist – days of uninterrupted contact with a master mind which acknowledged, as the poet himself admitted, none of the petty barriers which man, for his own convenience, had set up between alleged right and wrong. Lawrence had learnt why his host did not look well; it was loss of sleep, the price exacted by inspiration. He had a new poetic drama shaping in his mind which would scale heights that he had not yet attempted.

There was almost a touch of fever in the young man's dreams to-night – his last night but one. He had several. First he was standing by the edge of a sort of mere, inexpressibly desolate and unfriendly, a place he had never seen in his life, which yet seemed in some way familiar; and something said to him: 'You will never go away from here!' He was alarmed, and woke, but went to sleep again almost immediately, and this time was back, oddly enough, in the church where in his earliest years he had been taken to service by the aunt who had brought him up – a large church full of pitch-pine pews with narrow ledges for hymn-books, which ledges he used surreptitiously to lick during the long dull periods of occultation upon his knees. But most of all he remembered the window with Adam and Eve in the Garden of Eden, on either side of an apple-tree round whose trunk was coiled a monstrous snake with a semi-human head. Lawrence had hated and dreaded that window, and because of it he would never go near an orchard and had no temptation to steal apples . . . Now he was back in that church again, staring at the window, lit up with some infernal glow from behind. He woke again, little short of terrified – he, a grown man! But again he went to sleep quite quickly.

His third dream had for background, as sometimes happens in nightmares, the very room in which he lay. He dreamt that a door opened in the wall, and in the doorway, quite plain against the light from another room behind him, stood Augustine Marchant in his dressing-gown. He was looking down at something on the ground which Lawrence did not see, but his hand was pointing at Lawrence in the bed, and he was saying in a voice of command: 'Go to him, do you hear? Go to him! Go to *him*! Am I not your master?' And Lawrence, who could neither move nor utter a syllable, wondered uneasily what this could be which was thus commanded, but his attention was chiefly focused on Augustine Marchant's face. After he had said these words several times, and apparently without result, a dreadful change came upon it, a look of the most unutterable despair. It seemed visibly to age and wither; he said, in a loud, penetrating whisper: 'Is there no escape then?' covered his ravaged face a moment with his hands, and then went back and softly closed the door. At that Lawrence woke; but in the morning he had forgotten all three dreams.

The *tête-à-tête* dinner on the last night of his stay would have lingered in a gourmet's memory, so that it was a pity the young man did not know in the least what he was eating. At last there was happening what he had scarcely dared hope for; the great poet of the sensuous was revealing to him some of the unimaginably strange and secret sources of his inspiration. In the shaded rosy candle-light, his elbows on the table among trails of flowers he, who was not even a neophyte, listened like a man learning for the first time of some spell of spring which will make him more than mortal.

'Yes,' said Augustine Marchant, after a long pause, 'yes, it was a marvellous, an undying experience . . . one that is not given to many. It opened doors, it – but I despair of doing it justice in mere words.' His look was transfigured, almost dreamy.

'But she . . . the woman . . . how did you . . . ?' asked Lawrence Storey in a hushed voice.

'Oh, the woman?' said Augustine, suddenly finishing off his wine. 'The woman was only a common street-walker.'

A moment or two later Lawrence was looking at his host wonderingly and wistfully. 'But this was in Prague. Prague is a long way off.'

'One does not need to go so far, in reality. Even in Paris –'

'One could . . . have that experience in Paris?'

'If you knew where to go. And, of course, it is necessary to have credentials. I mean that – like all such enlightenments – it has to be kept secret, most secret, from the vulgar minds who lay their restrictions on the finer. That is self-evident.'

'Of course', said the young man, and sighed deeply. His host looked at him affectionately.

'You, my dear Lawrence – I may call you Lawrence? – want just that touch of . . . what shall I call them – *les choses cachées* – to liberate your immense artistic gifts from the shackles which still bind them. Through that gateway you would find the possibility of their full fruition! It would fertilize your genius to a still finer blossoming . . . But you would have scruples . . . and you are very young.'

'You know,' said Lawrence in a low and trembling tone, 'what I feel about your poetry. You know how I ache to lay the best that is in me at your feet. If only I could make my drawings for the Two Queens more worthy – already it is an honour which overwhelms me that you should have selected me to do them – but they are not what they should be. I am *not* sufficiently liberated . . .'

Augustine leant forward on the flower-decked table. His eyes were glowing.

'Do you truly desire to be?'

The young man nodded, too full of emotion to find his voice.

The poet got up, went over to a cabinet in a corner and unlocked it. Lawrence watched his fine figure in a sort of trance. Then he half-rose with an exclamation.

'What is it?' asked Augustine very sharply, facing round.

'Oh, nothing, sir – only that I believe you hate cats, and I thought I saw one, or rather its tail, disappearing into that corner.'

'There's no cat here,' said Augustine quickly. His face had become all shiny and mottled, but Lawrence did not notice it. The poet stood a moment looking at the carpet; one might almost have thought that he was gathering resolution to cross it; then he came swiftly back to the table.

'Sit down again,' he commanded. 'Have you a pocket-book with you, a pocket-book which you never leave about? Good! Then write *this* in one place; and *this* on another page . . . write it small . . . among other entries is best . . . not on a blank page . . . write it in Greek characters if you know them . . .'

'What . . . what is it?' asked Lawrence, all at once intolerably excited, his eyes fixed on the piece of paper in Augustine's hand.

'The two halves of the address in Paris.'

III

Augustine Marchant kept a diary in those days, a locked diary written in cipher. And for more than a month after Lawrence Storey's visit the tenor of the entries there was almost identical: 'No change . . . Always with me . . . How much longer can I endure it? The alteration in my looks is being remarked upon to my face. I shall have to get rid of Thornton [his man] on some pretext or other, for I begin to think that he has seen It. No wonder, since It follows me about like a dog. When It is visible to everyone it will be the end . . . I found It in bed with me this morning, pressed up against me as if for warmth . . .'

But there was a different class of entry also, appearing at intervals with an ever-increasing note of impatience. 'Will L. S. go there? . . . When shall I hear from L. S.? . . . Will the experiment do what I think? It is my last hope.'

Then, suddenly, after five weeks had elapsed, an entry in a trembling hand: 'For twenty-four hours I have seen no sign of It! Can it be possible?'

And next day: 'Still nothing. I begin to live again – This evening has come an ecstatic letter from L. S., from Paris, telling me that he had "presented his credentials" and was to have the experience next day. He has had it by now – by yesterday, in fact. Have I really freed myself? It looks like it!'

In one week from the date of that last entry it was remarked in Abbot's Medding how much better Mr Marchant was looking again. Of late he had not seemed at all himself; his cheeks had fallen in, his clothes seemed to hang loosely upon him, who had generally filled them so well, and he appeared nervous. Now he was as before, cheery, courtly, debonair. And last Sunday, will you believe it, he went to church! The Rector was so astonished when he first became aware of him from the pulpit that he nearly forgot to give out his text. And the poet joined in the hymns, too! Several observed this amazing phenomenon.

It was the day after this unwonted appearance at St Peter's. Augustine was strolling in his garden. The air had a new savour, the sun a new light; he could look again with pleasure at Thetis and her nymphs of the fountain, could work undisturbed in the summer-house. Free, free! All the world was good to the senses once again, and the hues and scents of early autumn better, in truth, than the brilliance of that summer month which had seen his curse descend upon him.

The butler brought him out a letter with a French stamp. From Lawrence Storey, of course; to tell him – what? Where had he caught his first glimpse of it? In one of those oppressively furnished French bedrooms? And how had he taken it?

At first, however, Augustine was not sure that the letter was from Storey. The writing was very different, cramped instead of flowing, and, in places, spluttering, the pen having dug into the paper as if the hand which held it had not been entirely under control – almost, thought Augustine, his eyes shining with excitement, almost as though something had been twined, liana-like, round the wrist. (He had a sudden sick recollection of a day when that had happened to him, quickly submerged in a gush of eager anticipation.) Sitting down upon the edge of the fountain he read – not quite what he had looked for.

'I don't know what is happening to me,' began the letter, without other opening. 'Yesterday I was in a café by myself, and had just ordered some absinthe – though I do not like it. And quite suddenly, although I knew that I was in the café, I realized that I was also back in *that room*. I could see every feature of it, but I could see the café too, with all the people in it; the one was, as it were, superimposed upon the other, the room, which was a good deal smaller than the café, being inside the latter, as a box may be within a larger box. And all the while the room was growing clearer, the café fading. I saw the glass of absinthe suddenly standing on nothing, as it were. All the furniture of the room, all the accessories you know of, were mixed up with the chairs and tables of the café. I do not know how I managed to find my way to the *comptoir*, pay and get out. I took a *fiacre* back to my hotel. By the time I arrived there I was all right. I suppose that it was only the after effects of a very strange and violent emotional experience. But I hope to God that it will not recur!'

'How interesting!' said Augustine Marchant, dabbling his hand in the swirling water where he had once drowned a piece of dark fluff. 'And why indeed should I have expected that it would couch at his door in the same form as at mine?'

Four days more of new-found peace and he was reading this: 'In God's name – or the Devil's – come over and help me! I have hardly an hour now by night or day when I am sure of my whereabouts. I could not risk the journey back to England alone. It is like being imprisoned in some kind of infernal half-transparent box, always growing a little smaller. Wherever I go now I carry it about with me; when I am in the street I hardly know which is the pavement and which is the roadway, because I am always treading on that black carpet with the cabalistic designs; if I speak to anyone they may suddenly disappear from sight. To attempt to work is naturally useless. I would consult a doctor, but that would mean telling him everything . . .'

'I hope to God he won't do that!' muttered Augustine uneasily. 'He can't – he swore to absolute secrecy. I hadn't bargained, however, for his ceasing work. Suppose he finds himself unable to complete the designs for *Theodora and Marozia*! That would be serious . . . However, to have freed myself is worth *any* sacrifice . . . But Storey cannot, obviously, go on living indefinitely on two planes at once . . . Artistically, though, it might inspire him to something quite unprecedented. I'll write to him and point that out; it might encourage him. But go near him in person – is it likely!'

The next day was one of great literary activity. Augustine was so deeply immersed in his new poetical drama that he neglected his correspondence and almost his meals – except his dinner, which seemed that evening to be shared most agreeably and excitingly by these new creations of his brain. Such, in fact, was his preoccupation with them that it was not until he had finished the savoury and poured out a glass of his superlative port that he remembered a telegram which had been handed to him as he came in to dinner. It still lay unopened by his plate. Now, tearing apart the envelope, he read with growing bewilderment these words above his publishers' names:

'Please inform us immediately what steps to take are prepared send to France recover drawings if possible what suggestions can you make as to successor Rossell and Ward.'

Augustine was more than bewildered; he was stupefied. Had some accident befallen Lawrence Storey of which he knew nothing? But he had opened all his letters this morning, though he had not answered any. A prey to a sudden very nasty anxiety he got up and rang the bell.

'Burrows, bring me *The Times* from the library.'

The newspaper came, unopened. Augustine, now in a frenzy of uneasiness, scanned the pages rapidly. But it was some seconds before he came upon the headline: 'Tragic Death of a Young English Artist,' and read the following, furnished by the Paris correspondent:

'Connoisseurs who were looking forward to the appearance of the superb illustrated edition of Mr Augustine Marchant's

Queen Theodora and Queen Marozia will learn with great regret of the death by drowning of the gifted young artist, Mr Lawrence Storey, who was engaged upon the designs for it. Mr Storey had recently been staying in Paris, but left one day last week for a remote spot in Brittany, it was supposed in pursuance of his work. On Friday last his body was discovered floating in a lonely pool near Carhaix. It is hard to see how Mr Storey could have fallen in, since this piece of water – the Mare de Plougouven – has a completely level shore surrounded by reeds, and is not in itself very deep, nor is there any boat upon it. It is said that the unfortunate young Englishman had been somewhat strange in his manner recently and complained of hallucinations; it is therefore possible that under their influence he deliberately waded out into the Mare de Plougouven. A strange feature of the case is that he had fastened round him under his coat the finished drawings for Mr Marchant's book, which were, of course, completely spoilt by the water before the body was found. It is to be hoped that they were not the only –'

Augustine threw *The Times* furiously from him and struck the dinner-table with his clenched fist.

'Upon my soul, that is too much! It is criminal! My property – and I who had done so much for him! Fastened them round himself – he must have been crazy!'

But had he been so crazy? When his wrath had subsided a little, Augustine could not but ask himself whether the young artist had not in some awful moment of insight guessed the truth, or a part of it – that his patron had deliberately corrupted him? It looked almost like it. But, if he had really taken all the finished drawings with him to this place in Brittany, what an unspeakably mean trick of revenge thus to destroy them! . . . Yet, even if it were so, their loss must be regarded as the price of deliverance, since, from his point of view, the desperate expedient of passing on his 'familiar' had been a complete success. By getting someone else to plunge even deeper than he had done into the unlawful (for he had seen to it that Lawrence Storey should do that) he had proved, as that verse in Genesis said, that he *had* rule over . . . what had pursued him in tangible form as a consequence of his own night in Prague. He could not be too thankful. The literary world might well be thankful too. For his own art was of infinitely more importance than the subservient, the parasitic art of an illustrator. He could with a little search find half a dozen just as gifted as that poor hallucination-ridden Storey to finish *Theodora and Marozia* – even, if necessary, to begin an entirely fresh set of drawings. And meanwhile, in the new lease of creative energy which this unfortunate but necessary sacrifice had made possible for him, he would begin to put on paper the masterpiece which was now taking brilliant shape in his liberated mind. A final glass, and then an evening in the workshop!

Augustine poured out some port, and was raising the glass, prepared to drink to his own success, when he thought he heard a sound near the door. He looked over his shoulder. Next instant the stem of the wineglass had snapped in his hand, and he had sprung back to the farthest limit of the room.

Reared up for quite five feet against the door, huge, dark, sleeked with wet and flecked with bits of green waterweed, was something half python, half gigantic cobra, its head drawn back as if to strike – its head, for in its former featureless tapering end were now two reddish eyes, such as furriers put into the heads of stuffed creatures. And these eyes were fixed upon him in an unwavering and malevolent glare.